Praise for *Selfish Girls*

'The story and characters felt both sharply real and ethereal at times, as though reading this novel enters you into a deep dream-like state ... Complicated women, with all their intricate elements, are my favourite people to read about' **Emma Gannon, *Sunday Times* bestselling author of *Olive***

'Abigail Bergstrom writes with so much vigour and colour and detail. *Selfish Girls* is an outstanding novel: pithy and singular, gloriously dark and compelling, a must read!' **Salena Godden, author of *Mrs Death Misses Death***

'Sisterhood at its darkest and its most beautiful – every time you think you understand, Bergstrom reveals a new, breathtaking layer' **Monika Radojevic, #Merky Books New Writers' Prize winning author of *A Beautiful Lack of Consequence***

'I'm not exaggerating when I say this is literally the best book I've read in YEARS. And that's coming from a Gen Z with the attention span of a cat' **Lucy Blakiston,** *Shit You Should Care About*

'*Selfish Girls* is *Little Women* meets *Bad Sisters*, and I adored it. With great empathy and precision, Abigail Bergstrom has created a family portrait that's richly detailed and deeply intimate' **Chloë Ashby, author of *Wet Paint***

'A masterclass in emotional storytelling. A searing, beautifully written portrait of messy love, buried pain, and the bonds that refuse to break. I couldn't look away' **Amie McNee, author and creator of @inspiredtowrite**

'Bergstrom writes with a beauty that bruises, capturing what it means to be a sister, a mother, a lover, a friend' **Hana Walker-Brown, multi-award winning journalist and author of *A Delicate Game***

'An exceptionally clever and moving portrait of the messy realities of sisterhood – it took my breath away' **Olivia Petter, award-winning journalist, author and broadcaster**

'*Selfish Girls* is bold and lean and enduring' **Maxine Mei-Fung Chung, author of *What Women Want***

Abigail Bergstrom is a celebrated author and publishing powerhouse who has shepherded countless *Sunday Times* and *New York Times* bestsellers throughout her career. She writes for national magazines and broadsheets including *ELLE*, *Sunday Times Style*, *Red magazine*, the *Telegraph*, *Grazia* and *Refinery29*. She reviews books for *Konfekt* and also writes the substack newsletter 'Something to Say,' offering writing advice and cultural commentary to thousands of readers worldwide. She is also the author of the critically-acclaimed novel, *What a Shame*.

Abigail Bergstrom

Selfish Girls

HODDER &
STOUGHTON

First published in Great Britain in 2025 by Hodder & Stoughton Limited
An Hachette UK company

The authorised representative in the EEA is Hachette Ireland, 8 Castlecourt Centre, Dublin 15, D15 XTP3, Ireland (email: info@hbgi.ie)

1

Copyright © Abigail Bergstrom 2025

The right of Abigail Bergstrom to be identified as the Author of the Work has been asserted by her in accordance with the Copyright, Designs and Patents Act 1988.

All rights reserved. No part of this publication may be reproduced, stored in a retrieval system, or transmitted, in any form or by any means without the prior written permission of the publisher, nor be otherwise circulated in any form of binding or cover other than that in which it is published and without a similar condition being imposed on the subsequent purchaser.

All characters in this publication are fictitious and any resemblance to real persons, living or dead, is purely coincidental.

A CIP catalogue record for this title is available from the British Library

Hardback ISBN 978 1 399 71948 3
Trade Paperback ISBN 978 1 399 71949 0
ebook ISBN 978 1 399 71950 6

Typeset in Bembo Std by Hewer Text UK Ltd, Edinburgh
Printed and bound in Great Britain by Clays Ltd, Elcograf S.p.A.

Hodder & Stoughton policy is to use papers that are natural, renewable and recyclable products and made from wood grown in sustainable forests. The logging and manufacturing processes are expected to conform to the environmental regulations of the country of origin.

Hodder & Stoughton Limited
Carmelite House
50 Victoria Embankment
London EC4Y 0DZ

www.hodder.co.uk

For my sisters, Amy and Nicola,
and for my mother, Lesley.

'What is this impulse in me to worship and crucify anyone who leaves me?'

Emily Skaja
Brute Poems, 2018

'Abjection is above all ambiguity. Because, while releasing a hold, it does not radically cut off the subject from what threatens it – on the contrary, abjection acknowledges it to be in perpetual danger.'

Julia Kristeva
Powers of Horror: An Essay on Abjection, 1980

Prologue

Red is a warning. The human body is almost entirely red inside yet there is no sign of it anywhere. Not one drop of red until something shatters and breaks. It's the canopy of hell. Caught red-handed, the things she had done that her family wouldn't forget. The colour of their school jumpers, crimson and wilting as they followed one another through the front door, cherry Tip Tops staining their lips. The streaks of sunburn, red, like a map of what had been forgotten. Ruddy shawls pinned with a daffodil for an *eisteddfod*. The inevitable revealed as she'd bitten into herself, peeling the skin down and around a nail.

Now red is the colour of an ending. Soaking through her cotton nightie, like lava scorching her sides, going into those deceptive corners of fear. The pain a vent, it comes from deep inside her. Feels like hands clutching around her womb and twisting in opposite directions. She moans as Noah tries to get her to sit up, pushes at his waist. She'd brought this on herself. Now he's on the phone listing the facts: age, what time it started, how far along she is, how much blood.

She rolls over, reaching for the back of the sofa where a hardened coarse towel has been thrown down; it would be a shame to ruin a good one. A wince masks her anger, which fastens itself on a different outcome as she feels for something coming out of her, blood on her hands. The foul smell as she pulls down her knickers. The sac of cells resembling hope falls from between her legs onto the floor. Why hadn't she thought to catch it? She cries out but it's not a sound she's made before. A maternal bellow: she'd needed to graduate to. And she knew it would linger with her now when she stared into the mirror, asking herself a question she could never say out loud: hadn't this been what she'd wanted?

Impromptu Dinners

October

'Ines Ivory?'

She doesn't register the name at first because it's not her real name. The voice seems to be calling these women held in a tension of their own making. She doesn't feel anxious; she can't feel anything. Competitive glances bounce off the walls of the narrow corridor, which is lined with green plastic chairs. They are deliberate in their discomfort, informing you that you're not to settle. She focuses on the red nails belonging to the voice, seizing around the clipboard.

'Ines Ivory?'

'Oh, that's me!' She lifts a hand and notices that the gesture signals frailty.

'Can everyone listen out for their names? We need to move quickly if we're going to see everyone.' The casting assistant draws her eyes over her. 'You'll be up next – follow me, please.' She disappears back into the room and the remaining hopefuls seem resentful that Ines's incompetence could eat into their shot.

She reaches for her bag then, hands shaking, shuts off her phone, the screen turning dark on a text exchange with Noah trying to convince her not to go, it's too soon, her body is still recovering. But she isn't as fragile as he likes to think she is. She *wanted* to do this, so she glides down the corridor, a paper plane in the windstream of her own determination.

Inside the audition room a young woman and a middle-aged man sit behind a table with bottles of water and pens spilling over yellow-lined paper. The brick walls are painted white and have signs with lists of names taped to them. The assistant hands the man Ines's résumé as he finishes reading something on his phone. She tries to imagine herself as the woman in the photograph he's just been given: pretty, distinguished, destined for something better than herself.

'Name please?'
'Ines Ivory.'
'Age?' He lifts his eyes to her.
'Twenty-eight.'
'Not at me, love, at the camera.'

Right, of course. She smiles and shifts her body, stares down into the hollow lens.

'Have you done TV before?'
'A few ads and a small role in a series that—'
'Great. So, this is a nappy ad for a new brand. You're a happy new mum overjoyed with your little one and an innovative absorbent technology. Any questions?'

She parts her lips to speak, then refrains. Hadn't her agent said shampoo? Feels for the back of her head, her mind hazy now from the excruciatingly early train she'd taken to fit in a blow-dry.

'Wake up – let's go,' the man chips, and his assistant flusters with the clipboard. It has lost its power in this new room, seems more like a life raft now under the harshness of synthetic lighting. The assistant reaches for one of the plastic babies piled on a table, placing it on the changing mat on the floor, which Ines hadn't noticed. She looks at the tiny red apples decorating the plush mat and kneels before it almost instinctively, cradling the baby, head against her breasts, which are still sore.

'No lines – we just need to see you with the product, put the nappy on, interact with the kid. Show us what you can do basically.' He pulls at his T-shirt, stretching it to shield his paunch.

Music starts playing and a new voice comes through the speakers, describing the environmentally friendly nappies to keep the planet happy and thriving, like your little one. Ines pulls at the plastic leg of the counterfeit child. Its toothpaste-green eyes look through her, head round and hard with a firm wisp of plastic hair, mouth rubicund and scrunched, like the arse of a cat, its countenance somewhat conniving.

She starts talking to the baby, holding it gently by the wrists, smiling, meeting her nose with the plastic, which smells tangy, chemical.

'There are no lines!' the casting director shouts against the overplay. 'Use the product.'

She reaches for the nappy, hands still shaking, and finds there's blood on them.

'Pick the kid up! Not like that. Christ, haven't you held a baby before?'

She tries to wipe it off, wipe it from the plastic limb she's just smeared as the apples start to merge into one, the mat soaking with blood, the doll's face disappearing behind a dark pool of red. The sound of white noise as she's carried back to herself, back to a wound with a freshness that makes outperforming it seem silly, and then this sensation again of drowning.

Her mind is blank as the heavy audition-room door slams behind her, anticipatory faces look up and there is an expression of surprise on the girl who walks past her. Ines can see she'll do a better job, looks more like a mother anyway. She feels the wetness of her lashes, wipes at her mascara, surprised by the evidence of feeling, black and smudged across her fingers. She reaches for her phone, turns it on as she strides decisively down the corridor. An email notification appears alongside a text from Mam: *How did it go?? x* She clicks on the mailbox icon and Emma's name floods her with relief until she realises what it is: an invitation to her niece's baptism. And she starts to laugh then, the sound leaving her body with the loud shriek that hits the low ceiling of the corridor, eyes of the still-hopefuls pressing up against her, deliberate in their discomfort, informing her that it's best you go now.

★★★

Dylan is rushing down the high street, pulling heavy bags brimming with tight chokers for narrow necks and chunky rings shaped like soap dishes. Her phone is ringing, and as she searches, the rope straps digging into her shoulders, she feels the vibration in her back pocket.

'Hello?'

'Did you want me to keep all your old school textbooks?'

'What?'

'There's tonnes of them yer – I don't know why you've bothered to keep them all.'

'Hi, Mum. Yes! I'm fine, thanks,' she couldn't resist the sarcasm, 'and how are things with you?'

'Sorry, love, it's a bloody mess yer – I'm just trying to get sorted. What about your elephant? Do you want him?'

'Flumpy?' She recalls the rainbow-coloured fur that smelt like bedtime.

'Yes, Flumpy. Are we keeping him?'

Mam had lived in that house on Laurel Road for her entire life; Dylan couldn't understand the sudden need for an industrial-scale clear-out. 'Do I need to decide right this second?'

A sigh down the line. 'Clara said this would be a healthy thing for me to do.'

Mam had been to three therapy sessions only to thank Emma and Kit for their generosity and announce: 'It was really useful, and I enjoyed it. Three sessions were plenty for me though.' And yet she often felt the need to namedrop 'Clara' in conversation, like some badge of honour but only for all the work she'd opted not to do.

'What about these Polly Pockets? They can go, surely?'

'Mum – I'm running around seeing stockists today. It's not a great time to make consequential decisions about which parts of my childhood to hold on to and which to forgo.'

A scoff. 'I don't know why you have to make everything complicated, Dyl.'

A man pushes past her. 'Look, I'm running late to meet Em and Ines.'

'That's nice.' Mam's voice softens. 'Try not to bicker, won't you?'

'We're adults now: we don't bicker.'

Mam's screaming silence sets off a rush of cortisol, warming Dylan's stomach with an old rage. She picks up her pace, says again that she has to go.

'It's great they've decided to move back, though, isn't it? I can't wait, all my girls home together again.'

This stops Dylan in her tracks as people rush either side. Her voice doesn't sound like her own when these words land in her mouth: 'Moving back.'

'Aye! They're coming in a few weeks, mind, to look for somewhere to live. It'll be good for her. She needs us – she's been having such a hard time. What with the miscarriage and ...'

Dylan knows Mam is welling up, can see her reaching for her charcoal bob as if to check it's still there, imbibing Ines's grief and rerouting it as her own.

'I can't chat anyway. There's loads to do yer – I can barely see the carpets.'

'Okay – bye, then.' Dylan collects herself and starts to push through the crowds. 'Wait. Mum?'

'Yes, love?'

'Don't you dare throw out Flumpy.' She hangs up, and the attachment to this old toy is self-revealing, like re-remembering your favourite colour by proxy. Dylan never placed a lot of importance in objects. When it came to her work the driving force was never the finished article – no matter the necklace or the earring, it was all merely decoration in the end. It was the process that held relevance: she liked what the pieces revealed. How, in coming from the same place, their imperfections and flaws were always different, each piece unique in how it fell apart and came together in her hands. Sisters were like that, and much like her pieces, something salient seemed to happen when they were all worn together.

★★★

It's been a while since Emma saw Ines. Longer still since they'd all been in the same room – likely eight or nine months, now that she thinks of it. Is that why she's nervous? She runs her hands over her suit to straighten it before sitting up taller in the high-backed chair. The waiter offers her a menu and she orders a bottle of white wine – they'll probably want the same. She feels her in the room before she sees her, lifts her head to the entrance where Dylan is withdrawing suspiciously from the hostess, a dozen bags thrown across her arms. She gestures she'd rather keep hold of them and Emma stands to greet her, which feels strangely formal.

'Sorry. Excuse me.' Dylan nips the backs of diners' heads as she makes her way through the restaurant towards her. 'This is fancy.'

Is that the first thing she can think to say? 'Not really.' Emma's defensive. 'It's just a hotel.'

'White tablecloths.' Dylan returns to the sentiment.

But Emma doesn't let this grate, instead starts unloading Dylan, placing the bags on the floor as she complains about people wanting to see everything before they'll commit to an order, unspooling the woollen scarf from around her neck. Emma pulls off her sister's hat and Dylan recoils at the infantilism in her gesture. 'You must be boiling in all this,' she perseveres.

'Of course she's late,' Dylan remarks, when she sits down, cradling her wine glass. Why is she wearing fingerless gloves? Emma resists the urge to tell her to hold it by the stem. That's when she sees Ines, in the reaction on Dylan's face.

'I'm sorry, I'm sorry, I'm sorry, I'm sorry – don't be pissed off at me. My audition ran late, okay?' She goes to Dylan first. 'Hi! Aren't you going to stand up and give me a hug?' She deflects the tension that's waiting for her here.

'Yeah, okay. Give me a second,' Dylan pinches, standing up.

Emma ventilates the awkwardness by interjecting: 'It's been ages, hasn't it? Busy lives. I'm glad we could do this, though.'

Ines embraces her then, mumbling something about the convenience of them all being in Cardiff on the same day.

'Well, I didn't just *happen* to be here. I drove up especially.' She smoothes the front of her suit again.

Ines validates this with a slight nod and something suckles on the angst. 'You'll be thrilled to know it's your time, Em.' She takes off her coat revealing herself. 'Trouser suits are finally in.'

Emma smiles curtly at the playful dig, and suggests she look at the menu. 'We've already decided what we're having.'

Ines asks the waiter several questions about the sides, if the tuna is cooked in butter and whether she could have that with the Dijon dressing instead. Once they've ordered, they turn their attention back to one another, how Dylan's meetings had gone with her stockists: good. How Ines's audition went: she was a little evasive on the subject. Emma doesn't flinch when it's her turn and neither of them goes beyond asking how Kit and the girls are. As Ines dominates the conversation, Emma thinks about bringing up the miscarriage. Watches her posture confidently with a swollen chest, breasts crushed by the strapless top that goes down past her waist over tailored trousers. She was used to this masking but it was always hard to see her youngest sister in pain.

'This horrible thing happened to me earlier.' Dylan reclaims the conversation. 'Do you remember the old lady on the raisin box?'

Emma shakes her head, tolerant of these wandering threads of thought.

'You know? The woman on Sun Maid raisins, that little red box. We used to eat them as kids.'

'What about her?' Ines asks, reluctant in tone.

'She's not old,' Dylan says earnestly, breaking the conspiracy. 'She's not old at all. At least not any more.' She draws up a picture on her phone and shows it to them. 'Look – she's really fucking pert and young. That means *we're* old.'

Emma laughs into her wine, and when Ines looks at the picture more closely, she's genuinely horrified. It's disconcerting how time can do this, shift familiarity into something unrecognisable. Ines signals to the waiter for another bottle. Dylan side glances Emma, as if annoyed: *I'm driving. I don't want it either.*

'How are you feeling, Ines?' Emma tries navigating towards what's really going on.

'Fine.' She sits up defensively and Dylan gives Emma a warning look: *Just leave her.*

But Emma feels overcome by this ambient anxiety generated by the three of them. The tension of a tight rope pulling – one side all childish glee cast in the humour of a shared childhood, yet it took only a second to lose your footing and find yourself in the chaos and uneasiness of those same years. Her sisters were both her resolve and pain point, and though she spent more time with Dylan, who came over and made an effort with the kids, she felt daunted by the idea of them all being back on home soil.

'It's official, then, or so I hear. You're moving back to Wales.' She watches Ines's shoulders tense, looking for the horror to be found in Dylan's open mouth.

'You're moving back?' Dylan steadies herself in the words, in what they might mean.

'Yes, we've just decided. We haven't really told anyone yet.'

'Noah told me.' Emma repositions her napkin. He'd also told her Ines wasn't coping and he wasn't sure how much more rejection she could take. He thought she needed to process what had happened and Emma had reminded him: it also happened to you.

'He didn't say anything to me.' Dylan finally pulls off the gloves.

'We haven't all lived in Wales since we were children. It'll be nice,' Emma offers and Dylan returns a closed-mouth smile: *Will it?*

She observes her sisters then, quick-footed in their conversation, not wanting to get stuck in the waterlogged marshlands of their childhood, both of them projecting into the future instead. And soon they will arrive there, at the desired destination, lucid in its disparagement of what they'd thought they wanted. Some great job, a child, a perfect studio they'd never been able to afford, inside which they'll realise they're still not happy. Still not those people. She wonders if she should warn them. Emma is the eldest, and she knew she'd never escape the chip on her shoulder that life had been harder for her because of the fact. Dylan was the classic middle child, the moderator, set on cementing herself in ease. And Ines, the baby, well, she'd always been the most dependent on them while being the most detached – Emma found this irritating. Though she'd never say so. And in always being one step ahead she can see exactly what her sisters are coming through. They have little consideration for this, so she keeps quiet, covers her glass when Ines tries to pour more wine and raises the other hand to signal for the bill.

1

Christenings

November

The baptism is held at the Methodist church where all the Wyn sisters were christened. The service must feel long to just about everyone, but most of all to Ines, who gets up midway through and walks back down the aisle. The congregation's eyes are on her, including those of her sister Dylan, which Ines can see rolling into the back of her head: *Do you always need to be so self-indulgent?*

In the church toilets, she hangs her head over a bowl, dry-retching into yellow bile-stained water, all that was left inside her. She starts to hear voices through the cloakroom window as people make their way outside, flushing her with relief: it's over. Emma's voice is the loudest, instructing her husband Kit to find Bun-bun, while he complains, searching the Tesla for the beloved rabbit. Their daughter Sunny is sobbing for her missing toy and Ines knows this feeling. Someone says what a beautiful day it is and when she looks up and out of the window from the toilet floor, she sees swallows soaring and dropping in the sky. She imagines the endless expanse of green surrounding the church and the thought asphyxiates her reality as she zooms out on herself. She hears Emma elongating her vowels as she talks to Kit's mother, the performance abrasive. It is a blessing that they rarely have to suffer their own extended family. She'd been surprised to see so many of them at the service; she could only assume it was a bid to balance the numbers against Kit's wide-jawed family. As kids she and her sisters had always been more interested in one another. It had carried them through and sometimes it had broken them up into tiny pieces, like the gingerbread men snapped apart for them to share as children.

A disapproving voice comes from outside the cubicle, filling the empty space: 'I can't believe you're hung-over, Ines. Today of *all* days.'

Surely a christening was a perfect day for a hangover, slow and boring, dulcet tones gathering around a beige buffet. But Mam hated them drinking. She had a limited perspective of their lives now, unable to acknowledge the full spectrum of roles that had befallen her daughters as adults. Ines assumed all mothers were like this, wanting to glaze their progeny in a childlike sheen to contain them in the version that was most recognisable to them.

She wished she'd gone home with Noah last night instead of dancing until God knew when. It was easier in London with her actor friends: contrived was what those people wanted. And that was better than stagnating in her watery bowl of feelings where she couldn't touch the sides. It had been light when she'd walked home barefoot. A flashback of kebab meat and the grate of her thumb against the polystyrene box. Her head out of the window as Noah drove them up from London this morning.

'You must be finished in there now, surely,' Mam persists, knocking more abruptly, engulfing all the oxygen left in the small church toilet.

Goosebumps proliferate on Ines's skin, swarming over bare arms as she traces this anxiety to where it has always lived. She pulls herself together, tucking away her unsightliness, swiping at the undesirable and the sickly throwback from the collar of her dress. She dabs her mouth with the coarse toilet paper and stands, readying herself as the version expected to emerge. She pulls back the chrome lock and catches Mam in motion, the cloakroom door held ajar as if she is about to give up and leave.

'Look at the state of you.' Her tut is so distinguished it echoes.

'I didn't drink *that* much. It's one of those undeserved hangovers that catches you off guard.' She glances at herself in the mirror – she looks awful – starts washing her hands in the basin. Mam says everything by saying nothing, taking her in under the LED strip lights, which she knows are only making her look worse. She closes the tap's water valve.

'What's the matter with you, love?' The cadence of her mother's Welsh accent is the first thing to have soothed Ines all day.

'Oh, you know . . .' She reaches for the right words to appease her, swallowing the thought that she'd be back living here in a month. 'He thinks it's going to help.' Her voice sounds strangled, suppressing a feeling she's worked hard to deflate.

'It'll be good for you both to be around family.' Mam reassures her. 'Emma and Dyl are looking forward to having you home, aren't they?'

But this isn't home, hasn't been for a long time. She holds on to either side of the basin, steadying her sway, managing not to retch. A tiny version of herself stands in her own head, spinning. They've been together for so long that it's difficult to see where one of Noah's goals starts and one of her dreams ends. They're part and parcel, all threads of desire looped back on themselves until it's impossible to decipher which ones are coming from her own heart.

Mam lets go of the door handle and places a hand on Ines's back. They look at each other in the mirror and she sees how their facial features layer onto one another's. Ines has always looked the most like her.

'Look, we'll all benefit from spending more time together, won't we? What with you and Noah getting married, you'll have your own family to think of soon, won't you? Trust me, you'll be grateful to have us all around then.' Mam takes a pale pink lipstick from her bag, knowing she'd already successfully talked Ines into it. 'You'll need a village. I didn't have that, of course, but you will.'

Ines observes the groove drastically worn down into the shape of her mother's Cupid's bow. Witnesses her excitement at having her youngest daughter back on her doorstep. Then again, she feels this terror of living, which she writes off as hangover angst. Tells herself instead that Wales is the right move, for both of them.

★★★

Outside the church, Emma discusses with Mam what the other guests are wearing.

'I don't know where she thought she was going.' Mam's nostrils pinch.

'I know. That's Kit's uncle's *third* wife. They're getting younger.' Ines emerges then and Emma's critical eye shifts to her. 'Why are you wearing black? I specifically asked you *not* to wear black.'

She looks down at the dress. 'It's navy.'

'Fuck off. No, it's not.' Emma looks for Kit, then spots him taking shade under a tree with his friends, their suits tailored and skin toffee-coloured from winters spent in the sun. Noah's there too, handsome but slightly out of place. He meets Emma's gaze and motions as if to slit his throat. She tuts disapprovingly but is amused. Watches him excuse himself with something that makes the other men laugh.

When he gets to her, he leans in to kiss her cheek. 'The service was lovely, Em. Congratulations.'

She's pleased by the affirmation, thanks him again for making the effort to drive up from London.

'We wouldn't have missed it, would we?' He turns to Ines, sympathetic, gliding his hand across her lower back and Emma envies their tactility. 'How are you feeling, babe?'

'Are you hung-over?' Emma goes for Ines. 'I knew you were.' Then, dialling up disbelief as ammunition: 'Is that vomit on your collar?'

Ines covers the offending evidence. 'Can you not attack me, please?' She puts her head into her hands like a child and leans forward. 'I really don't feel well.'

'No one's attacking you, drama queen.' Dylan joins the circle, and leans down to antagonise Ines's craning body. 'Just to clarify, though, that was you running out in the middle of the ceremony to throw your guts up?'

No matter how much she and her sisters grew up they would still meet each other as the children they'd once been, an impression that was as outdated as it was indelible. A swimming back to safety, or reassurance, to the version they had known most intimately.

'Emmie.' Kit interrupts her from a distance as he makes his way towards them with their daughter attached to his leg, lifting Sunny with each stride as he signals to her disapprovingly. She was meant to be sorting the photographer.

'Right.' She perks up. 'I am – yes.'

★★★

The photographer wipes his dank forehead with a hanky, reluctant to help Emma herd them for a family photo as she encourages Ines away from the wall and into the middle of the lawn. She feels the low hum in her body, the savage cadence that comes with her sisters. Her jaw tenses as she tells Mam to get off her phone, her attention then on Ines again, wondering about the black bags under her eyes, assuming she's not eating enough. Noah – who is lifting his chin to the camera – says something funny and Dylan erupts into laughter. Emma reprimands Sunny, coaxing her to give her best smile for the nice man and she retaliates by biting Kit's finger. He yelps in pain and Emma raises her hands to the sky with frustration. Baby Lilah is the only one to hold her composure on her big day and not ruin the photograph Emma so desperately wants to be perfect.

It is an effigy to their dislocation, to the natural disharmony characteristic of a family who, after spending long spells apart, trample their way back to informality. To Emma, they are an ensemble of ill-cast characters, somehow not quite in their right roles. But she decides she'll print and frame this picture and place it in the entranceway of her home, just to prove she isn't as uptight as they all claim she is.

★★★

Dylan can hear her niece Lilah crying, sick of being at the centre of the commotion. The reception is at the Tickled Trout pub that looks over the Wye valley. Sausage rolls sit alongside pastel Party Rings on trellis tables covered with cloths; people drink tired Diet Coke, lager shandy and Malbec from tiny wine glasses that hit their measurement marking. She observes young girls in their best dresses skid across carpets, laddering tights and competing with boys whose tiny limbs have been forced into suit jackets. People make polite conversation: *When was the last time I saw your little'en?* and *How's the new job going?*

Bored, Dylan goes to the bar where the lights in the frame overhead project down onto her stool. She orders a drink, and through the beer taps and shelves of glasses, she can just about see Emma on the other side of the bar, which services the adjoining function room. She's interrogating Noah on how Ines has been: not a lot better. On whether she's still seeing the therapist: she isn't. And how she's feeling about giving acting a break: she seems excited about it. He holds onto the brass pole running along the bar and pushes his weight back into himself. It's an adolescent motion. He's looking down at his feet as though shielding his guilt. And it annoys her that the family uses him like this, some oily rag to help clean up Ines's mess.

Dylan takes her drink and walks to the other side. 'What are you pair talking about?'

'Ines's audition. I just can't believe she didn't get it.' Emma sighs. 'She just can't catch a break, can she? And she deserves to. She's got the talent.'

'It's been nothing but audition after audition for the past few years,' Noah continues. 'She needs a break. It's killing her.'

'But it's her dream,' Dylan reminds them, 'and what is she going to do here? She's not Emma. She can't just do Pilates and live off her husband's money.'

'Oi! *That* family money is paying for the drinks, actually.' Emma goes to wrestle the glass from her hand and Dylan shrieks and slaps her away playfully. 'And did they accept your offer on the cottage?' Her face remoulds back to concern.

'That cottage near my studio?' Dylan straightens her back and brings her other hand to her glass.

'Yep. Old tenants are out already; we'll be in for Christmas. It's got a bit of land – the fresh air will be good for her.'

'You make her sound like a convalescing Victorian bride retiring to the sea.'

'Well, you don't really get how tough things have been.' His tone is a little off.

'Has anyone seen the baby?' Emma's unsubtle in her attempt to redirect the conversation. She cranes her neck, obviously searching for Lilah.

'What are you two thinking on the baby front? Have you talked about that yet?' Dylan presses, and that's when she spots her, Ines hiding behind a small chalkboard on the bar listing today's specials, ducking slightly to avoid being seen. Dylan considers outing her but is too amused at the sight of her baby sister who, after all these years, is still listening in on her conversations.

The Axminster carpet is being used as a dance floor where kids prance around, like leaping crickets. Dylan watches Ines, sitting alone at a table, necking her wine, wincing as though she's trying to remember how she likes it. She chews the edge of a cold pizza before getting up and discarding it in the bin.

'I saw that,' Mam says, accusatory, walking past them both with a gin and tonic. 'Try to eat something, will you?'

Ines would need to accustom herself to being exposed now, just as Dylan had when she'd moved back.

'Another shit show of an audition, then?' Dylan sidles up, making Ines snort wine through her nose.

'Fuck off.' Ines uses a shoulder to push her away.

'You didn't seem that positive when we had dinner.' Dylan pauses. 'You'll never top that flower you played. What was that for again?'

'A butter advert,' they remember in unison.

'Face tinged yellow, framed in a buttercup. God, you were cute.'

'Am cute. And that advert paid my rent for a year, actually.'

'How are you feeling about paying rent on a cosy cottage in Wales?' Ines doesn't appear to enjoy the assumption in Dylan's tone, but she can't help it. 'Not really where you saw yourself ending up, is it? Back here?'

Ines opens her mouth to defend herself, but her gaze travels over Dylan's head. She turns to see Mam dancing with Sunny. They watch and Dylan imagines that the same sensation is pulling in Ines. 'Maybe you're homesick,' she diagnoses.

'I'm not back for her.' Ines challenges her supposition.

'Mum's in a good mood.' Emma lands with the stench of stale smoke, Kit and Noah following her. 'I reckon it's because her favourite is moving home.'

'Well, if you can't beat 'em.' Kit pushes his glasses up his nose and removes his suit jacket to shake tight, awkward hips, better suited to holding him up as he conducts heart-valve replacements. Noah struts over to him, peeling off his own jacket and spinning it up in the air to reveal sweat marks on his shirt. He mouths, 'I love you,' at Ines. Dylan pulls her by the arm – she's a little unsteady on her feet – but they start singing the lyrics at one another, arms linking, and laughter sounding more like relief as they start to orbit around Mam.

1999

Two Years After They Moved to Laurel Road

Emma is twelve, Edi is eleven, Dylan is ten, Ines is seven

Emma looked out of the kitchen window, her furrowed brow reflecting back at her through the glass. She slumped back in Grampy's faded terracotta armchair, deflated, patent school shoes still on her feet, not quite touching the floor. Homework poured across the kitchen table where a biro had leaked, and Mam's wooden hairbrush lay abandoned from the morning, their hair still caught in it. Edi was pressed down on it too, half her face smothered on the wooden top, hair splayed out like an old black fishing net. She watched Emma carefully, knowing she'd issue instructions once she'd finished seething. The table took up most of the floor space, and they'd find themselves edging around it in an orderly queue to get to the fridge, which was awash with letters from the school to remind Mam about Christingle and Jeans for Genes Day. But it was Emma who would remember.

They were meant to be going for ice cream – Mam had promised. Only at the newsagent's a few streets away, but still. She'd forgotten, again, and hadn't been there when they'd got home from school. She always forgot things. They needed Edi to say something, anything, to break Emma's excruciating silence. Ines picked up the hairbrush and started brushing her hair.

'Let's go and play in the garden,' Edi said.

Emma, seemingly relieved by an interruption to her anger, shifted her bum forward so her feet could meet the floor. The rest followed, except Dylan.

Their garden was slim but long, with a large pear tree in the centre and a stone path that ran all the way down to a brown wooden shed. Emma, Edi and Ines assumed a circle around the tree, unsure what to do next, leaning awkwardly, slow and lethargic from the June heatwave. Sweat beaded on their foreheads, dampening identical hairlines as a wasp swarmed around a rotting pear that had fallen from the tree. Bored, Ines started batting it away.

'Stop it. You'll make her angry,' Emma scorned.

'No, you'll make it angry with your big fat frown.' She contorted her small wrists to push it away as it circled her head.

'Ines,' Edi spoke calmly, 'let's see if we can find that caterpillar again. It might have already turned into a butterfly.'

'Yes – Edi and I are going to look for the *caperpillar*,' Ines huffed, taking her hand.

Upstairs in her room, Dylan gently put her mouse back into its cage. Whiter than white, Cherry had been given her name on account of her red eyes. Mam hated her, but after it had happened, they'd each been allowed to choose one thing they wanted. Dylan said she should just be grateful it wasn't a tarantula. Cherry safely locked in, Dylan changed out of her uniform into an outfit that made her feel womanly. She came downstairs, emerging from the conservatory, cavorting her hips.

'Get that off, now!' Emma yelled. 'Right now, Dylan.'

'Don't be mean.'

'Take it off.'

'No.'

'RIGHT NOW.'

Dylan twirled in the skin-tight skirt, which clung to pointed hip bones and revealed bare legs through slits that ran up each side. The matching tank top had a thick turquoise strip that ran across her bony chest. Emma was in no mood, not after today's disappointment, and the fact that Mam wasn't there to intervene left her annoyance threadbare. Nothing could just be hers. Everything was at risk of being purloined by her sticky-fingered sisters.

Ines was still hunting caterpillars further up the garden, the sun streaming down, dark strands of hair clinging to her damp neck. Edi was in the shed. Having spotted her through the window, Ines pulled open the wooden door by its rusty lock. 'What are you doing, Edi?' she moaned.

She was sitting inside the dark hut on a small stool, among the broken Wendy houses, the discarded bikes with stabilisers, and an old Roses tin filled to the top with Grampy's marble collection. Ines saw that she was crying but this didn't surprise her. Edi was often found sobbing in the small corners of their home, encouraging them to join in, insisting they needed to grieve.

'What's wrong now, Edi?' Ines whined unsympathetically.

Her head was hanging down over cupped hands, and Ines could see she was holding something.

'Did you find the *caperpillar*?' She started climbing over the mountain of jumble, allowing the door to slam behind her.

There, cradled in Edi's hands, was a small hatchling. Its feathers were still shiny and its head was balding, not thick enough to conceal its flesh. Its claws were taut, gesturing to the air, its ebony beak open, revealing a blood-red mouth. Ines gasped.

'I found it just now by the fence; it must have fallen out of Glenys's tree.' A tear hit the down of the bird's feathers.

'What shall we do?' Ines asked obligingly. She already knew the answer, so turned her head to watch Emma pinning Dylan between her legs, the tank top pulled over her head.

Edi wheezed, 'We should bury him, give him a funeral.'

Ines held the door open for her sister. As they emerged back into the garden, their eyes had to squint to readjust to the brightness of the grass. She walked over to Emma who was clawing her skirt off a topless Dylan now, stopping when they saw the bird, which shut them both up.

'Not another one,' Dylan said mercilessly.

'We're burying it,' said Ines, matter-of-factly, dragging the shovel behind her.

Dylan remarked that it was just a bird and Emma gave her a heated stare.

'No, it's sad,' Edi said sharply. 'He died here and it's really sad. We should bury him.'

'Okay,' Dylan relented. 'Emma will dig, but I'm only coming to the funeral if I can wear her tank top.' She crossed her arms indignantly. Emma rolled her eyes and handed it to her, looking to Edi for instructions on what to do next.

Dylan was sent inside to search for Mam's black crochet table mats, which she eventually found in the drawer of the wooden dresser. She placed one over her head and handed out the rest to them as they knelt among the rotting pears. They waited for Emma to finish digging. The soil was dry, and it took all her strength to part the earth into a small crevice in the ground.

They circled around the hole and Edi said it would be nice if Dylan sang a song, which she did, making up the words to 'Ave Maria' from under her mourning veil. Edi then lowered the hatchling into the ground, and together they started to push the earth over it, their white hands becoming one as they spread the mud until the final feather was covered. They watched through the black patterned holes of their veils as Edi collected two twigs and used the black hairband on her wrist to connect them. As she pushed the handmade cross into the ground gently, they all sobbed together, grieving like she'd taught them to.

Once they'd stopped crying, they sat for a while, silent but for the insects swarming around decaying fruit and the sound of the radio coming from the neighbour's garden.

'Mam!' Ines squealed, jumping up and running back to the house.

Edi got up slowly and made her way sombrely back inside. Dylan followed, the sadness about the baby bird discharged by an eagerness to show off her new outfit.

'We're having chip butties, girls,' Mam announced loudly, so that Emma might hear from the overgrown lawn. 'What's the matter with you all?' she asked, catching sight of the tear-stricken faces.

They looked away, not wanting to get into trouble, Emma still sitting on the grass with her stubbornness.

'Em, are you coming in or what?' Mam shouted, holding the handle of the conservatory door.

She got up reluctantly then, pulling the black crochet mat off her head and collecting the others, which were scattered around the bird's grave. She took her time, carrying the shovel back to the shed before making her way down the garden towards Mam. 'We were supposed to be getting ice cream.'

Mam ignored this. 'What've you been doing out here?'

'A baby bird died. It was sad so we buried it.'

'Right.' She looked over Emma's head at the small mound of soil and sighed.

'It was Edi's idea,' she said defensively.

'Go and get cleaned up, and give your sisters a hand. I'll get the oven on.'

'But where've you been?' she pushed with her frustration.

Mam tapped her nose and told her not to pry. Emma did as she was told, closing the conservatory door behind her, placing the table mats back in the drawer as Mam stood looking out at the garden, muttering under her breath, then calling to them that she wouldn't tell them again. 'The neighbours will think you're odd as cod, mind, if you keep burying things out yer.'

Moving House

December

On the drive up to Wales, Ines doesn't say much, just stares out of the window while Noah sings along to the radio. They pass endless green hills only to find more green hills, lush and verdant landscape fertile for renewal, or something. The word 'slow' painted on the roads turns to 'ARAF', taunting her after they cross the Severn Bridge: ARAFWCH NAWR. The landscape is scruffy, fields full of sheep with red numbers painted on shaggy coats, as if they're making a political statement. She looks around at all the green she's agreed to: there are so many hills to die on. Perhaps this was all happening too fast. She looks back at their canvases in the rear mirror, bubble-wrapped and leaning against one another on the back seat – a diptych – splattered with acrylic one Sunday morning in a hung-over daze. It had been her idea and they'd fucked on the sofa afterwards, the black paint still drying on their hands. Ines had felt nostalgic this morning. Their warehouse flat seemed idyllic to her as she and Noah had finished loading up and she'd fingered through their memories, replaying them like vinyls. Noah had been climbing the walls there, sick of watching her cave in on herself on the kitchen floor. *Get up, Ines, please get up.*

    She'd heard him somewhere outside herself that night, pleading, as she'd crawled around on the tiles after another shitty audition, looking for her centre of gravity and positioning her body so that the room might give in and stop spinning. Her hands were wet and stringy with vomit. He had told her the next day he wanted to move home and she'd insisted he was overreacting. She'd been bartering with him for more time: once she'd graduated there was no exact need for them to stay in London and it had got harder to keep him there. He was right about some of it. She was wrecked from bending herself into unthinkable shapes to fit through audition doorways; she needed to recover something of herself. Even so, she'd managed to persuade him to hold out, let her try for a few more roles. He went quiet on the subject again for a while. Until one night they fell drunkenly into bed with a girl from her improv class. It was silly, really, hadn't meant anything. The girl had been sheepish the next morning, kissing them goodbye, pulling the heavy warehouse door behind her. Noah asked how the hell that could've happened, like he hadn't been there the whole time, and Ines paused to consider it, sitting up in bed next to him, a mug of coffee wrapped in her hands.

'I suppose I don't mind the idea of sharing you. In a way I've always had to.'

'I want to go home, Ines.'

And she knew that time he meant it.

They start driving through narrower country lanes, getting deeper into the rabbit warren. It's too late to back out. The surrounding houses are decorated with Christmas lights but in the daytime switched off, something about them doesn't add up. As they slow down at a junction, a reindeer on a lawn with a wide grin goads her with its red nose. When they pull up outside the eighteenth-century cottage, which is now her home, birds' nests are buried in the stone and ivy trained up its sides. Discarded terracotta pots have weeds growing in them and empty glass jars are lined with dark moss and filled to the brim with rainwater. Ines can sense Noah's excitement. She watches the feathered birds returning to feed their young, wonders if they do so out of love or obligation.

'This is us then, the new pad.' He twinkles as he puts his hand on her thigh and she looks down at it. They haven't been intimate since she'd lost the baby, and he'd been careful about how he touched her recently, as if she were some frail half-formed thing. But there's something suggestive about his fingers on her inner leg now.

'We'd better get our stuff out. The others will be here soon.' She turns her head, the condensation from her breath appears before her on the glass.

'You always say how much you miss them. Now you'll have them on your doorstep.'

But a wistful wish for spending more time with one's family isn't often something one wants to happen practically.

'This is going to be good for us,' he says, as they get out of the car. 'Look at all of this land.' He points across at the several acres they're renting with the cottage. 'I'm going to plant and grow our food, and we've got our own water supply. Here, come and see the well—'

'Sounds great,' Ines cuts him off, holding a pressing question: *And what will I do here?*

It was easy for Noah: he already had an established client base, most of which was based in Toronto and LA, meaning he could work wherever he wanted. She was pulling back from her career. She couldn't take the audacious prodding and poking, the 'Can we just see you with your top off?' and 'How old did you say you were again?' The limited range of parts with vacuous, dull-as-ditch-water lines in the shadow of the wryly complex characters she always saw herself playing. She was burned out by the dwindling insecurities that filled in her agent's excuses: 'They wanted someone a little more underdeveloped'; 'They went with someone who had more experience in horse riding'; 'They need someone less obviously beautiful.' She had sat in the lap of powerlessness, and she had crumbled.

It's freezing as they ferry the boxes inside. Ines takes some plants out and hangs a couple from the white hooks left by previous tenants, startling and lush against the bright white walls, yet constricted in the new space, having grown to fit different corners. Then there's the sound of tyres on the gravel. She stands on tiptoe to see out of the tiny window at the back of the cottage to the large drive. Emma is waving frantically at Noah through the windscreen while Dylan, in a hat and scarf, holds a cardboard tray of coffees somewhat reluctantly.

Another vehicle pulls up on the gravel. It's the removal people, whom she hears Emma immediately start to instruct. Thank God. She really needs them here today. Her bones feel heavy now – even unpacking the cutlery from bubble wrap exhausts her. She wants to tell them she's going for a lie-down but she needs to ask Dylan to put the bed together, so she goes downstairs to say hello, wondering if there's still time to convince herself of the future that's on offer.

★★★

'Did you bring a screwdriver?'

'Yes, I brought my screwdriver, Noah. It's part of the larger realm of my tool kit. Honestly, I don't know how you pair managed in London.'

Dylan walks to the other side of the bed, which is currently disassembled bits of wood and loose screws. She gathers her hair into a disorderly bun. Through the exposed sides of her khaki dungarees, Noah sees the folds of her stomach as she reaches down for the drill. Feels his ears getting hot. Perhaps he's nervous at being in a room on his own with her. He knew she was the least supportive of Ines giving up acting, but it wasn't for ever. And she had been so absorbed in her own work, she had no idea how badly Ines had taken losing the baby. It had been Emma who had checked in daily, sent flowers and bath salts in the post.

'Are you going to help, or will you just stand there gormless?'

He shrugs and offers her a plate of chopped fruit. She could always eat, always had a taste for more: more questions about how they were choosing to live, and always more men, which offers itself up to him as a conversation starter:

'How's it going with that Oliver fella, then?'

'Oh, would you spare me from regaling tales of my catastrophic love life?' She sinks her teeth into the watermelon, eyes dark like the seeds.

'It's only catastrophic because you engineer it to be.'

He resents how Dylan conducts herself in matters of the heart – much in the same way she's consuming that piece of fruit – voracious and feverish, abandoning it without a second thought. She wipes some of the juice from the corner of her mouth and lets out a laugh he recognises as forced.

'What?' There's irritation in her tone.

He shakes his head, and she gestures that they should get going, asks him to hold the other side of the bed. 'This place is so near my studio.'

It's as though she's saying this to herself and he can't decipher whether she thinks it's a good thing. He was looking forward to spending more time with Emma and the girls, to hanging out with Dylan more. He passes her another part, observing as the fallen wooden bones start to resemble a bed frame. Moving the conversation to her work, he congratulates her on the studio, telling her how brilliant it is to see her having all this success. He's unsurprised by the disclosure that she finds it a headache more than anything else: most of the famous people want to wear her designs for free. She's never been easily impressed. Then, with the modesty that has genetically bypassed Ines, she redirects the conversation.

'Now where do you want the bed?' She brings her hands to her hips. 'Let's move it into place before I fix the slats. Come on, I've got things I need to get done for myself today. Ines forgets, but I do have my own life.'

They lift it together, carrying it between the paint-chipped bay windows that look out over the garden backing onto a small wood. Noah lingers on the subject. 'Emma constantly shares updates and sends us links to all the press you're getting. She's probably got one of those colour-coordinated folders, you know, like she does for Sunny's drawings.'

'That would be a bit much.' She tucks some stray strands of hair behind her ears. 'Now concentrate.'

'Okay, where does this bit go?'

'That's part of the container the bed was delivered in.'

He can see she's trying to decipher if he's being serious. He places it down, deliberate in his gawkiness, and she laughs. But this time it's a noise from the deep concaves of her belly, a port key to the young girl on the swings with bulging cheeks. This sensation happens with all three of them. They can transport him back to those doe-eyed creatures, high off sass, giddy from Mr Salem's sugar-dipped sweets. Even as a kid he could see the rot inside them, a chaos that drew him in as he'd watched them at the front of the house through his nan's bedroom window.

She asks questions about the wedding, and he's underwhelmed by this small talk, deliberates whether they'll really get into it. His replies, deliberately clipped, can tell she's not interested in the questions coming out of her mouth. So, he downplays it, calling it an excuse for a party.

'It's not just a party, though, is it? It's a pretty big deal, getting married.'

'We've been together so long, we're practically married anyway.' But he can tell by the arch of her brow it's the wrong thing to say: 'I know what you think, DW, that I'm trying to paper over things with all this.'

'That's not what I said.' Her tone is sure.

'You don't need to.' He takes the drill out of her hand. 'Your thoughts are as loud as this bloody thing.'

'You don't have unlimited access to my mind.'

'No. Only your sisters have that.'

She snatches the drill. 'Gimme that. You'll hurt yourself.'

'I know what happened can't be fixed by some stupid ring and a party. But it's still the logical next step, for Ines and me.'

'And all I said is a wedding isn't *just* a party.' She makes out like he's overreacting and he stares down at the carpet, dissociating, thinking about his odd socks.

'I'm sorry,' she musters, and he wonders if she means about her hesitance around their engagement or about the baby. 'I am happy, for you both.'

He'd forgotten this need for their approval, one that kneaded into him whenever he was back in Wales. The Wyns operated from two stances: in denial of how intense the three of them were together; or in complicity, harnessing their swell to intimidate outsiders. Dylan picks up another piece of watermelon and bites into it, shrugs as if to imply she can't help it.

'Are you pair almost done?' Ines appears, loose-limbed, her slight frame holding self-consciously in the doorway.

'Ugh, yeah,' he says, unsure, looking to Dylan for confirmation. 'Yeah?'

She tells Ines she's done.

Ines pulls his attention to more crucial matters in the bathroom, like where he wants his toiletries to live.

★★★

'You got them a tree?' There is surprise in Dylan's tone as she walks into the living room and leans against a radiator next to Ines.

'Pretty, isn't it?'

'It's only an old one.' Emma plays down the gesture. 'We had a few extra decorations lying around so I thought I may as well bring it over. Kit likes to have real ones.' She tells the movers where she wants the sofa as she unwinds the cord from the back of the vacuum cleaner. 'You could help.' There's accusation in the suggestion.

'But I'm so tired, Em.' Ines mimics the stance of her eight-year-old niece and Emma looks to Dylan: *What's your excuse?*

Dylan rolls her eyes, starts moving objects around and asking Ines where she wants this and that, unimpressed that they're already fawning over her. Emma vacuums and polishes until the house smells just like hers. It's not long before all the furniture is spread across the cottage. The bare walls and empty corners emphasise how much bigger it is than their flat in Walthamstow. Dylan thinks their mid-century teak sideboard and low-set armchair look misplaced and suggests a second-hand furniture store where you can part-exchange things. Noah takes down the details; Ines doesn't say anything. Emma then lights the scented candle she'd bought as a housewarming gift. No one had bought Dylan a gift when she'd moved into her flat. 'I must have forgotten mine,' she remarks, and Noah throws a ball of bubble wrap at her.

They go into the living room and Ines draws her attention to their diptychs. 'We painted one each.' She smiles at them proudly. 'Aren't they something?'

'Bit cheesy, isn't it?' Dylan retaliates, and Emma frowns at her: *Can you try and make an effort?*

'Guess who painted which?' Ines continues. And Dylan is quick to say which is Noah's.

'How can you tell?' Ines asks, irked they've won the game.

Emma's eyes widen, high from playing house, flouncing curtains and setting lamps on side tables. 'We just can. This one is, well, it's . . .' She stands up, tilts her head in front of the canvas. 'It's unhesitating. It's rash and free-swinging but without trying to be.'

'And mine?' Ines asks pointedly.

Dylan's relieved when Noah interrupts them, before she's had time to give her opinion, which is that Ines's painting is all over the place, doesn't know what the fuck it's doing.

'A toast, then?' he says, a tray of glasses and a bottle of Moët tucked under his arm. 'To our new gaff.'

'Just a small one for me.' Emma dithers. 'I'm driving.'

The champagne cork pops and there's over-pour.

'What's left in here?' Dylan goes towards a box discarded in the corner of the room and starts to pull things out.

'No!' Ines shouts at her. 'Not that one.' She snatches the box from the floor, quickly gathering its contents: the tiny hand-knitted booties, a packet of soft cotton Babygros, one fluffy grey hippo.

'Shit.' Dylan presses the weight into her knees, tries to ground herself. 'Sorry, Inny, I didn't know.'

Ines storms into the hallway, and they listen to her throw the box under the stairs, slamming the door. Emma looks at Dylan disapprovingly: *Really?* She stands perfectly still, the hair on the back of her neck raised by the echo of what she'd said on the drive over: that Ines's denial wasn't healthy, wasn't helping her. When she comes back into the room, they awkwardly salute with their glasses, and not long after Emma says she'd better get back to the girls for bedtime. On the drive home Dylan tries to recover her guilt, pushing away the thought that it's possible some unconscious part of her had opened that box on purpose.

1999

Two Years After They Moved to Laurel Road

Emma is twelve, Edi is eleven, Dylan is ten, Ines is seven

They wore pastel bathing suits that tied at the back of their necks. Emma's was sugary-speckled pink, Edi's pastel blue, Dylan wore pale yellow, and Ines lilac.

'Right, come on, get in, Inny,' one of them urged.

'I don't want to get my hair wet.' Ines stood on the shoreline, hands wedged under her armpits.

Dylan was already sitting inside the yellow dinghy, holding the handles on either side, scowling as she was tossed about by the waves.

'Come on, get in behind Dyl.' Edi's costume was soaked up to her belly button.

'Get in!' Emma was flooded with frustration. 'Just get in or go and find Mam on your own.'

Ines looked back. Mam was still nowhere to be seen. She couldn't face wandering up to the bar where she might find her laughing too loudly at the Spanish waiter's jokes, smoking his cigarettes with the picture of a camel on them. All she could see were fat tummies turning pink and freckled faces biting into ice-cream cones. *On her own*, sang at her, the hot sand splattered with bright towels, homemade picnics, and orange bottles of sunscreen. She thought about wandering back to the cool box to start on the chicken-paste sandwiches. At least then they wouldn't be soggy.

'Oi, Poo Head!' Dylan shouted at her. 'Stop being a scaredy-cat.'

'Shut up,' Ines moaned, and everyone laughed as she made her way into the sea, squealing whenever a wave crashed against her chest and jumping up in a bid to stay dry.

'Hold it still,' she whined, as Emma and Edi battled with the boat, their hair gathered into thick clumps encrusted with sand. She rested a hand on Edi's shoulder to lever herself in, her bottom squeaking against the plastic inflatable as she jammed herself between Dylan's skinny legs. She reached out a hand to Emma, who lifted a foot onto the side of the boat and scrambled in. Last in was Edi, who took the plastic oars attached to its sides and passed them up, using her arms to lift herself in so they were stacked like cups.

'Move down now.'

'There's no room yer for me.'

'Push. Push. Push,' Emma encouraged, laying her head back against the boat.

Ines looked over the side, down into the water as it got deeper. Over the course of their adventure, they saw five big fish, five million small ones, a Coca-Cola bottle, and some seaweed. There were two almost-sightings of mermaids, one of which turned out to be more seaweed tangled with a dead bloated fish; the second remained an unconfirmed sighting.

'Still none, Emma,' Ines shouted back, as they made their way into deeper waters.

'Don't worry, we'll find some,' Edi reassured her.

'For God's sake! I'm doing all the rowing.'

'No, you're not.'

'Stop breathing on me.'

'You're on my side.'

They bickered like that for some time. Emma took her turn at rowing. Then Ines insisted on having a go, which meant they were in the hands of the tide and its intents. But eventually they came across exactly what they were looking for.

'There they are!'

'Where?'

'I can't see them.'

'Look – just there.'

Emma took the oar and manoeuvred the boat towards the smack of jellyfish.

'Oh, they're beautiful.' Ines gazed down into the water, leaning against the yellow dinghy, which was hot against her chin and smelt like salt.

The jellyfish twisted beneath the boat. Their gelatine bodies reminded them of the translucent aspic Mam would glaze over meat when people came for dinner. The creatures contracted and relaxed their bell-shaped heads. The uneven, wavy edges of their tentacles were joined by longer arms that drifted through the sea like shoelaces.

'They have no brain, no heart, no bones, and not even any eyes,' Edi mused.

'No heart,' Dylan pondered. 'They're like Emma, then.'

Emma pushed her so hard that she let go of her paddle, and Ines trying to move out of the crossfire let go of hers so it dropped into the sea. They watched them float down, hitting the rocky bottom.

'Ah, now look what you've done.'

'Emma should go in for them! This is her fault.'

'She could die.'

'Don't be dramatic.'

They argued about what they were going to do, how they'd get back to shore, and who should be the one to jump in to retrieve the paddles. They considered that it might be too deep, an impossible distance to hold their breath. Ines clapped and laughed, amused by the rigmarole as the dancing medusas with their clear bodies and speckles of neon purple glowed through the water. Then came a loud splash. Edi had dived in head first, palms pressed together, holding her breath and anticipating the prickling, stinging pain. Her arms contracted and relaxed, contracted and relaxed as she pushed herself further and further down into the expanse of the sea. But not having enough air, she retreated back to the surface, spluttering and coughing, and it was as if they could all feel the stings against their skin.

She took no notice of Emma brandishing an arm for her to grab hold of. 'You see. I told you, it's too deep. Get out, Edi!'

She gasped and filled her lungs, shot back down through the water and the sadistic smack floating around her.

There was a hysterical scream then, which drew their attention back to the shoreline to where Mam was making a commotion. She looked ridiculous, waving her arms around frantically like that. They could see the lifeguards starting up an orange speedboat, and it occurred to them then how small they seemed, like little Lego men.

The plastic oars were retrieved and they all pulled Edi out of the water, all eight limbs enmeshed and reaching for one another. She started to cry then, and they stroked the sore lashes that were red across her cheek.

Then the ecstatic groan of the speedboat's engine came up behind them.

'*¿Estan bien chicas?* Is anyone hurt?'

Later back at their apartment, where the tiles were white and the dead cockroach Ines had killed earlier that morning had birthed multiplicitous offspring, Emma got an earful from Mam. They couldn't afford holidays abroad; in fact, they'd never been on holiday before – Mam had won the trip at bingo. There was only one bedroom, but the sofa in the living room pulled out into an extra bed where Emma, Edi and Dylan slept. Ines would creep in at night so they could all sleep together.

Mam ranted as she soothed the stings with warm water and something that was 'extortionate' from the chemist. 'You were meant to be watching them. I don't know what the hell got into you.'

'It's not my fault,' Emma said, glaring down at the floor, cheeks plump with disgrace. And then, under her breath: 'You should have been watching *us*.'

Emma Wyn

1. When Emma is born she has jaundice. Mam jokes that she looked like one of those yellow rubber chickens used by comedians.

2. When she's five she refuses to eat anything that isn't baked beans on toast, and later in life when her therapist asks, she tells him, 'I've hated eating for as long as I can remember.'

3. At the age of seven Emma witnesses her father doing something so terrible to Mam that she starts drawing it in crayon on every piece of paper she can find until Mam starts hiding them. It's the first time she ever experiences shame.

4. She knows that sometimes when her sisters enter a new space, they all feel the chill at the back of their necks – sensing the remnants of those who have previously suffered in it – even though they don't like to talk about that.

5. She's seventeen the first time she ever has sex; the second time is a one-night stand and she hates every second. She marries the next man she sleeps with.

6. Emma still allows herself one cigarette a week, on a Friday after the children have gone to bed; she'll sit cross-legged and smoke in front of the fireplace.

7. She is the only one to have ticked all the boxes – marriage, offspring, mortgage – and she sometimes feels smug about that.

8. She knows one joke, about a deaf man losing his shoes, which she tells each year around Christmas time.

9. She will soon realise the baby in her nightmares isn't who she thinks it is.

1979

Gwendoline is ten

Gwendoline stood listening to the sound of her mam's breath. On each exhalation she could smell all traces of her childhood: the fatty batter mix from the cakes she'd made; the grass stain on her favourite Sunday-school dress; the clips she'd get around the back of her ear; and the sourness of being bathed once a week in dirty water, putrid and unwanted.

Her mam's dark hair fell over her face and she was hypnotised by the needle and thread moving in and out, in and out. Gwendoline lifted up the pocket she was attaching to her brother's jacket. What a good thing it was to be a pocket. She tried to imagine herself as one. To be useful. To be able to hold important things and be a home for them. She reached down with both hands towards her shoes, which pinched her feet, her hair falling towards the floor.

'Don't be idle, Gwendoline. Go, take yourself outside for a while now.'

'But it's raining.' She stretched back up, resting her forearms on the grey arm of the settee where she sighed, her breath warm.

'They're gonna get soaked,' her mam tutted, raising her eyes to the sound of the rain hitting against the window.

Her father, usually more obliging of her bored spells, had taken Llewelyn for a routine hospital appointment and she'd already played with her dolly all morning. She looked out at the heavy dark clouds, which seemed to worsen the pull for reassurance. And although she could tell she was the cause of irritation, was some line in a song her mam could never get out of her head – even if she wanted to – she couldn't bring herself to move away. So, she continued her approach, walking from the side of the sofa and sitting down next to her mam.

'*Iesu mawr!* Careful!' She sucked the tip of her finger. 'Look what you made me do.'

Gwendoline couldn't see blood, but leaned over as if to kiss it better and her mam quickly withdrew, disturbed by this gesture of affection. She couldn't think what to do so she continued to watch her stitching the pocket, burning with shame as she imagined the thread going through her skin, in and out, finally tying off her ache. Her need for closeness a reflex more than a conscious choice, she placed the side of her cheek on her mam's shoulder.

'Oh, for goodness' sake, Gwendoline, you're all over me.'

Then came the sound of the key in the front door.

'Ah!' The air flooded with relief. 'You're back.' Her mam got up quickly, discarding her stitching, making her way over to her brother. '*Mae fy machgen hardd adref!*'

Sunday Lunches

January

The carpets are red. Weren't they meant to be cream? The stairs are narrow and wooden like Mam's. The colours of her mind all shades she doesn't recognise. Music is playing upstairs and she's following the noise only a woman could make – gore and grime and fluid spilling out. She couldn't feel her own body. Was she in it? Perhaps she was in the other woman's body. She could hear a heart beating, the blood pounding all around her. The stairs stretch out ahead. She hears the woman sigh and smells the sickly, putrid death in her mouth. On the landing her waters have broken and the carpets are sodden; they squelch beneath her weight. There is light behind the bathroom door. She hesitates but the woman is calling to her. It's quiet and dark inside, and she recognises her childhood bathroom, the basin where she brushed her sister's teeth, the tub where they bathed together, wet limbs, and the smell of the soap they took chunks out of with milk teeth. The dreadful thing, though, is in the tub. She walks closer and the tub moves nearer. She looks over and a baby is face down in the water, a stiff figurine, like a doll, hovering on the surface, waiting to be played with. She must have forgotten she was in there.

Emma wakes screaming and someone is holding her shoulders and telling her to calm down. She is back in her body, her pyjama top damp, sticking to her back. Wet hair clings to the side of her face. Someone is saying over and over again: *It's just a nightmare, Emmie. Calm down. It's a dream.*

'Mummy ...'

She comes back to find herself in her marital bed where Kit's hands are clasping tightly at her shoulders. His eyes are wide.

'It's okay, Sunny. Mummy's fine. She just had a bad dream, that's all.'

Emma digs her nails deeper into the sheets: 'Where's Lilah?'

'In her cot, she's probably still asleep. Emmie—'

But she's up and out of bed, rushing the length of the landing that runs in a large square around the top floor of the house and straight into Lilah's bedroom to find her standing in her crib, trying to fit a sheep on the mobile into her mouth. 'Oh, my sweet baby.' She lifts her out, sleeping bag still attached at her shoulders, and draws her tightly to her chest.

'We're having pancakes,' Sunny announces from the landing.

'What?' She stumbles. 'Oh, no, you won't eat your Sunday lunch.'

'Oh, come on, don't be a bore. I haven't had a weekend off in weeks and Sunshine wants pancakes.'

Emma looks at her husband, holding hands with her daughter and sharing the wide-eyed expression he gave to her. He'd been working even longer hours at the hospital recently and she hadn't heard him complain once.

'You had another one?' he asks then, sympathetically.

She nods.

'Is Mummy crying?' Sunny asks, surprised.

'Oh, no, I'm fine, darling. It was just a nightmare.'

'Those are happy tears, aren't they? Mummy's excited about pancakes. Go downstairs and let the dogs out, Sunshine. We'll be down in a minute.'

Sunny looks at her mother cautiously and then back at her father before letting a grin rip, her voice shrill as she races down the stairs calling after Barney and Barley.

'You've got to do something about this.' He makes his way into the baby's room, tightening the belt on his dressing gown.

'I know.'

Kit takes Lilah from her and leans her against his shoulder. 'Why don't you take a minute to pull yourself together? Have a shower. I'll keep Sunny busy. We're all fine, Emmie. We're okay.'

'You're right, I'm sorry. Just give me ten and I'll come downstairs and start prepping lunch.' She injects lightness into her tone, and he sighs heavily, walking away with her baby.

★★★

A twenty-minute drive away, Ines lies in bed thinking about the seeds in the garden set to rest by Noah in their black beds and the roots that would be growing out of them by now, arms reaching through the soil. It had been only a month or so, but something had settled between them in Wales. She would sit, watching him garden, while she made pots of coffee and dressed in jumpers over short dresses, causing his gaze to revert to her. Noah loved to be in nature, and she'd always loved to be wherever he was. It felt like being back was working, which had taken her by surprise. She was drinking less – Noah had commented on it – and although she still felt her overall condition was of exhaustion, she wondered if something might be lifting.

She lies facing him, her dark hair sprawling across the pillow. 'I like the mornings here.'

'Me too.' He turns to face her.

'There's something comforting about the birds and the rabble of wildlife . . .' She grins. 'I also like it when you shout at the rabbits.'

'I've tried everything to keep them from that damn kale. I can't believe the fuckers got through the crop cage again. What a rip-off! I'm going to have to construct something myself.'

She kisses the frown on his forehead. She'd always liked that he was unflinching. He knew what he believed in and that meant by association she stood for something too. Obsessed with the natural world, he felt humans had tried to cauterise themselves, but he didn't see them as separate from it, rather a by-product. He was always rescuing small, injured creatures; she'd recently found a mouse housed in a designer shoebox, pressed up against the radiator in her bedroom: 'He needs to keep warm.' She liked how he ate edamame beans in their shell, the heads of prawns and didn't see an apple as finished until he'd consumed the entire core.

She tunes back in to him preaching about the privilege of being able to sustain themselves and grow their own food, how rewilding is a theory they can integrate across different parts of their lives:

'It's a way to reach climactic biodiversity. You can rewild anything. You can rewild a relationship—' he presses a finger to her head '— your mind—' he draws it to her breastbone, then gently runs it down over her soft, concave stomach '—even your body.'

'How do we do that?' she whispers, feeling warmth between her thighs.

'Let me show you.'

His hand moves further down her body, and she opens her legs. He kisses her mouth and gently moves two fingers up inside her as she moans. She pushes back her shoulder blades and lifts her pelvis. Pressing his face into her neck, he tells her she's wet, and he kisses her slowly along the side of her face until their lips meet. Pushing his finger into her mouth, she sucks making him draw a breath, satisfied by the feel of him hardening. They kiss more, hungry, pushing their bodies against one another. She is always like this with him: defenceless, wanting. Her body is quivering, and she makes the familiar noise when he pushes himself inside her; she knows how much he loves that noise. He rasps, pushing his way in and out, her legs wrapped around his waist, hands clasped.

But then something happens. A sudden collapse that brings her back, causing each thrust to hit a piece of her she doesn't want to feel, like the sharp jolt of sensitive teeth where bone turns soft. She resists his hot breath on her neck as the sensation travels further and further, under the lining of her stomach and up through her throat. She wants to tell him to stop. But he continues to traverse the warm surface of her skin and she's crazed he hasn't noticed she's not in it. But this resistance trapped in her body doesn't collide with her desperation for him. For him to yearn for her. To desire her more than anything else. She doesn't need to be aroused for that; she can succumb to ease instead. She tucks her head over his shoulder and relishes his soft, boyish moans until he finally collapses into the pillow. He moves his hand under himself and down between her legs, but she pushes at his shoulders. 'No, I'm okay, that was perfect.'

★★★

A ten-minute drive away, Dylan wakes up feeling dehydrated with a bruised soreness between her thighs. Her bed faces French windows that look out onto the river Severn. The tops of the windows are stained glass and there are numerous plant pots along the window ledges — some look livelier than others, more resistant to her neglect. She sits up in bed, pulls the mustard linen covers up around her to protect against the cold. It's one of those perfect mornings, sunny with a blue sky, cold and crisp, the river high along the bank. She looks down at Ollie, a freckled arm thrown across her waist, his red-blondish hair tousled, smelling like cucumber and salt — clean but lived in. And knowing she was going to do this — having decided on it weeks ago — didn't mean she took any pleasure in it.

'Got any coffee in?' He stirs, warm against the side of her body.

'What do you take me for?'

'Sent me packing like a zombie last time.'

'That must have been an excuse to get rid of you. I always have coffee.'

He doesn't take offence at this, has always appeared to enjoy her dismissiveness. She waits under her sheets, biting the corner of her nail, while he puts a pot on the stove.

Ollie is an engineer at BAE Systems. They'd met in the good old-fashioned way: Tinder. He has a good job and a nice family — not that she'd met them, but she'd seen evidence of their affection: drawings on his fridge from his nephew; cards from Mum and Dad congratulating him on his latest promotion; and enough photos of family holidays to suggest they were fairly regular occurrences. He's a good guy, a nice guy, a can't-believe-your-luck — quick, catch him — kind of guy. And she didn't know why he wasn't right for her, only that he wasn't. When he comes back with two mugs, he comments on how cold it is, looks around the room, which is a little messy. Then he picks up one of her jumpers from the floor and it strains across his body like his boxer shorts. He looks cute, adorable maybe. She should say it now.

He lies out on the bed facing her, asks again if she can turn up the heating.

'I told you it's on. The heat escapes straight through those windows. There's nothing I can do.'

'You could get them replaced.'

'I know,' she sighs, 'but windows are expensive, and at the minute I'm pumping everything into the studio.'

'You could use some jobs doing around here. Look at the cracks in your paintwork.'

'Excuse me.'

'I could come over and give the place a touch-up.'

'Oh.' Her belly clenches, the inevitable dawning. 'That feels a little above your paygrade, doesn't it? No. I wouldn't expect you to do that.' She pulls herself further up the headboard and leans back on it, readying herself.

'I want to do it for you.' He smiles at her. *Oh, no.*

'Ollie, I want to be honest here because I don't want to see anyone get hurt.' Her tone is more formal than she intends. 'I've said from the beginning I'm not looking for anything serious, haven't I? And I still feel that way. It's not a good time for me, with the business and—'

'You do know that plenty of people hold down a business and a functioning relationship, right? It's not one or the other, like.'

'I do know that.' Then she asserts, more simply, 'I don't want to be in a relationship.'

'But don't you want kids?'

She almost spits her coffee back into the misshapen ceramic mug she'd made.

'Because you seem broody to me; you're always staring at babies and talking about how cute they are. You're *obsessed* with your nieces. Aren't you eventually going to have to settle down if you want your own family?'

'Not necessarily.' Why do people use those words like they're appealing, *settle down*?

'But you could pick a person. Someone who suits you. Who's working towards building the same sort of life. And we're good together, aren't we? We could be great together. I don't get why you don't wanna give it a shot at least.'

Way to play at the heartstrings. Her move: 'I don't get it either.'

He places his hand on her thigh; her panic flutters. 'I knew this was coming,' he says frankly. 'I'm not an idiot. But I like you and, well, I could probably see myself falling in love with you.'

Each cell in her body tenses, and when he witnesses this recoil, he necks his coffee, says he should be getting off.

'Ollie,' she tries, as he paces the room, looking for the clothes he'd so passionately discarded just hours ago.

'That's not an easy thing to say to someone like you. Do you realise that, Dyl? You can be so, so cold ...' He scowls like that's her fault, not a default mode she can't find the off switch for.

'You're a great person.' She tries at warming. 'You know this isn't about you.'

'Spare me the it-isn't-you-it's-me chat, for Christ's sake.' He buttons his jeans in a retort.

'I'm just ...' She searches for the word, holding the coffee like a prop. 'Maybe we're not all cut out for monogamy.'

'If you know something's broken, how 'bout trying to fix it instead of relishing suffering?' he stings, then walks out of the bedroom and slams the door behind him. Only then does she feel the sweat in her palms, how tightly she's gripping. Relief rushes over her. He's gone. Thank God he's gone. She settles the mug on her nightstand and pulls the sheets over her pounding headache.

★★★

Emma is pushing for a Sunday roast to be a family tradition now that everyone lives within a short driving distance, desperate to carve out this normality for her own daughters. She'd spent a childhood wishing for ordinariness while she ate picnics constructed from leftovers in front of the TV, curtains blocking out the daylight. She sets about the kitchen preparing the vegetables, the skylight dappling rainbows across the spotless white countertop; is that too much garlic? She's concerned things will overcook if people don't arrive soon, irritated by the Play-Doh palace Sunny is constructing on top of her table design. She's laid out neutral napkins, petal-edged bowls and Kit's family's silver serving spoons that she can never quite think of as her own. The radio is on too loud, and Lilah is chewing one of the dog's toys. Kit is nowhere to be seen. The kitchen is her favourite room in the house, large and spacious with a huge island at its centre; when she'd viewed the property all those years ago, she'd known it was the one right away. Not because of its size and grandeur, but because it represented a commitment to a life you couldn't easily walk away from.

When she'd married Kit, his parents had been disappointed. It's not that they were ever unkind to her, but she knew what they thought. With their family crest, acres of land and seasonal ski trips, he could have done better. When they'd met, Emma was still living at Mam's in a more dubious part of town and was a barmaid at a golf club, studying social work. She understood quickly that her background ticked a box for him: he resented his mother's snobbery and general sense of superiority, so his wife would always be an act of agitation. And what she'd been looking for was someone who could take care of her. She fusses over her leg of lamb, smells the rosemary in her hand. They should have been here half an hour ago. Then the chaos in her chest – if she'd just allow herself to pause with it, she could drown. She wanted everything to be perfect, and what was wrong with that? She kicks this open can of emotion across her expensive kitchen tiles, busies herself with making the gravy and the mental to-do list of what's left to organise for the girls, keeping it compartmentalised, sorted, safe. The doorbell goes. *Fucking finally.* She wipes her hands on her apron and hurries towards the front of the house. When she opens it, she's greeted by Dylan wearing sunglasses, looking unamused, hung-over. She decides not to give her the satisfaction of an accusation.

'Where's Lilah? I could really do with a cuddle.'

There, confirmation.

'She's in the kitchen contracting worms.'

'I couldn't face buying wine but I got these.' She hands her some tired-looking flowers and Emma gestures for her to come in before starting the conversation where she typically does.

'What did you get up to with Oliver last night?'

'We ended things.'

Emma knows her expression will only provoke but she can't help herself.

'What? I was never interested in it being serious . . . He wanted to come over and fix my cracks.'

'Sounds reasonable.'

'I don't know who these men think they are.'

'Do you mean he wanted to help you with the flat?' She frowns. 'It could do with a lick of paint.'

'Stop looking at me like that.'

'Like what?' Emma's defensive.

'All pitiful and longing because I haven't got lost in the dick sand like you and Ines.'

This wasn't exactly accurate but Emma knew a sure-fire way to her sister shutting down was to poke at the wound she was still pretending wasn't there. She worried about her sisters. Perhaps then, if she could think the worst, it would never happen. She knew Dylan resented her for thinking she should want what Emma had, but the truth was she'd be happier if she could just find the right person.

'Well, at least the business is going well.' She nods at her encouragingly.

'Yeah, *at least* there's that.' Dylan's sarcasm sticks to the air like toffee. 'The perfect two point five family isn't for everyone, Em.' And then, under her breath: 'Especially when you make it look so exhausting.'

She shakes the carrots abrasively. 'I'm not uptight any more.'

'That's not what I said.' Dylan dips her finger into the honey on the tray and smiles, enjoying this thread she's pulled at.

Emma wants to say something, but she won't. She wants to say that if Dylan doesn't get her act together, doesn't start taking her future seriously, she'll be left scraping the barrel of avoidant and broken men.

Kit walks into the kitchen then, greets Dylan by kissing her cheek and takes the dog toy out of Lilah's mouth. Emma feels her sister's eyes on them as he starts to ask questions about lunch.

'What time did you say people were meant to be arriving again?'

'Oh, they'll be here soon.'

'How long has the lamb been on?'

'Only twenty minutes or so, love.'

She responds to his questions lightly, watching Dylan observe them in a way that feels deserving of permission, before reassuring him everything is in hand.

When the doorbell goes, she's relieved. Kit goes to answer it. The dogs gather excitedly as Mam walks along the hallway, their tails hitting against furniture. She gives them each a treat from her coat pocket as she emerges into the kitchen.

'Hello.' She smiles at Emma, like, *Isn't this civilised?* 'You look tired, love.'

Of course that's the first thing she says. Dylan pulls her sunglasses back down over her face and Mam lifts the bunch of ugly flowers off the counter.

'Who bought garage flowers?' she says disapprovingly, as if she'd raised them any better.

Dylan head lifts in the direction of Emma: *How does she know?*

'They're lovely.' Emma backs her up. 'I'm just going to put them in some water.' She fusses around in her vases cupboard, looking for the exact one.

'What's all that?' Dylan asks, as Kit carries in large black bags from Mam's car, placing them in the corner of the room before asking if there's anything else he can get for her.

'There's just one more, Kit. I've had my clear-out, haven't I? They're just the bits and bobs I thought you might want to keep, given I couldn't get a straight answer from you all. You can sort it out among yourselves. The girls might like some of it.'

Emma's attention turns to the jumble where Sunny is already riffling, Lilah curious, toddling towards her.

'You threw our things out without asking?' Emma presses her lips into a tight line.

'I sent you a text,' Mam says defensively. 'Dyl said you wouldn't care about most of it.'

'Is that what I said?'

'Oh, don't start on me, will you? I just got yer.'

Emma notices Dylan's body contort at this unfounded accusation.

'You haven't bothered with the stuff in years, have you? Most of it was broken or just rubbish anyway.'

The doorbell rings and Mam turns to go and answer it. Obviously, Ines is the last to arrive and obviously Mam unleashes unnecessary excitement as if the homecoming of the prodigal daughter is still novel. Dylan rolls her eyes and Emma's brow flickers, as she cuts the stems.

'Hi!' Ines's tone is high-pitched as she demonstrably unloads a box of craft beers into the double-door fridge. Noah steals Dylan's sunglasses off her face and puts them onto his own before kissing Emma's cheek. He's the only one to apologise for being nearly an hour late.

'Hey, is that Flumpy?' He nods in Lilah's direction.

'No.' Dylan leaps up. 'You can't have him. Where's that dog toy you just had?'

Kit guffaws, reminding Emma he's still there. Noah asks Mam how she's been, and they descend into exchanging gardening tips, which mostly consists of her telling him what he's doing wrong while he pours her some white wine without being asked. Kit asks Mam how she's getting on with the new alarm system he'd fitted for her, but she claims she's had to shut it off because the damn thing wouldn't stop going off. He's disappointed and the lack of gratitude nips at Emma. She watches then as Sunny finishes drawing eyebrows with a black felt-tip on Lilah, who sits patiently, mouth open.

'Subtlety never was a Wyn trait.' Noah pats her on the back consolingly.

They all get distracted by Ines, who takes centre stage, complaining about utilities not working at the cottage properly, which Mam entertains, diving into the minutiae while Emma exchanges looks with Dylan.

'Why don't you go and work with Dyl for a bit if you've got itchy fingers? You're no good at being idle, love. I know it's not what you want to do, but it's something, isn't it?'

Dylan looks around. 'Sorry, did someone employ a head of HR and not tell me?'

'She's your sister,' Mam challenges.

And what did she think that meant, exactly?

'How is the new studio looking anyway?' Emma changes the subject back to Dylan. 'It looks great in the photos you posted, but I need to come down and see it.' Emma tilts her body towards her, leaning over the island intentionally.

'Yeah. Still needs painting, but it's slowly coming together. I ordered all the new work benches yesterday.'

'It looks great.' Ines plants herself next to Dylan.

'You've seen it already?'

'Yeah,' Ines says casually. 'It's only down the road from us, isn't it?'

Emma's embarrassed at her flush of envy. She hadn't yet been invited. She goes in again, side-eyeing Ines: 'And what happened with that retailer you were telling me about on the phone?'

'We got the gig, actually.' Dylan bares her teeth apprehensively. 'They're taking a huge quantity. They'll be our biggest customer.'

'See. She's going to need more staff.' Mam nods, justified. 'The three of you could work there. Family business.'

Emma rolls her eyes and Noah lifts the sunglasses off his face as he says to Dylan: 'That's very cool.'

'Superb, indeed.' Kit tries again to make an effort, 'Emmie, pop some champagne in the freezer.'

This gesture warms her to him. She knows it's hard having them around more often. They were a hard nut to crack into when they were all together and Kit would sometimes get lost down the sides of their shared history. As she reaches up for the champagne, Sunny arrives at her side, handing her a case, nudging her to open it, and the realisation of what it is makes it hard to breathe.

'What?' Mam tries to read her. 'Oh.' She looks down. 'Yes, that. My old vanity case.'

'It's not yours. It's Edi's,' she says, her sisters pooling around her. 'Just a minute, Sunny.' She wipes a layer of dust off the leather, placing it on the island. She can sense Mam feels uncomfortable as she fiddles with the clasp. It pops and she opens the lid. Folded inside is Edi's yellow mohair cardigan. She picks it up, burying her nose in the softness. It still smells like poppies, even after all this time.

'Her lipstick,' Ines says affectionately, removing the lid to reveal a pink stump.

'And her charm bracelet.'

Mam, helping Lilah dress her dolly, corrects Dylan: 'That was your nanna's.'

'Oh, for fuck's sake!' Emma yells, seeing the time on the oven. Everyone looks to her with surprise. 'The fucking lamb!'

★★★

Selfish Girls

The meat is a little overdone but nobody says so. Except Kit, who tuts at it. The rest of them drain the glass bowls of mint sauce, passing around roast potatoes, tucking into the cauliflower cheese. The vegetables are the last things to go, and Noah is the first to say thank you for all Emma's hard work, to which the rest of the table concur between mouthfuls.

'Are you still thinking of looking for a job, Em?'

This is the first question anyone has asked her all day.

'She doesn't need to work, Gwen,' Kit says, resting his chin on his hands and using his tongue to dislodge something from his teeth. 'She can enjoy being at home with the girls while they're still young and want us around.'

Emma distracts herself by taking a napkin and using it to wipe the gravy off Lilah's chin.

'Maybe she wants to do something for herself,' Mam pushes back. 'It's hard work being stuck at home with kids all day.'

'It's not that hard—' Emma feels the heat in her face '—and there's Beata,' she says, defusing the discussion.

'Still, you said you wanted to do one or two days a week, something to keep skin in the game, until they're both in school.'

'And you've talked about volunteering,' Ines joins in.

Kit turns to her, like it's the first he's heard of it, which Emma supposes it is. 'I don't know. I need to think about it. Kit and I haven't really discussed it yet.'

'Look at those squirrels going wild in your garden!' Noah loudly redirects them.

'Oh, those, they're taking over.' Emma grasps the opportunity. 'Getting confident, too – one bit Kit the other day.'

'I love squirrels.' Dylan smirks.

'Nobody loves squirrels,' Kit ripostes.

Noah winks at Emma and she offers a soft smile, grateful for his deliberate distraction. More wine is poured, beers are drunk, and there's laughter around the table, which dissolves the tension she can see running, like veins under everyone's skin. Noah and Kit take the piss out of one another, and she understands it must feel intimidating in the shadow of another brother-in-law who had trodden the passages of their childhood. Emma thinks at least twice that Ines looks noticeably better, happier. Maybe Kit was right: everyone is doing okay. It feels good to have them all around her table again. She glances at the vanity case. It's like having a famous person in the room, them all pretending they're not there while it offsets everyone's energy.

The smell of the cardigan had lifted out an old memory, one that had oddly come to her last night as she'd pulled the joint of lamb out of the freezer. She tries again to push it back to wherever it came from, opting for martyrdom, insisting on doing the dishes once everyone else is full and satisfied.

2000

Three Years After They Moved to Laurel Road

Emma is thirteen, Edi is twelve, Dylan is eleven, Ines is eight

Dylan pushed open the door lightly and called out to her in the dark room. There was no response. She lingered in the doorway, contemplating closing it and leaving Mam to marinate. But it was upsetting everyone, especially Ines, so she readied herself to go inside, letting the door close behind her. She stood in the darkness, just listening to Mam breathe, slow and rasping, like a whale skimming the surface of an ocean.

'Mam?' she whispered.

The curtains were drawn, and Dylan couldn't see her face, just a mound of floral bedding and the outline of a human body encased in feathers. It smelt stale, but there was also a sweetness to the residue that fell over the room, still, so still. Dylan wanted to reach out and touch her, to sit on the bed and wrap herself around her back. But she knew better. Mam didn't really like being touched.

After no acknowledgement that Dylan was in the bedroom, she tiptoed across the faded rose carpet and around to the other side of the bed. Her dark hair was lank, her grey school skirt stained from tinned spaghetti earlier in the week. She found Mam's face then, saw her eyes were open, staring ahead into nothingness. Mam didn't look like herself when she was like this – blank expression, muscles drawing down her face, the deadness behind damp eyes that showed signs she'd been crying. But everyone was worried because she hadn't eaten anything in days.

'Will you come downstairs now? We'll make you some tea and toast . . .'

Mam stared into the distance.

'What if we bring it upstairs?' Dylan bartered, shifting her weight and clasping a hand to her forearm.

Everyone hated Mam's 'sad spells', the heavy weight that pulled her down to the bleak pit of herself. As if there was a rock tied to her feet, plunging her deeper. Swept away in the tides of her own condemnation, drowning in the depths of her despair, sweat beading her upper lip, Mam would give up struggling and let it become part of her.

Dylan walked closer, brought her face near, her hair falling on Mam's, but she didn't so much as wince. 'Please? We don't like it. We need you to come back. Em won't be cross, she promised. And we'll still help take care of Ines until you're feeling better. Just say something, Mam. Just get up now.'

Downstairs, Dylan joined the others on the living-room carpet, their uniforms creasing around their bodies, white socks smelly and browning on the soles.

'What did she say?'

'Is she getting up?'

'I'm hungry.'

Emma held Ines's foot in her lap and drew circles on it lightly with her finger. They had carnation-pink kiss prints on their foreheads from Edi who had taken Mam's lipstick out of her handbag and tried it on. She sat forward on the sofa hopefully, but Dylan shook her head. She looked for Cherry, who was making her way across the floorboards in a hamster wheel their neighbour Glenys had given them.

'She's still tired. That's all. She needs rest.' Edi tried being constructive. 'Come on, let's make dinner again. It'll be fun.'

'It wasn't fun last night,' Dylan moaned.

'Or the night before,' Ines added.

Edi pulled the sleeves of her cardigan over her wrists. 'Stop being grumpy. We can make it fun if we want to. Why don't we have a midnight picnic?'

Emma snorted at this suggestion. 'With what?'

Edi wandered into the kitchen, and Emma followed her around the table to the fridge-freezer where she pulled out cold, empty white trays containing nothing except a concrete leg of lamb, some ice trays that smelt like meat and the remaining bag of peas from yesterday's makeshift supper. Ines came in next, followed by Dylan, who shook her head remorsefully at the half-empty bag being held up as the solution.

'We'll make a feast,' Edi insisted.

They started putting bread into the toaster, and Dylan got the butter from the scant fridge that had nothing left to offer but sticky marmalade jars and an old tube of tomato purée. Ines sat on a stool at the island and yawned loudly, resting her chin in her hands. It was late, and the sound of her belly rumbled in everyone's stomachs. They all formed a production line, pouring frozen peas into a bowl, buttering toast and putting more bread in the toaster. Edi took a blanket from the sofa and laid it on the living-room floor where they sat to eat their picnic: a side plate with two slices of well-buttered toast and some warm green peas in the middle. They ate with their hands, giggling, licking butter off fingers and catching stray peas, putting one or two in their mouths at a time. They talked about school, silly things their teachers said, and whether to watch a film. Instead, they lay across one another on the large red blanket, old and bobbled. With crisscrossed limbs and satisfied bellies they started to quieten and slowly drift off. All except Dylan. Unable to relax into the furrow of sleep, she thought only of Mam, stuck at the bottom of the ocean, and all alone. She pulled herself gently from under Emma's head, lifting it with both hands and resting it on a cushion. She got another blanket and laid it over Ines, who always felt the cold.

'Stay here,' Edi whispered, half waking.

But Dylan shook her head.

She went upstairs to Mam's bedroom to pick her scabs. She hadn't managed to finish her toast; every happy thought she'd ever had was sucked out of her and strangled in the weeds. She sat down on the bedroom carpet, legs stretched out in front, as if attaching the rope, pulling it tighter around her ankles. Then she collapsed into the waves, letting them pull her asunder, washing over her as she sank into her sadness and a deep sleep on the floor, lonely still, but closer at least to Mam, who stared through her from the bed.

Dylan Wyn

1. Dylan is born in April and has a sun, moon and rising sign in Scorpio, which means she's a 'Scorpio Stellium', except she doesn't believe in star signs.

2. The first time she bites Ines, Mam takes her hand and bites down on it as hard as she can, ensuring she never thinks to do it again. It's the first time she ever hates her.

3. At the age of eight her biggest problem is that Emma insists she has to be the stupid crow every time they play princesses in the garden.

4. When she's fourteen Mam finds a spliff in her bedroom drawer, which she still to this day claims was for medicinal use.

5. At sixteen she is the only one who thinks it's sweet when Mam puts rape alarms in their Christmas stockings.

6. She thinks men wear rings when they're in a phase of self-exploration and makes a mental note to keep a wide berth.

7. Despite having her own washing machine, she makes fortnightly trips to the launderette to people-watch and escape prying thoughts of her next collection; she tells herself this doesn't mean she's lonely.

8. When asked what the secret to her cooking is she always gives the truth: sugar.

9. Falling in love is one of the most painful things she ever does. It will happen to her only once.

1982

Gwendoline is thirteen

Gwendoline started riffling through her sock drawer, wiping the sleep from her eyes — it was today. And she'd be waiting for an eternity for this day to arrive. She'd hidden it there because it was somewhere she would never look. Having squirrelled away loose change from running out to return the glass milk bottles when paying the milkman, saving the odd pennies her father had given her and Llewellyn to buy sweets every other Sunday, she'd finally saved up. She knew she was going to love it, felt confident about that. Her mam would have to be receptive to a gesture that opened its mouth and passively yawned kindness.

She pulled out the dark green socks and gently pulled them apart, using the two pads of her fingers to hold the tiny charm in place. It was a message bottle, and it would be like a secret between them. An unspoken thing no one else understood, like how they loved one another. She ran across the landing to their room, her feet collecting dust off the brown carpet, pulled open the floral curtains that were made by her mam's stubborn hands and discouraged tuts. But they weren't there.

'Llewellyn?' She wandered into his bedroom, his curtains already drawn. '*Daaaad?*' She remembered then he was on shift. With the tiny bottle still pressed safely in her palm, she went downstairs to the kitchen, which was empty with no sign of anyone having had breakfast. Strange. Maybe they'd gone to the shops to get bread. Llewellyn usually slept in, but if he'd had a bad dream or a disrupted night's sleep, mam might've taken him for a walk to calm him down.

She sat and waited for them to get back. It was all she could think to do: she sat and waited, sat still in her nightdress, sat for the entire day. The miniature bottle clutched hot in her hands, the condensation puckering against the glass with disappointment.

'*Shwmae?*' The door went, her father's voice sang, but she sat, frozen still. 'All okay, *cariad aur*?'

'It's cold in 'ere, love,' he said, walking over to his terracotta armchair where she was sitting. 'You should've put the fire on.' And then: 'Where's you-er mam, then? 'Ave you 'ad a nice day?'

She stared ahead of herself, still clutching the bottle, wondering if the message inside it was cruel. And seeing she was upset then, he sat down and put his arm around her where she collapsed into his dark police uniform, the heavy wool coarse against her face, her arms stretching around his back, like mercy, registering a need to breathe as the tears streamed down her cheeks.

When they finally got back from their day out, Gwendoline was already up in her bedroom, her dad having sorted tea. She creaked open the door slightly to listen, and there was Llewellyn, standing across the landing, happy to see her like always, waving at her from outside his bedroom. Her big brother who had been there long before she or her father had. And even though Llewellyn would never surpass the mental age of an eight-year-old, he knew and understood something she fundamentally didn't: their mam. She lifted a finger to her lips then and he copied her, his chuckle brusque as they stood blowing kisses back and forth, distracting themselves from the screaming downstairs.

'No. That's not right, you're out of order. For Christ's sake, Edith, it's Mother's Day; she's just a nipper still. Why do you have to be so bloody cruel to 'er?'

Interventions

February

At the theatre, Emma shouts, 'FUCK,' as she throws her phone into the pile of costumes and lets out the mother of all internal screams. Sunny is grinning, a bowed arm swinging her around the clothes rail as she reminds Emma they're not meant to swear.

'I know. Sorry. It's just your nan better get here soon.'

Backstage is always hectic, with its stench of glue guns and hairspray, and the flickering attention spans of little girls wearing lipstick for the first time. Emma had stabbed herself late into the night, sewing countless black spots onto a garish red cape, as Kit groaned at her to turn the light out. Then, in the morning, she was met with another ungrateful performance from Sunny, who insisted she wasn't in fact a ladybird. Initially she took no notice, instructing her to stand up straight as she tried to adjust the scalloped collar. It was only when Sunny broke down in tears that Emma finally went downstairs to retrieve the newsletter from the fridge. FUCK. She was right. She was a honeybee. It was her friend Ellen who was a ladybird. How could she have got that wrong?

She recollects this feeling, angst rancid as she'd stood at the school gates as a child. The hair on the back of her neck raised. Fear blocking her throat. She had walked them all to school for the first time. Grampy had a tooth infection, had been up all night and could only get an early emergency appointment. She remembers it vividly, Dylan gasping as she let go of her hand, Ines trying to hide, squirrelling herself behind her. The four of them, throbbing thumbs in red school jumpers and grey school skirts while the rest of the playground ran about in dresses, jeans and T-shirts. It was non-uniform day and she had forgotten. How could she have? The boys in Dylan's year started pointing and laughing and she retaliated by sending Emma daggers.

'I'm sorry. We – we can go home and change quick.'

But the bell was already ringing and they were being ushered in by teachers. Her frail little body full of panic and a sense of responsibility that was too big to belong there. Ines started to cry when her teacher pulled her away, gently reassuring that they might find something in the lost-property box. But Edi had held onto her arm tightly. Even though Emma had got it wrong, let them down, made them feel even worse than they already did. *It's not your fault, Em. Doesn't matter anyway. It's only a stupid non-uniform day. Who cares? We won't have to pay the one pound fifty now.*

To this day, Emma hates getting things wrong – and not because she's highly strung but because it puts the fear of God into her. Dylan had been hollowed out by her asking for help that morning. But no one ever seemed to care when she – struggling with two kids – was up against it. When Emma had asked Ines for help, she'd somehow been roped in to giving her a lift to the train station. Ines had been vague about what she was doing – Emma suspected a lavish day out with friends, resenting that she couldn't even taste her own freedom. No bottles to sort or nappies to pack, no buggies to drag up escalators or leaking snack boxes to excavate from the bottom of a handbag. Then a flashback of her purging earlier that morning. The guilt following through afterwards at leaving her children sitting at the kitchen table while she reappeared dewy-eyed, hoping they wouldn't notice. She looks at the ladybird costume, regretfully clinging to its hanger. How much of her was repetition? The same patterns and cycles and thoughts that she poured varying perspective into.

Mam's flustered when she walks into the changing room, hanging the honeybee from the rail before straightening her jumper purposefully. 'What do you think, love?'

Oh, thank God. She thanks her again, disregards the conflict knitting together in her chest, encouraging Sunny to change as she dawdles in front of a dirty mirror with dead light bulbs around it, no pace about her. 'Come on!'

'The girls, they're thriving, Emma. Try not to worry so much, eh? Loosen up a little. Don't take it all so seriously. We all screw up as mothers. It's part of the act.'

Selfish Girls

Emma bites the inside of her mouth. She knows what's getting to her. It had all started with Edi's vanity case. For years she'd had a well-rehearsed version of how this conversation would go: she'd played it out and turned it over in her mind. She'd say something along the lines of: *We've never really spoken about what happened.* And Mam would stand perfectly still, as to not to give herself away. But Emma would be able to tell from the slight upturn in her mouth that she was nervous. She'd reply with a one-word answer, something clean and simple that would deter the conversation from moving forward. So Emma would have to try again, but only very gently, saying something cordial and pale, like *Perhaps we should.* And they'd sit then, or perhaps Mam's breath would come heavy down the receiver as they talked calmly, composed. And Emma would finally ask the question. The one she'd always wanted to ask, not admonishingly, it wouldn't scold. She'd say it gently. The train of thought is interrupted by the Tannoy, which calls for group three to make their way quietly to side stage.

'That's Sunny. I need to take her.'

'Here, you don't want that cape going to waste mind, let me see if I can revive it.'

And Emma carries on walking, Sunny's hand in hers as she hears Mam start to rip out her stitches. And Edi's voice all the while coming through: *Whatever happened, it wasn't your fault.*

★★★

A short walk away from Dylan's studio, down a slim under-passage smelling of human piss, there's a pub with a fruit machine and amber ale on tap. They'd arranged to meet for a drink, and it's only while she's sitting waiting for them that she realises how much she likes having Ines and Noah back. When Noah walks in, he's by himself. Sees her, gives a half-smile, and she gestures to him that she'd like another half. When he arrives at the table, she asks where Ines is.

'She had an appointment in London, something to do with the wedding or, no, maybe it's about a dress for the engagement party.' He shrugs, setting down their drinks. 'I lose track. Disappointed it's just me?'

She says of course not, it's good to see him. It was comforting how he'd sunk so effortlessly back into this environment, validating her own choices. Not like Ines, whose skin visibly itched when they talked about Sunny's birthday and renting a house together down in Tenby. She asks how his day has been.

'Oh, you know, roasting a chicken and writing average prose. The usual.'

They talk about his book, the one he's been writing for several years, some complicated kickback at his mother. He laughs as she relays the panicked call she'd received from Emma that morning and the small talk thaws into the familiar pitter-patter of their age-old friendship. They stumble back onto Ines. It was a strange thing, for your sister to marry your best friend, but Dylan had resolved to let parts of him go. Because it was appropriate. Because, after a while, they'd all had to grow up. And because, from the moment Ines was born, Dylan had known that she would never love anyone or anything quite like she loved her. Gazing into her bassinet when Mam and Dad had brought her back from the hospital – she squealed and snuffled like a piglet – Dylan had pushed her index finger into her mouth, feeling for the gentle firmness of her gums as she started to soothe. She learned quickly how to take care of her, understood when she needed pacifying and when she just needed to scream the house down.

'Where've you gone?' He angles his head, searching for her.

'How's she doing?' She coughs from the back of her throat.

'Better. A lot better.'

'Do you think you'll try for another baby?'

'Christ, there's a question.'

Then this burning taste, something like a burp, blocks her throat from finishing what she was trying to say.

'Part of the reason we've moved back here, isn't it? We want the family around us when the time comes.' He leans back in his seat and it's distasteful how sure of himself he is. How wilfully blind he could be.

She considers being honest with him, reinforcing that Ines isn't ready for a child, that the first was an accident. Remember? Not something planned. But her loyalty to Ines overrides the inclination. And it wasn't that Noah pushed her into doing things she didn't want to do. That was Kit's remit. It was more that Ines sloshed around in the things she wanted and didn't want, as if asserting herself was beyond the realms of her control. And that was her own burden to bear, not something her sisters could keep protecting her from.

'I think I owe you an apology,' she says peaceably.

'Oh, really?' He lifts the collar of his jacket. 'That's a first.'

'Hardly a first.'

'Name one other time you've apologised to me.'

'I said sorry for getting you suspended.'

'I tried to warn you it wasn't a good idea to go into school still pissed from the night before.'

'I said sorry when I wrote your car off.' She bites her tongue teasingly then is distracted by a group of boys on the table behind him: they're celebrating something – one has two pint glasses attached to his hands with masking tape.

'That was my first ever car, DW. Mum was furious.'

'Don't look at me like that. I said I was sorry. What did I snap again? The wishbone or something? Who knew a car had a wishbone?'

He titters into his pint and when he looks up, they hold each other's gaze until she decides to let go. 'Back to my apology, then. It's just we've all been so wrapped up in Ines, how burned out she's been, how hard she took the miscarriage. And I don't know if we ever asked if you were okay.'

'You did,' he says matter-of-factly. 'And you let me have the last Yorkshire pudding the other day, a pity pudding.' He shakes his head. 'You're better than that.'

'I am – you deserve more than a Yorkshire pudding,' and then, more gently: 'You lost a baby too.' She watches as the sadness seeps in to find all his corners, sees the boy he used to be, in a perfectly ironed school uniform, always a pocketful of change for sweets, and the familiar image endears her to her old friend. That he had always wanted what was best for all of them. But then there's a flash of Ines in her mind's eye, the horror on her face when she'd seen the test was positive, throwing it into the bin, washing her hands vigorously as if to undo the immutable fate of a blue cross before calling to tell her.

'The doctor said there's no reason why it happened. It was just one of those things.' He shakes his head.

Now that she's allowed herself to do so, she can see his pain writhing in microscopic detail. He's always wanted to be a dad. He holds his head in his hands and she rubs the back of his neck, brushing up against the pools of curls at the nape. A lad from the other table returns to his friends' applause with a tray of sticky black shots.

'It'll happen when it's meant to.' This feeling hardens in her gut, but she worries, if voiced, it could sound more like jealousy. 'Just be careful, Noah. You know how she can be.'

Therapy, I

Kit smiled politely at their therapist, a foot resting on the edge of his knee, looking occasionally at his watch, which seemed to evoke something for Avril, who picked up her pen and jotted it down. He had never been late to a session. He wasn't afforded such incompetence: you can't be ten minutes late to a heart attack.

'I'm sorry.' The door swung open. 'I had to give Ines a lift to the station and then Beata forgot her key and I've been trying to sort Sunny's costume. It's been a nightmare day. The show's this evening.'

She says this as though he's blissfully unaware, hadn't been kept up all night by her profanity and the sound of her needle tying off her frustration.

Kit smiles at her. 'It's fine.' He's just conducted two heart-valve replacements and been called in for an emergency consultation. 'You're here now.'

Avril suggests they start by taking three deep breaths. She has extraordinarily large teeth, looks serene in the way one could only by dedicating their entire personality to being calm. Her grey hair perfectly parted, falls equally on each shoulder, and she looks as if she might float off her chair at any moment. He hopes she will so he can get back to work.

'I think it would be helpful this week to reflect on, and perhaps explore again, why you're here. I want our work together to be directional and I wonder if we're missing a thread.'

Characteristically abstract. Why not lead by example and tell *them* something directional for once – something they could use?

Emmie looks at him and he says, 'You can go first.'

Avril writes something, her pen scratching at his patience. Perhaps he should have been more assertive. And really this was the last thing he needed, another woman sliding him into a Petri dish as if he were a new bacterium of man.

'Sorry, are you married?'

'Kit!' Emmie acts as though he's being boorish, not picking up the £150 bill.

'No, it's just I don't think we've asked. And one would assume—' he looks back at the therapist '—if you're offering couples counselling . . .'

Avril nods at him, unflinching.

'Well, that you would be married, or have been in a marriage.' He looks back to Emmie for support but she just shrugs at him.

Avril looks stimulated by the unconscious swerve. 'Sometimes we can use deflection as a coping mechanism.'

Jesus Christ. Isn't everyone a globule of coping mechanisms just trying to get through the bloody day? Isn't that what being human is? He was simply asking for some clarification on this woman's authority to take a scalpel and open up the chest of his marriage.

'Right.' He searches the room for framed certificates but, of course, there aren't any. He straightens his tie and brings his other foot to the floor. 'Well, I suppose we're here to connect, to understand where the other is coming from, and try to find more compassion for one another.'

Avril nods encouragingly. 'What sort of things in your relationship do you think might benefit from compassion?'

'Well, we might start with work. You know your life isn't *that* hard, Emmie. All you have to do is sort the girls – and I'm not saying that's an easy job. But that's it! No back-to-back nights on call—'

'That's *it*, is it?' She looks at Avril as if he's mad. 'Is it a competition?'

'Only when you make it one.'

She folds her arms, visibly dispirited. 'But I didn't.'

'Do you sometimes feel like it's a competition, Kit, or do you feel that Emmie is competing with you?'

He considers this. 'It's more that she always wants to catch me out.'

'Oh! This is about the school-gates conversation, isn't it? I knew you'd bring it up.'

She's going to sulk now. Avril's eyes are widening with interest – finally something to get those incisors stuck into.

'I told you I didn't want to play the game,' he says.
'But you did. And, of course, you chose Amelia.'
She's still insulted, but he'd had to choose someone.
'And who is Amelia?' Avril enquires.
'Oh,' Emmie scoffs at his pettiness, 'we just had this silly little conversation the other day about who we'd ...' she pauses '... *you know*, out of the mums and dads at school.'
It sounds even more undignified when she puts it like that.
'Who you'd want to sleep with?' Avril's pitch ascends as she seeks clarification, adding weight to the conversation, like she's paid to.
'And I said I didn't want to play,' he reaffirms his innocence.
'Yes, but you did.'
'You forced me into it.'
'And it was so obvious you'd pick Amelia ... I'll tell you who you should want to fuck.'
'Go on, then, tell me.' He raises his eyebrows at Avril, leans back on the sofa.
'Wendy.'
'No.' He screws up his face, revolted at the idea. 'I don't want to sleep with Wendy.'
'Wendy is *incredible*. And she's such a great mother.'
He looks back at Avril, as if to say, *Help me. Please help me.*
'Let's try to keep the conversation focused on you both for now, shall we? How are things with your own sex life?'
'What sex life?' he jests, then turns to register the hurt on her face. 'It's just hard, with the children, and Emmie's family are always coming over unannounced. They're very ...' he treads carefully here '... well, they're intense women and it's as if—'
'What's your problem with them?' She shifts her body to face him.
'Emmie,' Avril interrupts. 'Let's allow Kit to finish.'
'They don't like me. That much is abundantly clear. And now her youngest sister has moved back and they're all over us like a rash. Hung-over, floundering on our sofas. It's as if they intentionally provoke me with their loose sarcasm and all these secret jokes from their past.'

'And do you feel excluded in this dynamic?' Avril dissects the tissue she's just found in the corner of her sleeve.

'Everyone feels excluded around Emmie and her sisters – even their own mother.'

2000

Three Years After They Moved to Laurel Road

Emma is thirteen, Edi is twelve, Dylan is eleven, Ines is eight

Dylan leaned against the front of Mr Salem's newsagent's, one foot against the window and the other in front of her, pelvis sticking out so the denim shorts wouldn't rub against the sunburn on her thighs. A child impersonating an adulthood she hadn't yet experienced, she chewed with her mouth open, blowing a bubble and popping it against her chin to distract from the raw sensation of her skin. She geared herself up, pulling her shorts in at her waist, before walking into the local shop, which smelt of sugar and printed newspaper. Endless rows of penny sweets had brown-paper bags hanging next to them, shelves were packed with magazines, and there were two large refrigerators with a row of ice creams and lollipops on top of bags of frozen chips.

'How's your mam doing?' Mr Salem asked. He was sitting on his stool behind the counter, as always, in a washed-out shirt and small spectacles perched at the end of his nose, thick hair coming out of his nostrils.

'Fine.' Dylan blew another bubble, reluctant as they all were to ever give anything away.

A boy entered the shop then, and they turned to look at him. He was skinny, his hair curly, and he stared at Dylan before he started leafing through the magazines.

'It's been a while since she's been in,' Mr Salem butted in again.

Dylan ran her finger over the glass top of the refrigerator, applying enough pressure to make a squeaking sound. The boy stole a look at her over his shoulder. She raised her chin and glared back, as if to say, 'What's your problem?' He reached for a comic and flicked through it absentmindedly.

'If she needs, tell her I can send Ali around with some groceries.'

She stared at the back of the boy's head, unable to tell if she'd seen him around before.

'Girl! Are you listening to me?' Mr Salem raised his voice at her.

'Yes,' she said, her hands on either side of the refrigerator, messy hair lank and hanging in front of her.

Mr Salem tutted and muttered something to himself, turning to the doorway behind the till. It was covered with a curtain made of brightly coloured plastic strips. He pushed them aside with the back of his hand, and they fluttered out of his way. This was Dylan's chance.

They arrived at the till at the same time, and the boy gestured for her to go first. She placed her items on the counter and curtsied at him playfully. Mr Salem sat down again on his stool and removed his glasses, letting them hang from a cord around his neck. Dylan counted the money.

'Is this everything?'

She continued to sift through the warm metallic-smelling coins in her palm.

'Girl – I said, is this everything?' he repeated, maintaining eye contact as he nodded towards the black-and-white CCTV.

There was stinging at the back of Dylan's throat, then came this intense heat all over her body.

'You're lucky I know your mother, or I'd call the police. I just got these fitted. I've had enough of people stealing from me. We're an honest family, running a business like everyone else on this street ...'

He went on, but she didn't register any more of what he said. She was too busy tuning in to the boy's thoughts, feeling the sensation of his gaze behind her, her pink crop top sticking to her back. She sank her hands into her shorts and pulled out two sachets of strawberry Angel Delight and some packets of white candy cigarettes, placing them on the till with a disgruntled sigh. Mr Salem shook his head and rang them up.

'No, I'll just take these.' She motioned at the bread, the tins of beans and the tube of discounted toothpaste. She paid Mr Salem and left, her humiliation hanging in the air.

★★★

'Hey, wait for me! Hey – wait!' The boy ran faster and grabbed at her shoulder.

'Get off me!' She pushed him away with so much fervour that he fell back, an Angel Delight flinging itself onto the asphalt. Then his bottom came to meet the pavement.

She looked down at them both, the dry summer air expanding in her lungs.

'I got your sweets and that, for you and your sisters,' he explained.

She put her hands on her hips suspiciously. 'How'd you know I have sisters? Have you been spying on us or something?'

'Yeah,' he said defensively, and then, 'Well, not spying, my nan lives on your road.'

Laurel Road was a long street with large Georgian houses at the top and smaller 1950s terraces at the bottom, where they lived. Their Grampy's house was number seven, the same house Mam had been brought up in. He had asked Mam to move back in after their dad left, saying he could give her a hand and help look after the girls. They barely remembered anything of their father. In the few images that existed, he held them as babies in hand-knitted blankets and smiled into the camera as though there had been some happiness. Emma remembered him most because she was the eldest but she rarely talked about him; whenever she did, they'd all gather around her quietly. Dylan could still remember his smell: petrol, oak and stale cigarettes.

'What number do you live at?' Dylan asked distrustfully.

'Eighty-seven.' The boy was still sitting on the pavement as he handed her the candy cigarettes.

'There's four of us,' she said, counting through the packets.

'Well, I got you three.' He looked cross. 'You should be grateful I did that.'

She grinned at him then, and put the packets of candy sticks into her carrier bag before giving him a hand up.

'I'm Dylan.'

'I'm Noah.'

'Noah what?'

'Ingelton.'

'Are you posh, then?'

'No.' He looked unsure. 'I don't think so anyway.'

'Hey, do you wanna go to the park?'

He followed her there, answering all her questions about where he came from, what school he went to, and whether he could eat five pears in under two minutes. She and her sisters all could. He was delighted by her interest in him. Noah had never met anyone like Dylan, knowing instantly he was in a tide he'd never out-swim. They shared his penny sweets on the swings, and he didn't seem to mind that she ate most of them, just watched as she pushed her feet into the ground, leaning her back flat, stopping every now and again when she thought of a new question to ask him between chewing a red liquorice stick.

'I have to go now, Noah,' she announced, out of nowhere, 'but it's nice to meet you. Thanks for the laces 'n' that.'

And before he could suggest they walk home together, she was gone. Off like a gazelle, bare legs leaping through the long grass, that blue carrier bag her new tail.

That night, when Dylan got home she wrote in her diary: *Today was an important day. It's the day I met Noah Ingelton.*

The others were curious as to where she'd been all that time and hungry for their beans on toast. She told them all about him and Mr Salem, and Edi told her off for talking to strangers. Dylan remonstrated, saying she'd only talked to Mr Salem and one neighbour, which meant they weren't strangers at all. Emma protested too. If any of the others had gone AWOL, Mam would have slapped the back of their legs. But Mam wasn't there, not really. Ines didn't say anything, just watched Dylan carefully, noticing a change in her that she couldn't yet locate.

The following Monday, they all had to go to school, and as Dylan sat in her form group, swinging on the back legs of her chair, Noah walked into the classroom.

'Ah, yes, you must be Noah. Come on in, please,' Miss Lee said.

Noah was different, and the class picked up on it straight away. He moved with confidence, with an air of having done things others hadn't yet. They understood there were two types of being different:

one that offered glimmers of something people wanted, like him, and one that made them feel uncomfortable, reminding them only of something they wanted to forget. Dylan sensed that she and her sisters were like that, their feral nature reminding the other kids of their own animalistic capabilities, which were intentionally being ironed out of them.

'Everyone, this is Noah Ingelton. He's new and will be joining our form group. I'd like everyone to make him feel extremely welcome.' Miss Lee looked for a space for him to sit, and Dylan was the only student sitting alone.

She was bullied by the boys, and the girls in her class didn't want much to do with her. Why did she never brush her hair? Why did she never have the right kit for gym? She made them feel uncomfortable, and they couldn't be honest with themselves about why.

'Yes, over there, next to Dylan,' the teacher directed him. 'I'm sure she'll make you feel extremely welcome, won't you, Dylan?' This was said with a warning look that brought her chair down to the carpet.

'Sure, Miss.'

Noah beamed at her, a smile that saw his mouth curl up on one side. Every eye in the class was on him as he strolled over and dropped his backpack onto the table, sliding himself into the seat.

'You don't wanna be hanging out with her. She stinks!' a boy whispered loudly, from behind his hand, and the girls erupted into giggles that sounded more like hisses.

Miss Lee pretended not to hear and told the class to settle down so she could call the register. Dylan sank back in her chair, feeling this familiar heat in her body again, too embarrassed to look Noah in the eye.

★★★

Noah thought Dylan made everything more adventurous, while Dylan didn't think too much about Noah at all. She simply made the most of a willing friend for as long as it lasted, knowing from experience that her luck ran out faster than other people's. Since that day in the classroom, they had been inseparable. They went on bike rides after school or met in front of Mr Salem's, where Noah used his pocket money to buy them sweets. They made each other laugh, and during break time, Dylan got bullied less because the other girls had taken a liking to Noah. It was in the toilets, out of sight, where things got crueller.

'What's that on your face?' Noah let go of his bike frame, dropping it onto the grass.

Dylan just shrugged and carried on looking for sticks around the forest floor, wedging any she found into the nook of an old tree under its low-hanging branches. It had been her idea to build a den in the woods.

'I found this. Thought it could be good. We could use it as a door maybe.' She showed him the plank of paint-chipped wood.

Noah looked again at her busted lip, and she felt embarrassed. She didn't want his pity: she knew it came from a place that supposed her inferior.

'Are you going to help or what? Or are you just gonna stand there dilly-dallying?' He was already late and was meant to meet her here ages ago.

'What's dilly-dallying?'

'I don't know. Mam says it.'

Noah felt in some way responsible for the bullying, and Dylan let him. Not because she wanted him to feel bad, but because it took the burn out of the humiliation that it had been going on for some time, long before he'd arrived. That he thought it was because of him was better than her being hated for who she was. Besides, it might mean he'd hang around for a bit longer. He started helping her construct the den, wedging branches wherever they would fit.

'What does your mum say about it?'

'Not a lot. Here, you're making a mess,' she berated him, starting to undo his efforts, laying all the sticks out in a line on the mud, gauging the stability of each.

'Tell me what happened.' He picked at her again.

'I told you, it's not a big deal.'

She had a large bruise, the force of which had popped several blood vessels, making the white of her eye a violent red. She reminded him of a vampire but he didn't want to say anything that would upset her.

'You should tell your mum.'

'I'm not a grass.' He couldn't understand how difficult things were at home for them.

'It's not about being a grass. Look at what they've done to your face. You shouldn't let people hurt you.'

She considered this for a moment, wondering how it must feel to have such an outlook on life where pain inflicted was unacceptable and not a prerequisite. Everyone the Wyn girls loved had hurt them.

'How does she think you did it?' he pressed.

'Who?'

'Your mum!' He was losing patience.

'Are you gonna collect sticks or are you just gonna keep asking me dumb questions?'

'I don't want to be the reason for you getting stick at school, DW.' He withdrew into himself, and she sighed, frustrated.

'You wanna get over yourself, Noah Ingelton. We're meant to be building a den, but if you're going to keep on about this stupid bruise, you can clear off, right?' She went and sat on the grass next to Cherry's portable black cage, wedging a finger in at her. 'Don't sit here,' she said sharply, as he came towards her. 'You'll get sore legs. Honestly, who has an allergy to grass? So stupid.'

'You think everything's stupid.'

'Stupid grass.'

'Stupid face.'

'Stupid mouse.'

They laughed into one another.

'I don't wanna clear off,' he said. 'You're my best friend. I love making things with you.'

'Don't go making us bestie bracelets or anything.' But the grin on her face gave her away.

She lay back on the grass next to him then, breathed in the pine from the needle-covered pathways, telling him that the moss was the most beautiful colour ever in the world. His favourite was black, which she said was predictable, watching him then as if he was making a mental note to be more surprising to her next time.

He opened the rucksack of stuff he'd brought for the den, pulling out an old rug he'd taken from his grandmother's airing cupboard, some plastic cups and a bottle of dandelion and burdock. Dylan had brought two fabric foldable chairs and an old woollen blanket with some fluorescent yellow spray paint she'd found in her Grampy's shed.

'Here, sit on these.'

She propped up the chairs as Cherry stood on two feet and pawed at the bars at Noah, who was making a fuss of her. He also had a few comics, some gum, the candy sticks they all liked, and blackberries from his nan's garden, which kept him in good favour with Cherry. Dylan took a stick from the box masquerading as a cigarette packet and put it into the side of her mouth. They sat like that for a while, as if mimicking an old couple, him reading his comic and her watching the birds overhead playing together in the trees, skipping across the branches until she said indifferently, 'All right, then, yeah. You can be my best friend.'

★★★

A few days later, so early in the morning that it was almost still dark, the Wyn girls were all creeping down the stairs in their faded nighties, their hair matted, breath still musty. Emma was in front, and Edi was whispering loudly to Dylan, who was jabbing her elbow into Ines to tell her to be quiet. They didn't want to wake Mam. They never slept well, less so after it had happened. They had perpetual dark rings under their eyes, which Mam would sometimes cover with her concealer if they went somewhere important. They went straight to the kitchen and started making toast, removing lids from sticky jam jars and peering inside.

'She doesn't like jam.'

'She does.'

'There's something wrong with it.'

Edi was outside in the garden picking the poppies their Grampy had planted. She handed one to Ines, their milky sap sticky on her hands, the flowers' heads hanging heavy, nodding in the breeze coming in through the conservatory. Emma stood on a chair, reaching up at one of the brown wooden cupboards for a vase to put them in. They placed the poppies, tea and toast on a tray, and Emma was silently nominated to carry it up the stairs to Mam's bedroom. Edi went first, pushing the door open gently, stepping from daybreak sunlight into the dark where the curtains were still drawn.

'Mam?'

'Are you awake?'

'Happy Mother's Day.'

They stood and looked at each other, waiting for permission to be given. Mam rolled over, a crumpled face emerging somewhere from within the floral duvet. She squinted at them, as if the smell of toast was making her queasy. 'What time is it?' She let out a disgruntled groan.

They reminded her again what day it was, stood, waiting to be invited onto her bed, a sacred place reserved for a high fever or a particularly bad nightmare.

'Up you come, then.' She patted the quilt, arranging the large pillows behind her, which sank as she leaned into them, forcing out white feathers. Ines placed a cushion on her lap so Emma could finally put the tray down.

'What's this?' Their mother picked up and inspected the folded piece of paper, which let out an explosion of glitter. 'Arrgh, what a mess!' Then quickly she forced a smile, seeing she had disappointed them. She nibbled at the edge of the black toast, burned and smothered in Branston pickle.

'It's your favourite,' Ines reassured her, leaning over Mam's waist.

'The jam was mouldy,' Emma added, with a very slight shrug.

'I'm going to have a clear-out of that fridge today; needs doing.'

'But it's Mother's Day.' Emma was unimpressed, the only one still standing. She scowled, and Mam winced as they took the tray, passing it along to one another, until Emma set it on the floor. It was unnerving how they always moved in convoy, travelling around the house together, checking for one another's blind spots. As if they drew in the same breath, their lungs expanding in unison.

The night before, Mam had gotten cross because she was trying to have a conversation with Dylan about her new friend, only to find they'd all been listening in. Her relaxing bath interrupted as their legs dangled from the toilet seat, a head poking around the door asking if they could get in with her. And it was as if the thought choked Mam then, as she forced down the sweet pickle. They were everywhere, all of them, all the time. She reached again for the card they'd made:

To Mam
Happy Mother's Day. We Love You Very Much.
YOU ARE THE BEST MAM IN THE WORLD.
Emma xx Edi xx Dylan xx Inny xxxxxxx

'We were all meant to put two kisses,' Dylan informed her.

Mam smiled then and looked down at the drawing, considering the four pencil-drawn figures, who they were, what they wanted.

'It's us,' Ines said, pointing at the picture, curling her warm body next to her. 'It was Edi's idea to make you a card.'

Mam nodded, and Dylan finished off the toast – feeling the need to make it go away. Then they discussed all manner of exciting things they might do together that day.

'How about the circus?' Edi stood up on the bed.

'Or the swimming baths? And we could go swimming in the river!' Ines enthused.

'No, I don't think so, girls. It's too cold.'

'The farm, then?' Dylan offered a compromise.

'It'll be packed at the farm today. No, if you don't mind, I feel like doing something a little more low-key. Mother's Day is meant to be about relaxing, isn't it?'

Emma's suggestion won in the end: a sofa day, popcorn and back-to-back films so none of them had to get dressed. Money was tight with Mam needing to take so much time off from the chemist, and Emma didn't like the idea of her feeling guilty about that.

'And a Chinese takeaway later,' Mam finished, bringing the conversation to a close and ushering them off her bed, proposing they choose a film to watch while she got sorted.

They plodded down the stairs one after another, hands attached to the banister, underwhelmed and minds all in different places. They pushed the sofas and turned them in on each other so they would all have a better view of the TV, laying blankets over the carpet before running upstairs to get the duvets and pillows from their own beds.

They bickered over which film to watch until Edi suggested they each select one to give to Mam, who would have the final say. Then they sat and waited for her.

When Mam eventually came downstairs, she was fully clothed, wearing pale pink lipstick.

'Where are you going?'

'Can we come?'

'I'm off to the shops.' She busied herself looking around for her handbag and pushing her hair out of her face as she searched for her keys. 'We need popcorn and sweets and crisps! Mouldy jam isn't going to cut it. And I think I've had my fill of pickle for the day.'

'Shall I come?' Ines tried again, sitting with her brown bear, turning its eyes in circular motions, loosening the plastic from the fabric.

Edi stood up and wiped herself down demonstratively but Mam insisted they were having a pyjama day: there was no need for them all to get dressed. She'd nip in the car now and be straight back – it would be quicker than all of them going – and when she got back, she'd choose one of the VHS tapes laid out on the kitchen table.

They stared at the closed door after she'd pulled it shut behind her, fear wrenching their stomachs, thinking of her ambling slowly in the supermarket, drawing out sanctuary from a day full of their expectant faces. On some level, they understood their intensity, how it suffocated her, left her unnerved. The hollow longing inside them was like a black cavity in her mouth; it went on and on, deep and boundless.

As more time passed, they grew more disturbed by Mam's absence. The house was quiet but for the deep hissing of pipes after intermittent toilet flushes and Ines's sighs as she gazed up at the clock, having recently learned how to tell the time. Edi said she knew a brilliant game they should all play, and her hands started bobbing in their periphery, gathering up some air as she started to mime, moulding it into an imaginary ball. She patted the ball down as if it were a lump of sand, her hands continually moving until she winked at Ines and lifted the invisible energy like a volleyball, hitting it with the palm of her hand. Ines jumped up on the sofa immediately, catching it straight away, then threw the invisible ball to Emma, who caught it with one hand while taking a bite of her apple. She bounced it up and down on the palm of her hand before throwing it full speed at Dylan, who put it into her mouth and swallowed it. They froze, shocked at her insolence, unsure how the game would continue. But then there was a loud belch, which made them roar with laughter as Dylan acted out a dramatic vomiting all over Edi. So, Edi reshaped it once more into a ball, padding it down before throwing it to Emma, who turned it into a kiss and blew it back at Ines, who again ate it before squatting down and pretending to poo it out. And they played like that until Mam got home, passing between them what they couldn't stand to hold.

Ines Wyn

1. Ines is the youngest sister, which means she was destined to be ruined.

2. It's well established by the time her teeth come in that she's Mam's favourite; it's thought this is because she's the most like her.

3. At five she resents Dylan and Edi for getting to be the crows when playing princesses in the garden while she endures the penance of shopkeeper.

4. She falls in love with Noah Ingelton aged nine, standing on the doorstep at number seven Laurel Road.

5. She is so homesick in her first year at drama school and cries into her mobile phone so much that the water damage breaks it, twice.

6. A year later, she makes the mistake of confessing to her sisters that she's never masturbated and has to engage Mam when Dylan won't stop sending sex toys to her halls of residence.

7. Ines likes comfort, clear skin, lie-ins, when the conversation is about her, and pushing herself so hard on a spin bike that she's almost sick – the sensation always invoking a sense of pride.

8. If forced to choose, her favourite sister would be Emma.

9. One day she will be a successful actor.

1983

Gwendoline is fourteen

'Bloody hell, Gwendoline, it's a bloody mess in yer. I need to get started on tea.' Her mam ripped a cushion from behind her back and started pummelling it theatrically, feathers dispersing for mercy.

It wasn't a mess: it was clean and immaculate because that was how her mam always kept things. Gwendoline arched around her so she could still see *The Red Shoes* playing on the television. It was better when she watched it at Angharad's house because her family had a colour television. Now she was having to imagine the shoes were red.

'You need to tidy your bedroom, please.'

'Done it,' she said, biting into a slice of *bara brith*.

'Well, you need to go and do your brother's, then. They'll be yer soon.'

'They won't be for hours, Mam. Why do you invite people over when it makes you like this?'

'Just do as I say.'

She told her mam she'd already cleaned Llewellyn's room, staring ahead, engrossed in the black-and-white figures on the screen.

'Well, push the hoover round, then.'

Gwendoline inoculated this request with a forced sigh.

'You're an idle girl, Gwendoline Wyn. Idle, just like you-er father.' Then she beat the last of the cushions, collected a half-drunk mug of tea and the cracked plate, and marched back into the kitchen.

Gwendoline sighed again, getting up to press pause on the video player. She walked into the kitchen and, without making eye contact with her mam, opened the cupboard under the stairs and pulled out the dark-orange Hoover, sulkily pushing it around. She could see her auburn hair in the corner of her eye as her mam leaned through the living-room door: 'Don't forget to do under—'

'Under the rugs, yeah, I know. *No such thing as sweeping it under the carpet,*' she assumed an impression of her, enjoyed the rich cackle it set off. See, she wasn't just like her father: she was like her, too.

When she'd finished, she wrapped the cord around the back of the handle in a circular motion and put the Hoover back in the cupboard. Then she went over to where her mam was preparing the food, picked up a knife and starting cutting an onion.

'Ah, Gwen, look a' this now.' She took the pregnant bell pepper that had been cut in half and showed it to her. 'You see yer, look, that's it's *babi.*'

She leaned over and saw the miniature bell growing in the belly of the red pepper, just underneath its seeds.

'Sweet, isn't it? You were like that once, a tiny little thing growing in *fy nghroth*. Do y' know what it means to find that in there?'

She handed the pepper back to her mam, who put her arms around the back of her and squeezed, just the once.

'Means abundance. There's more ahead than you think.'

Mother's Day

March

Once she's finished, she wipes her mouth and lies down on the bathroom floor, pressing her face against the Italian porcelain tiles that resemble polished concrete. The built-in storage allows for nothing unseemly to be on display, no dried residue gathering at the bottom of toothbrushes, no brightly packaged shampoo clashing with the sandy, neutral tones. She'd hand-picked everything: the marble countertops; a ludicrously large seashell; and that extortionately priced designer chair, the one nobody ever sat on. The one she'd had to convince Kit to buy. She'd been so particular about the details, though, her home the one place she could make choices. But in moments like this they feel rudimentary, and she finds herself wondering what she really wants, which means she makes way for an unhappiness that swings like a pendulum inside her. Good day, bad day, tomorrow-will-be-better day ... her life comprised of these strokes of uncertainty. Everything so tightly held. But even with this level of scrutiny, the removal of any trace of chaos, she can still smell manure from the nearby farm, can taste the acidity in her mouth. She looks up at the small cracks on the ceiling, dust gathering on the windowsill and the scuffed skirting board from Sunny's motor car, which she'd been told isn't an inside toy. Hears Edi's voice then coming from inside her, the vanity case still downstairs, out of Sunny's reach: *You mustn't do that, Em. You shouldn't hurt yourself.*

Kit walks into the bathroom, takes one look at her and sighs. Emma feels the guilt curdle, like off-milk, lumps of indignity gathering on her surface.

'Today isn't about you, Emmie,' he says, doing his tie in the mirror.

She nods, the mascara wet around her eyes. She'd chosen these tiles from a catalogue.

'You should enjoy these days with the girls. They're fleeting. We're going to blink and they'll be off in the world. Can't you try to make today about them for once? Make memories with your kids instead of indulging in your own self-loathing?'

Emma sits up and pulls her legs into herself, resting her elbows on the knees of her cream linen suit, which is still spotless, the floors cleaned by their housekeeper before anyone can see. Yet for a moment she had been vile.

She doesn't realise he's left the room until she hears the front door slam. The vibration shunts her back into her body and footsteps are making their way up the stairs as Sunny calls for her and the baby is crying. How long had the baby been crying? She stands up, a little unsteady on her feet, holding onto the his-and-hers basins. Pinches her cheeks in the mirror, then strokes the stray hairs into place, smiling at the evidence of herself stinging at the back of her throat.

★★★

Ten minutes' drive away Dylan is in her studio staring at the two patch tests on the wall. One, a moss colour, the other is a green that edges towards mustard. Mam had decided on the first shade, was set on it in the way she always seemed to know what was best for Dylan, not a moment's hesitation. But she still isn't sure.

'It doesn't matter,' she self-scorns. 'Just make a decision.'

She's been here since six a.m., sitting at the bench peg clamped to her desk, smoothing down the metal and using the polishing wheel to test the finishes she could get on the chokers she'd had cast, seeing which gave the battered effect she wanted. She always designed with lost-wax casting, building her moulds around models she could soften in her hands like putty. A kid with a ball of Play-Doh. The wax would take on her fingerprint, which she'd sometimes leave in the metal, some evidence of herself.

At first Dylan had had a rented bench, then gradually her own small studio. It struck her that this large stone building, with its wide-set windows facing onto fields, barns, worn-out tractors and hay bales wrapped in black bondage, was indicative of her success. But success wasn't the driver, wasn't what pushed her: it was merely a consequence. And though she'd spent all those childhood years longing to get away from Wales, it didn't take long for the restlessness that came from being away to fatigue her. She was surprised by how quickly she found her way back to the locus of this need that didn't have a name. A longing made bearable closer to home.

She turns her attention back to the choker. Making jewellery tunnelled her away from this emotion, casting it into something she could hold in her hands. The motive was motion, bending back the metals and using her flame torch to solder parts of herself back together, feeling and metal colliding. Something gets jammed, the metal crunching until it snaps.

'Fuck you,' she whispers, under her breath.

She picks up Edi's charm bracelet, which she'd taken from Emma's under the guise it might proffer some inspiration. Fiddles with the small atlas charm and then the message bottle, wonders if the tiny piece of paper inside has a note written on it. She can smell the scent of poppies when she hears Edi's voice in her own head: *Go on. Dare you.* She takes some pliers, and, careful not to damage the paper, crushes down on the tiny glass bottle, watching it disintegrate into pieces. She takes the tiny scroll and curls it back on itself:

> *The art to life is not controlling what happened to you but using what happened to you.*

She scoffs and sets it on the bench. She wasn't a person who wanted to control anything. Had learned very early in her childhood that life was a merry-go-round of chance. Any other proclamation was to take nihilism and beat it down to a meagre denial. The success she's having in her career isn't happening because she is more talented, a visionary artist, a better jeweller than others she knows – it's happening because it just *is*. Those around her are bemused she isn't better at decorating herself with the accolades, but she's aware they've only brandished themselves upon her through happenstance. She knows she's smart, not in an academic way but in a fast-on-her-feet sort of way. She didn't have the luxury of humility or the confidence offset by a good education: girls like her had to barge their way in to retrieve what life had left on the table. She was reactive even as a child, angrier than a kid should be, she now realises.

She feels the recklessness in her body then, the sensation old, beating like a drum against her nerve. Her fists close and her arms crush into her ribcage as she contracts into herself, recalling throwing a cup across the room, reaching for a lamp and chucking it with all her might as it crashed onto the floor, knocking things over, reaching for a discarded shoe and hurling it at the other scuffmarks on the wall. And when she ran out of things to throw, she'd grabbed for the door handle, opening it and slamming it, opening it and slamming it, over and over, until she heard Edi shouting: *Stop it, Dylan! You're going to get us in trouble!* Then later, after she'd calmed down, it was always Edi by her side, encouraging her to make amends, steadily lending a hand as she started to piece the broken lamp back together, trying to use a Pritt Stick to fix something of Emma's before she could find it. Both of them sitting on the carpet with what had broken inside her, trying to put life back together again.

She looks around her studio. Wonders if she should be more impressed with her lot or whether she should want more. She knew she wasn't concentrating, her mind elsewhere, reeling over Ollie, how everyone seemed to place her love life on the table, as if it were the centrepiece of her existence. Mam had been unashamed in her judgement, as usual: 'Oh, for God's sake, not again, Dyl.'

Ines and Emma were texting more regularly, as if she needed checking in on. Asking humdrum questions: 'How are you feeling today?'; 'How's it going over there?' Strange, she thought, that they should be so absorbed in her relationships, attentive to the minutiae that bore such little weight to the metal hook sunk in their own mouths. She didn't want what either of her sisters had, didn't like how Emma's energy was shifty around Kit, defensive or perhaps protective of him. Mam had noticed it too, reassuring her that she was keeping an eye on her, reminding her: 'Relationships aren't easy, Dyl.' But it was more than that and the disingenuous crust around Emma's placation pawed at her.

And don't get her started on Noah, rotating around Ines like the waning moon, always a hand on her lower back, allowing her to steal his funny jokes and announce them around the table more loudly. Ines had never been funny. Beautiful, yes. Thinner than Dylan, always. But never captivating in wit. She knew it would mollify them if she gave in and joined their quest to construct a false sense of permanence around another person. But as much as anything else she didn't want to give them the satisfaction.

'I'm woefully unsurprised you went green.'

His voice startles her. 'You scared me.'

'You always tell us to let ourselves in.' Noah scratched the back of his head. 'You Wyns, you're a walking contradiction.'

'Yeah. In case you've failed to notice we're not the same person.'

It was scurrilous, his inability to discern those little girls from the different women they'd grown into. The Wyn sisters – wild and untethered with untidy black hair and sticky long limbs, who moved around in symbiosis, making it hard to discern where one arm ended and another leg began. Like an arachnid, assured it won't hurt, rousing a wince as they moved across the palm of his hand. Noah would never know what his life might've been like had he never met them. But Dylan understood better than anyone: there was something about them that Noah recognised, something that was knotted within himself. He'd chosen to be ensconced within them, and that was to remain in Ines's shadow.

He tells her then that he's here to drop off the sideboard she'd wanted. It didn't really work at their place. She's surprised he'd picked up on her interest: Ines hadn't entertained her delicate suggestion to take it off their hands.

'How much do you want for it?' She sets the ruined choker down on the bench.

'Don't be silly. We're family.'

'Technically not yet.'

He sighs at her then, pushing his tongue into the groove of his cheek.

'Sorry. I'm being a bitch. I'm due on my period and I'm just so tense. The state of the studio—' she looks around at the mess, piles of boxes, clear bags of stock discarded everywhere '—and I can't make a decision about the stupid paint. There's so much I need to get sorted. All these benches need to be up by Monday so people can get to work. We've got this massive order we need to meet now and— What?' She glares at him, as he raises a single eyebrow at her. 'It's overwhelming.' She folds her arms in on herself.

'Yeah. That, and it's Mother's Day. You all get weird on Mother's Day.'

She realises then that he'd escaped Ines's anxiety only to ricochet into her own. 'How's she doing?'

'Yeah, a little tense,' he offers baldly. 'Like you.' He looks as if he's taking in her mental in-tray, reading through the innumerable anxieties she is trying to file away. Making a mess with all those things she doesn't want to look at.

'Resoundingly and respectfully, it has to be the moss green.' He directs his head at her swatches.

'Right. Yes, moss. Good.' A decision made.

'Now where do you want these work benches set up? Over here?'

'You don't have to help.' She gets up, resistance curved into her stance.

'Ah, but I want to.'

★★★

Back at the cottage, Ines is in the laundry room, folding their clothes, enjoying the flowery scent of the detergent and pondering how strange it is that they have an entire room now just to do laundry in. She loves folding Noah's clothes, knows she's not been much of a housewife since they moved in – rarely cooks and is terrible at cleaning – and wasn't that her role now? Somehow folding his T-shirts feels like an intimate act: only she would ever have the task of washing something he'd look to wear at the weekend, and it felt like a reasonable way to love him. She puts another load in, feels for the fabric-softener bottle, which is empty, throws it into the recycling box and looks up at the top shelf where there are several more. Noah had a thing for ordering in bulk, liked getting value for money. She tries, but it's just out of reach, so she puts her knee on the worktop and levers herself up with her hands. Taking down one of the white bottles, she sees a box behind the row. She can't make out the writing so she moves a few more bottles to the side: 'BABY W' is spelled out in handwriting more familiar to her than her own. She'd wondered where it had gone, knew he'd moved it from under the stairs to somewhere it wouldn't be easily stumbled upon.

    She edges the box out and brings it down from the shelf with her. Opens the lid, and takes out the grey hippo, which she instinctively brings to her nose. It's so soft. She thinks again about Edi's vanity case, how they'd sanctified her, kept her alive in a box of treasures. But there had been no baby. What would it be like to have one here now? Some toddler to chase around, those ugly gates on the stairs to protect them from falling. She was meant to wish things had been different. It was hard to consider, but perhaps being back in the countryside would make more sense with a baby. Without one, the slow pace feels superfluous. She picks up her phone and refreshes her emails, looking for auditions, but her brain doesn't register. Instead it thinks only of blood. Think of something else. Yellow: yellow butter melting on warm toast; buttercups held under her sister's chin; a plastic slide leading into a swimming pool; the mohair cardigan Mam used to wear; Edi. She reaches for her. Feels the disorientation again, reaches her hands down to the worktop, steadying herself. Then, crunching her stomach over as if in pain, she places her head on the worktop as her mind's eye finds their soaked sheets from that day.

    She'd slept in, the pregnancy making her so tired. When she'd woken up and looked down, it had soaked through her bedclothes. Such a dark red it was almost black. Then that deep wrenching pain – she can still feel it now if she tries, punishment. Noah had tried to get her up, said they needed to go to the hospital. None of it had felt real, not even the pregnancy. As she'd tried to get up she'd felt the bleeding getting heavier. She remembers sitting on a towel on the sofa while he'd called their doctor. Doubled over, feeling something coming out of her, blood on her hands. She'd pulled down her knickers and the sac had fallen out from between her legs. She daren't look at it, her peripheral vision revealing that it was about the size of a blood orange. She went back to their bed and lay down. How long had she stayed there? Until the sheets were completely soiled with clots and parts of herself.

Noah had wrapped another clean towel around her. That was when the ambulance had arrived, people around the bed, two female paramedics speaking softly to her and asking clear, pointed questions that Noah answered. Unlike the doctor at the hospital who had only looked at him when he'd said the baby was gone. Of course, she'd worked that much out for herself. She starts to cry then, alone in their new laundry room with a clean smell that takes her back to the happier corridors of her childhood, before the loss that bent them in on themselves.

She hears Noah call to her then as he rushes into the laundry room where she's leaning over the dryer. He lifts her up, holds her by her elbows, tries to steer her face at his, telling her to look at him. He's always wanted his own family. Surely she could give him that. After she'd lost the baby, Noah started going on all these drives. Said he'd needed to help a mate with something, or needed to pick up some equipment. But he'd always come home empty-handed. At first she'd wondered if he was having an affair, which was ridiculous: Noah would never do something like that. Then one evening it had started to snow. She hadn't left the house in days, and when she'd walked over to the window to look at it settling on the streets outside, she'd seen him. Sitting in his car, his body heaving, diabolical, reeling. Grieving away from her.

'What's wrong?' he says, pulling her back to him. 'Tell me, what's the matter?'

'Nothing.' She smiles through her tears, the smell of detergent bringing her back to herself. She wraps her arms around him. 'I'm all right.' Then, over his shoulder, the words congregate: 'Let's have another baby, Noah. It's time.'

★★★

Emma watches Dylan through the gates as she pulls up the gravel pathway behind Ines who has one foot outside the driver's side, aggressively wrangling her fob, pointing it towards the gate that separates them from Emma's driveway.

'Try it again now,' Emma calls to her, and Dylan winds down her window: 'You don't need to get out of the car, dickhead; it's Bluetooth.'

'It's not working.' Ines strains, forcefully hitting the button.

Dylan rolls her eyes and Emma watches her reach for her own fob from the glove compartment. Immediately the gate opens. She beeps her horn to tell Ines to get back into the car.

They park and follow Emma into the house, then straight through to the kitchen.

'Oh, you're here already!' Ines says brightly.

'You sound surprised.' Mam sits at the island, drinking the tea she'd just made for herself.

'Happy Mother's Day!' Dylan hands her a bouquet of impressive white flowers and Emma tries to remember the last time they had all been together for it.

'They're lovely, Dylan. Not a very original Mother's Day gift,' she says, as if teasing, 'but thoughtful. Thank you.'

'Here you go.' Emma pushes a wrapped gift across the island, somewhat hesitant.

'What's this?' Mam opens it up suspiciously. 'Face cream.' She attempts to read the label, reaching for the glasses on top of her head. 'Crème Régénération Intense ... Oh, anti-ageing, is it?' she says, clearly less than impressed.

'Crème de la Mer! Jesus, Em. Mum, do you have any idea how much a jar of this stuff costs?'

She reminds Dylan that she's not into the *fancy stuff*. 'You know me.' She tilts her chin. 'I'm happy with what I get from the chemist, suits me fine, and I get a staff discount.'

'Well, it's a lot better than your stuff from the chemist,' Emma gripes. 'Rich, too, so use it sparingly.' She reminds herself then, for the second time since Mam has arrived, that one day her mother will be dead and the guilt of directing that tone at her will resonate as insufferable.

'Sorry, Mam . . . I feel so bad.' Ines's voice comes wilting and child-like. 'It's been so full on, with the move and everything.'

Emma side-eyes Dylan. *She moved three months ago.*

'Don't be ridiculous, love. I wasn't expecting anything, was I? I'm just happy you're here. It's so special having you home, isn't it, girls? Makes a real difference. To us all.'

Ines grins and Emma continues taking laundry out of the basket, folding it onto the counter, forcing herself to breathe slowly.

'Have you got any gin?' Ines opens the fridge.

'It's a Sunday.' Emma stretches a Babygro as if wringing a neck.

'So . . .'

'I thought we were going out for a pub lunch?' Dylan airs, as if only just realising there'd been a change of plan.

Mam was meant to text her, but instead informs Dylan that she doesn't feel like it, that she'd much rather spend the day here and, anyway, Em had offered to make them lunch. Emma offers a manic smile: *That's what I've been told I'm doing.* Dylan folds her arms, realising she'd overdressed, and Emma watches Ines run her eyes over her, clouding something not wanting to be seen. Emma can't believe they're still in competition over their outfits after all these years. Of course they are. All they have to care about is who looks better. They don't have school fees to sort, costumes for a dance recital to magic from thin air.

'Where have you put Edi's vanity case, Em?' Ines asks. 'I'm assuming you're just keeping hold of that, are you?'

'What's that supposed to mean?'

'Can we just leave Edi for today, please?' Mam bites, and Emma wonders if they should be making more of an effort.

'Look, why don't we go and sit in the garden? It's a nice day, isn't it? And there are heaters if we get cold.' Emma knows they're all mismanaging one another's expectations on how things are going to be now they're living in such close proximity. Perhaps Kit was right. Maybe they are spending too much time together. She was hoping they'd eat out at the White Hart and she'd get back at a reasonable time: she had things to do, like crafting an elephant's head out of papier-mâché and administering nits shampoo after the letter she'd got on Friday about a breakout at school. Unlike Ines, who seemed only to watch daytime TV and wait for her skin to wrinkle in a hot bath. She watches her sister pouring the gin. Perhaps a little loosener isn't a bad idea, something to dispel the tension. She'd recently read how the heartbeats of audience members synchronise at the theatre, the rhythm of their hearts speeding up and slowing down together, beating harmoniously. And it had made her think instantly of her own family: Mam the production, the three of them feeding off her comfort or displeasure, heart rates shooting up or enabled to settle down together.

They go out into the back garden where she's already thrown sheepskin rugs onto the back of expensive garden furniture, the long table decorated thoughtfully with individual purple hydrangeas placed in small vases, which only she admires. Ines makes a toast, to Mother's Day, and a laugh compresses through her mouth. They pull their chairs in closer and sit like that for a few hours, chatting about the wedding, the engagement party, and then the hen. Emma can't recall if she'd been this self-indulgent as a bride. Probably. She was younger then too – naively believing it to be a day that held more importance than any other. It was easier to build stories about your life, much harder to sustain real memories.

She hears the gate go and her heart sinks as Beata appears with Lilah and Sunny, who has purple smudges in the corner of her mouth from whatever she's just eaten, some of it encrusted on the front of her dungarees. She'd never have time to make the elephant's head now. Sunny shows Mam her front tooth, which is starting to come loose, and asks, 'Where do babies come from, Nan?'

'Well, that's a fascinating question, actually,' Mam obliges.

'Not the whole story, please.' Emma's gentle warning goes unacknowledged.

'Babies come from little eggs that are kept inside their mam's wombs – in their tummies, see. So, when I was born, in my mam's belly, I already had your mummy's egg and your aunties' eggs inside me. And when you were in your mam's belly, you already had all of your little baby eggs inside you. And on and on it goes like that ... a spiral of life.'

'And a spiral of trauma!' Dylan adds.

'So, I have lots of little babies inside me?' Sunny looks alarmed, feeling for her stomach.

'No, that's not quite right, babe.' Emma rolls her eyes playfully at Mam.

Ines goes to pour everyone another drink. Beata offers to make the girls something to eat and keep them occupied a little longer. Emma allows herself to lighten. Shrieks of laughter spool like electricity around the garden as Dylan does a trip back into the house for more ice. They sit dusting off old memories, deriding the ridiculous things they've done to one another over the years, like when Emma had a bad stomach on the train to Cardiff and Ines opened the lavatory door, announcing loudly to the train, 'IT STINKS,' as Emma scrambled for the close button and what was left of her dignity. Dylan's eyes crease as Ines recounts the story, and she wipes away the tears of laughter. The outdoor heaters blaze orange and the mood is like silk, the unsettled cadence between them rediscovering its rhythm.

Emma announces she's hungry and should make a start on lunch before it's teatime. Mam offers to give her a hand, lifting herself up and taking in stray cups and glasses.

'I'm cold,' Ines complains, waiting for another of life's problems to be solved for her.

'There's a box of blankets over there.' Emma goes and gets them one each, laying one over Ines who titters as she wedges the blanket under her legs and tucks it behind her back. 'There – all *cwtched* up.'

In the kitchen, Emma stands over the grill waiting for the salmon to darken, the lemon cuts perishing under the heat.

'No wonder you're starving. You look *very* thin.' Mam pinches at her waist and she bats her away. 'What have you eaten today?'

'I'm not starving.' She flits about, wiping the surfaces. 'In all honesty, I want to try and get something into Ines, try to sober her up a little.'

Mam makes light of this. 'It's probably the last time she'll be able to have a few drinks for a while.'

Emma stops what she's doing, waits for an explanation.

'They're trying again,' Mam says.

'News to me.'

'She only told me today.'

Emma rinses the cloth and the remainder of the pesto hits the sides of the sink. 'Have you spoken to her about the miscarriage?' Ines had refused to talk to Emma about it, which is strange, given her usual verbal diarrhoea on matters that place her at the centre.

'No. I haven't.' Mam pulls the salmon from under the grill and starts laying it out on the chopping board.

Emma readies her knife. 'I'll do it,' she says short-temperedly, taking it from her. Then she realises she's hit a sore point. She apologises, telling Mam she understands it might be difficult for her.

'Why would it be difficult?' Mam layers the salmon into the pasta.

Emma picks up a wooden spoon as a prop, something to do with her hands. 'Well, it's something you've been through first-hand, isn't it? It was my worst nightmare when I was trying for the girls.'

Mam stops what she's doing, her overgrown bob brushing her shoulders as she turns her head, looking at Emma like she's lost it.

'You had a miscarriage, when we were kids.' As if she needs to remind her of such things.

'Er, I think I'd know if I'd had a miscarriage, Em.' Mam uses her body to push her aside, starts serving the food into the ceramic bowls Emma had laid out. 'I had a termination.'

Emma feels the anxiety shooting through her body, can't tell if it belongs to her or if it's Mam's. But then Dylan walks into the kitchen, a blanket wrapped around her shoulders like a scarf, Ines stumbling behind her. She jerks her head at their sister and Emma nods: *I know, I'm on it.* 'I've made pasta,' she says vibrantly to Ines.

'Right,' says Mam. 'I'm just going to pop to the loo. Lay the table, Dyl.'

'I don't eat salmon.' Ines wedges herself onto a stool.

'Well, we haven't put salmon on yours.' Emma can feel Dylan's eyes on her from across the room as she lays out the cutlery: *Don't, it's not worth it.*

'Why are you looking at me like that?' Ines hiccups, necking the rest of her gin.

'Don't you think you've had enough?' Emma sharpens.

'All right, boring.'

'It's not a case of being boring. It's just a case of not getting blind drunk every time you have a glass of wine.'

'Fuck you.' Ines's teeth graze her bottom lip.

'Don't speak to me like that, not in my house.'

'Oh, well, if it's such an imposition I'll just leave, shall I?' She pushes the blanket off her shoulders and it falls to the floor.

Mam walks back in on the commotion. 'I've only been out of the room two minutes. What's happened now?'

'Emma has asked me to leave.' Ines centres herself as the victim.

Emma laughs at this performance, trying to discredit it.

'It's fine. I'm leaving anyway.' Ines grabs her handbag and walks out of the kitchen, down the long hallway towards the front door. Mam calls that she should stay.

'I'll have to drive her, won't I?' Dylan huffs at Emma like it's her fault, picking up a bowl and quickly spooning mouthfuls of pasta.

Mam rummages in a cupboard for some Tupperware, tells her she can pack some for her to take.

'Don't bother.' She puts on her leather jacket and Emma jumps slightly when the door slams.

Mam looks at her, raising her eyebrows as she pushes a bowl across the island towards her, starts eating her own. 'Their loss. It's actually pretty good.'

Emma offers a flat smile, then blows on her fork, her appetite gone with her sisters.

'Shame, we were having such a nice day.'

'We never have a nice time on Mother's Day,' she lashes out.

'Right.' Mam puts her bowl down and starts putting the pan and her cutlery into the sink.

'Don't. It can all just go in the dishwasher.' She can feel herself getting angrier. 'It isn't my fault she's a brat.'

'I never said it was.'

'Well, why do you all look to me to manage her?'

Mam sighs and starts folding the blankets, signalling that she, too, is leaving, returning them then to the blanket box outside as Emma watches: she'll take them out again as soon as her mother's left and refold them all, properly.

2000

Three Years After They Moved to Laurel Road

Emma is thirteen, Edi is twelve, Dylan is eleven, Ines is eight

Ines was leaning against the door, her face scrunched in outrage. Damp towels were strewn across the bathroom floor, and Emma's makeup bag was filling the washbasin.

'But it's not fair. I want to come too,' she whined.

'Mam took you earlier and you're too young to come with us tonight,' Emma replied, her hands moving in synchronicity behind her head as she plaited her own hair. 'You wouldn't have fun. The rides are all too big – you're not allowed on most of them.'

'I can hold your coats,' Ines bargained, twirling herself into the towel hanging behind her.

'I don't mind waiting with her,' Edi reasoned. 'I don't like the rides either.'

'No, Ines.' Dylan leaned forward on the toilet seat. 'You can't come. You're too little.'

'Keep still, Dyl.' Emma held her by the chin to keep her face in position as she drew black wings on the hoods of her eyelids.

'Can you do ones like that on me too?' Ines pleaded, her life dependent on it.

'No, Ines,' Dylan barked, and Edi sat on the side of the bath, uncomfortable with the conflict.

The May Day fair brought excitement and possibility to their village, where nothing ever happened. Bright yellow and red posters were in every shop window on the high street, plastered on lampposts and bus stops. The common was transformed, covered with fairground stalls and a Ferris wheel with lights and swinging seats. Sugar-high candyfloss hung in clear plastic bags, and there was a constant smell of grilled sausages. The wails from the rides could be heard through their bathroom window, pouring in with the pollen from the hazel trees, whose long yellow catkins hung like the streamers decorating the maypoles – a soundtrack for all the fun Ines would miss out on.

'Mam, please, can I?' she shouted, from the top of the stairs. 'Can I go? I am big enough, I swear.' She stood on tiptoe. 'The kids from my class go!'

'Why don't you just take her, girls?' Mam shouted back. Then, with more frustration in her voice, 'She wants to go with you. Don't be cruel to her.'

'No,' Dylan hit back. 'She can't come.' She looked to Emma and said, as though this was final, 'She isn't coming.'

Ines glared at her with a loathing that oozed through her body, thick like warm treacle. She always got left behind, stuck at home with Mam, whose moods couldn't be relied on.

'Is Noah coming here?' Edi asked, and Ines's ears pricked up.

'No. We're meeting him at the fair.' Dylan side-eyed Ines, taking another punch at her disappointment.

Ines had never met Noah, not in real life, but she'd read all about him in Dylan's diary, which was kept hidden in a shoebox under her bed. After all these months, she'd developed a strong sense of the boy, shy yet willing to please. She knew about the trouble he'd caused for Dylan at school, how she'd been beaten up in the girls' toilets. She knew about the comics and the stolen candy cigarettes, and she knew all about their secret den in the woods. She was only biding her time to unleash the information on Mam to get Dylan into as much trouble as possible. She hated how they talked about him, in hushed giggles, with a knowingness she'd wanted to join in. And she hated how he'd pulled Dylan away, made her secretive, creating instability. It only made Noah all the more interesting – a new plaything her sisters had, like a mouse hiding under the sofa she was waiting to maul.

'Move, then.' Dylan clipped her with her shoulder on the way out of the bathroom, and Ines finally lost it. Started chasing her down the stairs, wailing, 'You're such a cow!' Leaping from the fifth step onto Dylan's back, plunging them both down onto the floorboards.

'Bite her back,' Edi and Emma riled. 'Rip her hair.'

'What's going on?' Mam came rushing in. 'Stop it! Girls, stop it now!' She pulled Ines off, blood hot in her face, spitting and possessed by a hatred whose depths only a sister could incite.

'YOU BITCH. I hate you! I hate you!' Dylan yelled back, small marks imprinted on her cheek, makeup reduced to black smudges.

Mam dragged Ines away as she continued to kick like a wild dog with a locked jaw.

Dylan stormed upstairs, where Edi ran a flannel under some warm water and pressed it to her face. 'Are you okay, sweetheart?' Dylan winced. 'Sorry, does that hurt?'

Dylan clutched angrily at her ripped top. 'She's not a baby any more. She needs to control herself.' Then she felt for the toothmarks in her cheek. 'If I did that to her, I'd be grounded for ever.'

'Why can't you just let her come?' Edi tried. 'You know she hates being on her own.'

'Just 'cause we're sisters doesn't mean we have to go everywhere together. I don't want her to come. I'm going to the fair with my friends.'

'*Friend*. You only have one.' Emma gathered with them in the bathroom, looking to Edi unhappily, not sure what to do as she listened to Mam telling Ines off downstairs.

'That may very well be the case, but I've told you, I don't know how many times, I will not tolerate violence in this house. I don't know why you need to fight like lads, the lot of you.'

Emma looked back at Dylan, who was sitting deflated on the edge of the bath, and felt sorry for her. 'Do you want me to help you find a new top?' she offered. 'You can borrow one of mine.'

Emma's bedroom stank of sickly peach blossom and cheap hairspray. The bed was still unmade, and there were board games precariously piled on top of her wardrobe. She traipsed over to it and opened the wooden doors, where everything was hung immaculately and in order of colour. Her hand hovered until she removed a moss-coloured top, hanging from its small ties.

Dylan's eyes dilated. It was Emma's favourite, and she'd slap them if they ever tried to steal it.

'Just this once,' Emma stated firmly.

Dylan removed her bra, which had once been Emma's, then pulled the top down over her small breasts. The fabric was delicate against her skin, the sleeves clinging tightly to lithe wrists.

'There. Now, let me fix this.' Emma lifted her by the chin again, but this time used her thumb to gently smudge the green eyeshadow across the upper line of her wide eyes. 'You look so cool. Better than before.'

Edi nodded in agreement from the bed.

In the kitchen, Mam was still talking down Ines's demons as she sat sulking at the table, her legs dangling from the chair.

'I wish you'd all just get along,' she entreated Emma. 'You really won't take her?'

Dylan arched herself forward, outraged. 'You think she deserves to come after that performance?'

Ines started shouting at her, and Mam raised both arms to separate them. 'All right,' and then again, more loudly, 'I said all right! Stop it. Just stop it, both of you.' She was upset. 'Ines, you and I are going to have a nice evening to ourselves. I'll take you down the shops and we can get some sweets and a film from the video man. Anything you like.'

Ines held onto the back of the chair with both hands and moaned helplessly. Edi looked to Dylan again, creating space for her to reconsider.

'Right, come on, then, let's go,' she said, collecting the house key from the bowl.

Edi and Emma readied themselves behind her, and just as they were about to walk through the porch, Mam called to Dylan, 'This Noah chap, he can come for tea next week, right? If you're gonna be spending all this time with him I'd like to meet him.'

Dylan scoffed.

'I'm you-er mam. I have a right to know.'

'Fine.' She opened the front door.

'Wednesday,' Mam stated, following them out. 'Now stay together; look after one another!'

Emma smiled at Mam placidly. 'Bye, Inny, we'll bring you back something, I promise.'

When she closed the door behind them, Mam walked over to Ines and sank down to her knees. 'There, come on. Don't let her see she's upset you. We'll have a nice night, us two, won't we? And we'll soon find out all about this Noah.'

★★★

They walked down Laurel Road at the bottom of which large green mountains met with the sky, and there was a field with black and brown cows that sat down to tell you when it was going to rain, which was always. But today they were standing proud, chewing the hedgerows, their tails swishing behind the low stone wall, and Dylan felt excited for the evening ahead. They passed the working men's club where people flowed out on the street drinking pints of ale and smoking. A woman they recognised shouted after them about Mam: *Tell her I was asking after her, mind! Ta-rah now!* Mrs Rogers's shop had a new window display with hanging tea towels that pictured scenes of towns like Powys and Betws-y-Coed, and bread bins and canisters with SIWGR, COFFI and TE written across them. Emma complained she was hungry as they approached Lucky Fish Bar, the Chinese takeaway with its laminated menus facing out, but Dylan insisted they ate when they got to the fair.

Noah was standing in front of the Ferris wheel, where they'd planned to meet, with a strange expression on his face. Dylan wasn't like the other girls and it was odd to see her with a face full of makeup when usually she had stains around her mouth from the last thing she'd eaten.

'Why are you staring at me like that?' she asked defensively.

'What've you got all that on for?' His tone was slightly mocking, making Edi and Emma giggle; Dylan didn't reward them with a scowl.

'Don't be an idiot, Noah. Buy me a hotdog?'

They wandered over to the food stalls with their large yellow signs that read CHEESY CHIPS and CHIP BUTTIES in large red letters, the smell of onions on a black grill with tall mustard and ketchup tubes, sauce hardened around their spouts. Noah paid the woman wearing a white hairnet as Dylan recounted the story of Ines and how much of a cow she'd been. He listened intently, as if understanding the importance of it to her. They went on ride after ride, and once they'd run out of tickets, Noah bought more with the money his nan had given him. Edi tried to help Emma win a goldfish for Ines. Dylan stood back stubbornly, eating her second hotdog, refusing to partake in the peace offering.

'Slowly, not too fast now,' Edi instructed.

'Try for that one there,' Noah pointed.

Emma tried again, her tongue circling her lips with concentration, aiming her ping-pong ball into the narrow-necked jar.

'Here, want me to try?'

She handed the last ball to Noah, and he threw it up gently, watching as it splashed into one of the jars. They jumped up and down with victory and Dylan looked around the fair distractedly while they picked out a black-and-orange fish with tall floating fins. Emma lifted it proudly as Edi fingered the bag, introducing herself to the newest member of the Wyn family.

★★★

Back at the house, Ines sat cross-legged in front of the TV, with Mam sprawled on the sofa behind her. Bored of the film, she went upstairs to Emma's room and started trying on her clothes, drawing thick messy flicks on her eyelids. She thought Dylan was spiteful – Emma and Edi shared everything with her. She stood in front of the mirror, doing impressions of Dylan that grew more vicious as the night darkened. Then she went to her room and sifted around for her diary under the bed with its pointless plastic lock and key. Disappointed to find no new entry and bored of the same old material, she landed on the map, symbols coloured in green and red, a bright yellow door, and embarked upon a new idea: the den. That would teach them. She wasn't some stupid kid: she could have her own adventures. She tiptoed through the kitchen and out of the front door, leaving Mam snoring like a freight train.

★★★

Selfish Girls

They arrived back from the fair excitable but worn out, ketchup abseiling down Noah's T-shirt, the girls' hair wild from defying gravity.

'Mam?' Dylan called. 'We've brought someone to meet you.' Perhaps if she met him now they could avoid the embarrassment of having to invite him over for tea, and Ines would be more subdued not expecting a new visitor.

Noah wandered around their kitchen, pawing at random items as if he was in a museum.

'Put that down,' Emma chided. 'That's our nan's. My mam will 'ave you if you break it.'

'Sorry.' He placed the vase on the table and stumbled back awkwardly, holding his hands behind him.

Mam appeared in the kitchen then, stretching her arms and yawning. 'I must have drifted off. Oh, well, forgive my manners. This must be the infamous Noah?'

Dylan flinched. 'Mam, don't.'

'It's lovely to meet you, Mrs Wyn.'

'Oh, Gwen – please. You'll age me calling me tha'.'

'Where's Ines?' Edi asked.

'Look, we won Ines a fish.' Emma held it up for approval and received a reluctant nod. It was just another thing to look after.

'She's probably taken herself to bed.'

Edi looked to Emma: didn't seem likely. Emma trotted upstairs, the fish still in hand, as Dylan lingered with her candyfloss.

'Would you like a squash or something, Noah?'

'No, thanks, Mrs – Gwen,' he corrected himself. He stood there, looking around curiously, hands still tied behind his back, sensing some discomfort in the room.

'She's not here,' Emma shouted from upstairs.

'She must be,' Mam said, throwing discarded cups and plates into the sink.

When Emma came back down, Mam looked as if to say, *Well?* But they were in agreement. Ines definitely wasn't there. Mam checked again in the living room, opened the tiny downstairs bathroom just in case, looked between the pipes, then opened the drawers of the dresser, like she might be hiding where the plates lived, scratching her head as if the answer to where she was should be in there. After searching the house high and low, unease slowly spiralling into panic, Mam grabbed the torch from the kitchen drawer and picked up the receiver, turning the rotary dial with her finger several times to call the local police station, words materialising a worst nightmare: *My eight-year-old daughter has gone missing.* Yes, it was out of character. No, there was nowhere else she could be. They didn't have anyone else, only each other. Emma went next door and knocked on Glenys' door, coming back to inform the rest that she was getting into the car with Ned to help look for Ines. She was probably down the street, playing with those kids.

When the policemen arrived, Mam knew the officer because he'd worked with Grampy and she'd also gone to school with him. He searched the house first as if they were stupid, like Ines might be hiding under one of the beds, which she wasn't because the spaces were crammed full of their stuff. They asked if there had been any issues recently, *anything that might have set the girl off.* Mam told them about her tantrum over the fair and Dylan lowered her eyes.

'She's eight, Matthew,' Mam screeched at him. 'She can't be out in the dark on her own at night; anything could happen. You need to tell your officers to go out and look for her.'

He wrapped his arms around her easefully, as if he was familiar with holding her, and she quickly shook him off, aware of everyone's eyes on her.

'Look, Gwen, I'll do everything I can, all right? We've circulated the details to everyone on duty. I've radioed in her description, and there are officers looking for her at the fair now, right. Do you have a photo I can take with me?'

'I think I know where she's gone,' Dylan murmured then, the room turning to look at her, at what she was holding limply in her hands. 'It's my diary. She's been reading it again, and the map's gone. I think she's gone to find our den.'

★★★

'I think we should go back, Ines.' Edi pulled her cardigan down over her hands. 'It's getting dark now.'

'Go back, then.' Ines marched on ahead, deeper into the embrace of the woods she knew so well.

As they'd walked through the village there had been the occasional whiplash of a passing car, the religious reprise of the local choir drifting out of the town hall. But the night had quietened since then, but for the distant drum of the fair and its faraway hollers of thrill.

The woods smelt like pine and the kick-up of dust from playing tag. Ines could taste the sweetest of tree swings and all the nuclear-coloured Tip Tops they'd eaten there over so many summers.

'You're gonna get in so much trouble,' Edi warned.

'It'll be worth it. I can't wait to see her stupid face when she knows I've been to their secret den.'

'Let's come back tomorrow, then,' she appealed. 'In the daylight?'

'Shush, Edi! I can't remember which way.' She scrabbled about for the map drawn in crayon: it made less sense to her now that she was here. Edi followed quietly behind her. There was only the sound of their feet crunching over dead leaves and branches as they passed through the thick pine trees. 'What was that?' Ines looked around nervously, growing afraid, the tree-lined passages becoming denser and more unknown, the branches scratching at her bare legs. 'Tell me a story, Edi.'

'Okay ... well, once upon a time, high up in these hills lived the great mountain Plynlimon and her three daughters. Plynlimon was mam of all the mountains and the highest points in the whole of Wales. When she straightened her back, she awakened all the creatures in the woodlands and forests. She stretched her strong arms, which were covered with cragged rocks but she was so big they looked like tiny little shells from the sea. And when she opened her mouth wide it was filled full of grass from the endless lands she'd watched over since the beginning of creation.'

'I think we're lost, Edi.' Ines felt the softness of fingers interlinking with hers.

'When mighty Plynlimon awoke that day she gazed upon her three daughters, but her eyes, which usually had the depths of the deepest sea, were completely empty and dry. Wye, Severn and Ystwyth asked their mam what they could do to help her. How could they fill her eyes with all the power and strength of the sea? Plynlimon said, "Daughters, I have reared you from the bogs and nurtured you in my marshes. You were born in the mountains but you must each follow your destiny and have your own journeys." And the daughters cried out. They were so sad because they didn't want to leave their mam behind but all their tears still weren't enough to fill Plynlimon's eyes.'

'Look, the river!' Ines let go of Edi's hand.

'Ystwyth, the smallest of the sisters, was brave and eager to meet with the sea. She wanted to hear the gulls screech, to see the colours of coral, feel the soft, silky head of a seal and become one with great beauty. "Go forth," said Plynlimon, "and receive the blessing of your mam and the mams who came before me." Ystwyth set off in haste, and as quick as that a river was born.'

'Look, there it is!' Ines ran excitedly to the bank and pointed across the river to the wooden door. It was the one she'd read about in Dylan's diary, spray-painted yellow, just like the map said.

Edi's voice quickened. 'Then the second daughter, Severn, stepped forwards. She wanted to see the creation of mortals, to understand their wisdom and to become one with great creation. "Go forth," said Plynlimon, "and receive the blessing of your mam and the mams who came before me." And Severn waded into herself, and just like that another river was born.'

Ines could feel the freezing cold water soaking into her trainers as she wobbled across the large pebbled stones, taking sharp breaths as the water started to soak further up her jeans. 'I just want to see inside,' she urged, and Edi's voice stayed close.

'The eldest of the daughters, Wye, lingered, seeing first that her sisters had gone safely. Then she kissed her mam's cheek and made her graceful wish to remain a part of the lands offering protection and a home for the river creatures, a steady passage for those who sailed her. She wished to become one with great Nature. "Go forth," said Plynlimon, "and receive the blessing of your mam and the mams who came before me."'

The water came fast then, rushing past Ines, applying force against her legs, but she had played in this river a thousand times before. 'It's cold,' she shivered, 'but it's not too deep. We can make it across.'

'Don't you want to know the end of the story? Wye glided into herself and began her journey down to the sea. And all three daughters became rivers, flowing through the darkest woods and spreading out to the brightest shores. Currents raging against themselves until their passage became smoother so that they met with one another, together, and became one with the sea.'

'EDI!' Ines called for her in the dark. It was almost pitch-black now; the only light source was the river's reflection of the wide yawning moon waking up to something precarious.

Edi's voice grew softer: 'Plynlimon's eyes began to fill and fill, rising with blue waters as her daughters joined this endless cycle. These three winding sisters returning to where they came from,' she whispered in the darkness, 'to the mam of the mountains, to Plynlimon, back to me.'

Ines tripped and screamed, falling and tumbling with the current, hitting her back against the rock, shrieking with the shock of the freezing water, ice-cold in her lungs, the river rushing through her as she tried to scrabble with her feet for its bed. She pushed to the surface crying out, the rapids filling her eyes and mouth, gasping for air under the surface until eventually she felt herself calming, floating through the shape of her name in her sisters' mouths, lungs filling with water.

Then hands were grabbing at her pink sweater, pulling her up to the surface, Emma wading in behind Noah and crying out to her. Blue and red lights, sirens and the blurriness of figures emerging on the bank as she coughed and spluttered, the river pouring back out of her.

'It's okay, I've got her.'

When Noah reached the side of the bank, he handed her to an officer as she tried to scrabble back to him. Back to this new sense of safety, transplanting itself away from her sisters and into this stranger, who was like some swell she had always known.

★★★

This was the angriest Mam had ever been, pacing around the doctor, prowling, ready to pounce on blame. Dylan lingered behind them, meek for once, as Emma flattened a plastic cup from the water cooler.

'Can I see her yet?' Mam asked, her voice cracked against the back of her throat.

'Almost, Mrs Wyn,' the doctor replied.

'It's Miss Wyn. And what does "almost" mean? She's my baby. I just need to know she's gonna be all right.'

'Miss Wyn,' the doctor corrected herself, 'we're going to keep Ines in overnight. How long she'll need to be in hospital is indeterminable at this stage, but she's showing signs of aspiration pneumonia, which is very serious.'

'Is she going to be all right?' Emma whimpered.

'We've given her antibiotics to help fight the infection, and she's on an IV. What she needs now is to rest. She's incredibly fatigued. If you wait here, one of the nurses will come and get you. Mum, you can come in and see her but it's better if the rest of the family wait here.'

As the doctor disappeared, Mam stretched her hands backwards then ran them through her hair, tugging at herself as if wanting to feel something else.

'This is your fault.' She turned on Dylan, eyes dilated with terror.

Emma tried to referee: 'Mam, wait—'

'Now you can shut it 'n'all.' Mam turned back to Dylan. 'Why do you always have to be so cruel to her? She just wants to be like you. Can't you see that? She dotes on you, but all you care about is looking cool in front of some kids at school. You're a selfish girl, Dylan Wyn. Do you yer me? She could've died!'

Dylan spoke up over the despair writhing inside her: 'Wa-wasn't it you who was meant to be watching her?'

Everyone in the hospital waiting room felt the slap as it came hard across her face.

1984

Gwendoline is fifteen

She was walking home from school with her best friend, Angharad, and as they turned onto Laurel Road, Gwendoline saw some of the neighbours gathering on the pavement. She took in the ambulance that was pulled up on the kerb outside her house, lights still flashing. She started to run.

The front door was open and she could hear her mam howling as she sprinted through the kitchen, almost tripping over the medical bags. There were paramedics in fluorescent jackets. Angharad hung back, standing in the living-room doorway as Gwendoline dropped to her knees next to her brother. Her mam sat further away, near the fireplace, legs sprawled underneath her. She was praying, begging God over and over again: *Please don't take him. Not this time. I'll do anything, please. Please don't take him from me. Not yet.*

Llewellyn's bare chest was white and exposed, and Gwendoline winced each time they shocked him. His whole body lifted off the living-room carpet with the electricity that pulsed through him, like an exorcism. The paddles were too big for his small body, and all she could think to do was count in the defibrillator with the paramedics: six, seven, eight, nine, ten. His body lurching up off the carpet again, his eyes still closed, enduring his own lifelessness.

'Come on!' one of the paramedics said, frustrated, and it was then she knew they were losing this battle.

It went on for some time, until one said they had to call it. A reluctant nod, her mam's howling intensifying as she pushed the paramedic out of the way and lifted the top half of his body into her, rocking him back and forth like a baby, still bargaining with God. But Gwendoline knew God didn't make deals with people like them.

They called the time of death, and the panic flooded through her. She hadn't realised she was screaming until Angharad's arms had come tightly around the back of her. 'I'm sorry.' She held on tightly. 'I'm so sorry.'

Gwendoline thought how appalling an apology was for death. An insignificant stop-gap in the face of such gaping loss, as it slowly set into her: a creeping realisation reconfigured who she was now that he wouldn't be here. Wouldn't ever be again. She reached for her brother's hand.

'We're so sorry for your loss,' said one of the paramedics, starting to pack his equipment, like the job was done.

Easter

April

Noah now realises that Ines is just humouring him. He'd seen her relief when, instead of disappearing off into his studio, he'd suggested they do something together this morning. Ines hates hiking yet she'd feigned enthusiasm, filling water bottles and overextending ideas about where they should go – just another of her performances. She was totally unaware of what he'd found last night, and he had asked himself if he was culpable, if he had gone along with it, pretending her last-minute trips to London were for the wedding even after reading the emails about auditions from her agent on their shared iPad. One for a new family drama – she was clearly excited about it.

He decides they're going to hike the Black Mountain because it's more challenging and, if he's honest, he wants to see her struggle. Wants to take pliers to these fabrications and abstract them from her, lay them out one by one and watch her squirm. Looks forward to the face of innocence she'll deploy as she feels for her back-footedness.

They start their ascent and she lags behind, refreshing her social-media feed and winding herself up with posts from her drama-school friends.

'They're *all* on set or on stage and they just can't shut the fuck up about it.' She pushes her phone back into her pocket and indulges in a post-scroll deflation, the walk only exacerbating her frustration.

Noah ignores her. If she wants an acting career she should just be honest about it. He couldn't care less, as long as she isn't drinking herself into oblivion because of it. She pulls her jacket around her more tightly to signal her discomfort, a state he's assumed responsibility for since she was eight years old. It smells like sticky pine and manure, and he knows all she really wants is a gin and tonic, some opportunity to go somewhere worthy of her Margiela Tabis that 'are being held hostage in their box'. But they aren't: she just sees it that way. He encourages her to try one of the blackberries, which she does, but only to appease him. They come across a rotting carcass trapped in the bushes and he's captured by the scene.

'Gross!'

He looks down at the fetid sheep, its skull starting to emerge, looks back up at Ines, who brings her palm to her mouth, her tongue pushing out the berries, dark saliva running down her chin, and he feels the same repulsion.

'The brambles have barbs, see.' He snaps one off and hands it to her. 'Here, on their tendrils. They come out and point backwards so the only way for an animal to move when it gets barbed is further into the bush. Sort of eats it up.'

She straightens her back, reviewing the carnivorous bush.

'Poor thing would've died of starvation.' He puts his head closer to the rotting animal. 'Yeah, most likely. Now its nutrients will go back into the ground and they'll end up feeding the plant. Isn't that clever?'

She says *gross* again, like he didn't register her antipathy the first time.

'It's not gross,' he snaps. 'It's the natural cycle of things. You'll rot and disintegrate into the ground, too, one day.'

'I'd rather be cremated.' Her arrogance walks off ahead of her.

'But cremation is like the final fuck-you to the planet.'

'You sound so naive sometimes, do you know that?' she spars. 'So outdated.'

'I'm not a trench coat, Ines. I'm a person.' His mind transfers to the foetus and the practicalities of where it had gone, some chemical waste bin, or perhaps it, too, had been cremated. She forces a sigh and starts walking faster, grass lashing against his shins as he follows her. 'Why did you tell everyone we were trying for a baby?'

'Uh, maybe because we are? And who's everyone? Since when did you have an issue with me talking to my family?'

He'd read that sometimes miscarried babies were buried or cremated together. 'Are we, though?' He rushes in front of her, starts walking backwards so he can look her in the face. Her eyes do an involuntary backflip.

'What is this about?' Impatience is her best posture now.

'For Christ's sake, for once in your life be honest. Not just with me, with yourself.'

She stops then and looks at him, her expression witnessing this version of herself being dismantled in his eyes. She isn't just failing at being who *she* wants to be: she isn't who he wants either.

'Your contraception,' he says then, as her insolence takes up space in his body.

'I don't know what you're talking about.' She goes to overtake him, but he speeds up.

'You see, it's this tiny pill you pop in your mouth every morning and it stops you getting pregnant. I found it in your makeup bag last night.'

'Don't be so condescending. You sound like your mother.' Then, of course, she redirects: 'Why were you going through my stuff?'

He starts laughing. 'That's seriously it, is it? Not even a fucking apology. Of course not.' He shakes his head. 'I should know better.'

'For what?'

He can see she's spiralling, trying to discern her next move. 'We've been trying for a baby, like what the fuck?' And her face now is like she's the one who's been betrayed. 'You should've told me if you'd changed your mind.'

'I didn't say I changed my mind. It's complicated, Noah. I don't know, maybe a part of me is afraid it'll happen again.' She sinks her hands further into her coat pockets, trying to make herself and the lie smaller.

'You promised this lying would stop. You said, when we moved back, things would be different, but you just can't help yourself, can you? The auditions you've been running back to London for? God, you must think I'm fucking daft.' He feels like giving up, turns and starts walking back down the splayed grass forming a pathway.

'I'm here, Noah,' she shouts after him. 'Can you not see I'm fucking here? Smelling the cow pat and trekking up fucking mountains, watering your garden every day, and I'm trying my absolute best not to go mad in this deafening silence. I'm not in London, chasing auditions or booking jobs. I'm here – with you. Like you asked me to be.'

Her voice enacts pain but he doesn't turn to witness the show, albeit convincing. They had both been miserable in London. He keeps walking away from her. Faster, back down the trail, and he can tell she's crying now, knows she'll do anything to placate him. She calls for him to stop and the heavy wind distorts her voice. He can tell she's getting closer, feels her grab at his shoulder.

'I didn't want him. There! Are you happy now? I never wanted the baby. I thought about getting rid of him before the miscarriage even happened – I thought about it all the time.'

This new information is infecting his thoughts but he shakes his head dismissively, and she looks like she's about to lose it.

'Don't you get it?' Truth of another kind, iridescent and flecked across her skin, as he takes her in. 'I didn't want him and then he died.' She shrugs helplessly. 'I didn't want him and then . . .'

But it wasn't her fault. He tells her it was always going to happen, regardless of whether or not she wanted him. It's just one of those horrible things that happen. He takes her by the shoulders and her hands hang listlessly. 'It wasn't your fault, Ines. You mustn't blame yourself.' She doesn't believe him.

'Why can't it just be us?' she screams as she pushes against his chest. 'Why are you never satisfied with it just being me?'

He's washed away from himself then, the bad guy once again, running out of options when it comes to what's best for her.

★★★

Emma puts out her arms and reaches for the warmth of Kit's body under the covers, feels him wince at her cold hands as she draws herself in to his back, taking a deep breath at his nape.

'We had better get up soon.' He taps her wandering fingers, which settle on his chest.

'Not yet . . .' She groans. 'They're still asleep. Let's stay here for a while at least until one of them wakes.'

She feels his body tense. 'I've things I need to get on with. There's not a lot of space for downtime, is there?' He draws back the covers. 'Not when you insist on inviting them over all the time.'

It was true: the last thing she wanted was a houseful of people but she'd offered to host Easter months ago. She watches him pick up his phone, a thumb sifting through it. She strokes his chest but he continues to look for distraction from her desire that's beating between them through the sheets.

'Do you know, not one of them texted me to say happy birthday last week?'

'Mum did.' She sighs unsympathetically. 'They're just busy.' She rolls onto her back. 'And I don't invite them over *all the time*. It's Easter Sunday.' They'd spent it with his parents last year.

He pretends not to hear her. Gets up and goes into the en-suite, turns the shower on. Leaving her legs crushing together, feeding off anticipation and the urgency between her thighs. She gets up, goes into the bathroom where she watches him shower. The water falling off his back and the comforting smell of shampoo. She pushes her nightie off her shoulders, shields her breasts with an arm as she pulls back the shower door and steps inside.

'Did you say you got prawns in the end?' he asks mindlessly, eyes closed, rigorously scrubbing his skull, one eye open then, some acknowledgement that she's there, even if uninvited.

'Uh-huh.' She reaches for the soap and massages it into his shoulders, running her hands across an almost hairless chest, firm from cycling back and forth between home and the hospital.

'What are you doing?' He turns his body away, finishes rinsing his hair.

'Washing you.' Her lips part.

'I'm not one of the kids.' He laughs a little, as though the intimacy embarrasses him.

She steps softly over the reluctance, pushing herself up against his back, showing him what she wants.

'Oh, stop it. You're acting like a teenager.' He washes off the soap, pushes past her still dappled with suds and the shunt of the shower door feels cruel.

She is left alone with her body, with the mass of dark hair she never trims, breasts hanging lower as she takes in all its lacerations: the smiling Caesarean scar beneath her paunch; the incision across the web of her left hand from cutting into frozen sausages as a kid; her appendix operation a thickset zipper. She is fighting to get into this body of hers as she stands under the pouring water but it won't have her. She turns off the hot tap and lets the freezing water dispel her humiliation, gasping for air as it stifles her yearning, letting it run cold.

Later, after Emma has finished the prep for lunch, she wanders around the garden hiding small eggs for the hunt. She thinks she'll have just one. But it doesn't quell the angst rippling under her skin. She looks for a tree-sheltered corner, then, somewhere she's out of sight, forces five or six more into her mouth. She doesn't stop to taste the sweetness, ramming the pastel-coloured wrappers into the front of her apron. She knows she needs to get hold of it – it's getting worse. She'd already had teeth bonded to repair the damage and can't face having that conversation with Kit again.

'Mummy!' Sunny's voice comes for her. 'You said we weren't allowed to eat any till after lunch.'

She looks back up to the house, sees him by the bi-fold doors, tuning into the commotion.

'She's eating all the eggs!' Sunny exclaims, like she's some traitor, not the woman who actualised that snitching mouth with her own flesh.

Kit sidles down the lawn towards them and she wipes at her mouth hectically, tells Sunny she had just one, that she's been too busy to have any breakfast. 'Shall I do that?' He takes the handful of eggs from her, then the bucket out of her hand. She dips her head with shame as he says to their eight-year-old, 'That's naughty, isn't it? Greedy Mummy.' He continues then to do the job she's proved incapable of, distributing them around the flowerbeds where she'd planted the begonias, fisting seeds into soil. And Sunny, some part of Kit too, roaming behind, learning to enjoy the turning of a cold shoulder.

She carries this feeling when everyone arrives, throwing coats and jackets across sofas, discarding glasses of prosecco on radiator covers, teacups cast away and misplaced. Kit has to shout over loud music and the giggling protests of the kids, whom Noah is winding up, while Mam distributes a large bag of chocolate eggs. Dylan and Ines squabble over which one they want – as usual – never stopping to ask which one Emma might like. Mam makes her annual squawk: 'Don't bicker over them or next year I'm buying everyone the same.'

And for a fleeting moment it's as if this life never happened: no one got married, started a business, moved out, or developed any semblance of independence. A tumble down a rabbit hole in a collapsing of time. Here she is, still standing on the sidelines waiting for whatever's left. And perhaps life is simpler when her sisters' wants are intertwined and overtaking her own, as if they were still passing that invisible ball around, sidestepping the damage in a collective trance. How immutable the scars were.

'Rather than saying that every year, Mam,' Emma's voice sparks from the corner of the room, 'why not actually do it for once?'

Dylan and Ines stop laughing and frown with a shared brow: *There's no need for that. What's the matter with you?* But that's an easy position for them to take, isn't it? So unfairly distributed is the load.

She gets through lunch by focusing on making three different versions of the same salad, two separate dressings, dairy-free for Ines, milky and thickset for Kit, who doesn't once offer anyone a drink. When everyone has finished their prawn linguine he suggests they play cards, but Sunny demands the Easter egg hunt she's just eaten all her spaghetti for. Dylan checks her watch again, and Emma hopes he'll stand her up. It wasn't fair – the male pursuit of her was constant, their affections unceasing.

'Who would like dessert?' She distributes spoons, an internal smirk warming her belly when no one offers to help.

Dylan cuts over her as the doorbell goes, 'Now who could that be?' getting up from the table. Sunny follows, Lilah tottering after them.

'Who is it?' Ines asks, confused, and Kit rolls his eyes as if to say, *You'll see.*

Emma places the pudding on the table and decants the custard she's warmed into a porcelain jug. 'I made a rhubarb and apple crumble.'

She's upstaged again, this time by a giant bunny, who walks through the kitchen, an empty wicker basket looped over his arm. Mam finishes what's left in her wine glass and picks up her cigarettes, readying herself to go.

'Look at that, kiddo! The Easter bunny has made a special visit.' Kit gets up to shake the bunny's hand – what a dick. Lilah, the only one of them she could still stand, stays clutching its leg and pressing her head against the soft fur.

Dylan hands out the small pink buckets and Sunny squeals with excitement.

'No one wants dessert, then?' Emma pricks.

'For goodness' sake, if you're that bothered why don't you just polish it off?' Kit forces a laugh, but the tension roots itself.

'Right. I'll try a little, with cream, please. Thanks, Em.' Dylan smiles weakly at her but it's laced with superiority. She has no idea what it takes to hold down a marriage, the sacrifices that need to be made. None of them do.

Dylan takes the bunny by his arm, laughing as she leads him out into the garden, and Emma stifles an urge to say something mean.

'Who's that exactly?' Noah asks, ever discreet.

'It's Dylan's new piece.' Kit's helping himself to the crumble now, and Noah's peeve buckles in for the ride.

'Whatever happened to Oliver?'

'Bit the dust.' Ines dips her finger into the custard.

Emma asks her not to do that: it's unhygienic. She can feel Noah's eyes on her, prying for more information. 'It's Dan,' she obliges him. 'You know, he owns the White Hart. Apparently he was already renting the costume for the kids at the pub, said it wouldn't be a problem to pop in for an hour.' She raises an eyebrow. 'Nice of him, isn't it? To be fair, he's quite hot, underneath all that fluff.'

Kit squints at her with distaste, and Ines inflicts further judgement: 'Eww, Emma. I mean I know you don't have *great* taste, but even so.'

Kit drops his spoon and it clangs against the bowl.

'I'm kidding, obviously.' She winks. 'Lighten up, Kitten.'

'Funnily enough I don't care for the opinion of a failed actress. And I've asked you several times now not to call me that.'

Ines is insulted, and Emma doesn't understand. They used to get on.

'He's just joking,' she defends him, while mollifying her sister.

Noah tilts his head distractedly, watching Dan racing Lilah and Sunny out on the lawn, as he says to no one in particular: 'What a strange way to try to impress someone.'

With some help from their aunts, the hunt is completed, but during the count, Emma insists they're divided between the girls equally, which leads to an eruption of tears from Sunny. Lilah sits on the grass, eating her finds with total separation from the situation. Kit admonishes her decision: 'It's unhealthy to construct a falsity of fairness. No one will share their earnings in real life. That's a fact. They need to learn the fundamentals of life.'

'I disagree. I think it's important they learn to share, Kit.' The addition of his name is lit with aggression. She notices Mam's still not back, decides to go and find her – she's not the only one who could use some time out.

When she opens the front door Mam's where she expects her to be, sitting on the bench, smoking.

'Can I have one?' Kit's thick coat drowns her as she lingers for permission, tucking her hands under her armpits.

'You know I don't like you smoking.'

Emma tuts and helps herself to the packet. They sit together quietly, bathing in a nicotine-induced peace.

'Kit seems a little tense today.'

'Don't start.'

Mam puts out her cigarette in the gravel at her feet.

'He's doing long hours at the hospital.'

Her silence is a gut punch.

'Do *you* know what it's like to be a cardiologist? It's exhausting and stressful – we can't expect to understand.'

'You always make excuses for him.' Mam shrugs, turning away from her.

'And you're always so judgemental of him.'

'I don't think that's fair.'

Emma hadn't noticed until now how drawn her mother looks.

'I understand that being a mam takes a lot from you.'

'I give it willingly,' she hears herself say, snide. 'I mean, I'm happy to.' Something unnameable cinches in the air between them.

Mam says she needs to be getting back: she'd promised she'd check in on Glenys and has left washing on the line. 'Looks like the heavens are about to open.'

But Emma knows she's been in bed all week and that getting herself here today had been a struggle.

'I'm fine,' Mam says, reading her mind.

'I'm sorry you're not feeling great.'

Mam closes her eyes and smiles peaceably, treating her depression like Emma might a stye or a gynaecology appointment – undesirable but sometimes unavoidable. They stand up off the bench and Mam wraps her arms around her in a tight hug, which surprises her. 'I just want you to be happy. We all do. And it's easy, you know, to become a martyr in it all. But there is something brilliant about showing children you have needs of your own. It's a good lesson to impart, especially to girls. It'll teach 'em to assert themselves.'

She's irritated by the accuracy of the assessment, how much alike they seem in that moment. But she isn't Mam, would never do what Mam did. Emma nods and watches her get into the car, left with a sadness that starts to form as if it's her own. She can't bear the thought of her in that house all alone.

★★★

'Will I see you this week, then?' Dan asks a second time, as she's showing him out.

'Sure.' Dylan holds her nonchalance, but it surprises her how much she wants to. She hasn't fancied anyone like this in ages and his smell is like knowledge in her body. She kisses him, pulling him by his bunny costume into the downstairs toilet, pushing the door closed, pinning him against the tiles. Her hand makes its way to his groin, teasing. He tries to kiss her but she pulls her head back as she presses herself against him, moving her hips. He's grabbing her arse, rough and groaning. Together, they keep rotating, until he makes a noise she covers with her hand, finishing herself off.

'What are you doing?'

Dylan freezes when she hears Ines's voice coming from the hallway. Turns, pushes at the door and sees Noah guiltily sprinting back, a tea towel and glass jug in hand. 'Nothing. Sssh,' he whispers. 'Go in there.'

He pushes her back inside the kitchen and Dylan tells Dan it's time to go.

'I was spying on DW.'

They can hear him from the front door.

'Why?' Ines sounds amused.

Dan awkwardly sidles out, as she hears Ines reminding Noah that she's a big girl and is perfectly capable of looking after herself. She closes the door and composes herself in the sentiment.

'Dan from the White Hart!' Ines says to her triumphantly, as she strides back into the kitchen, still a little flushed. 'He's actually quite cute now. Surprising.'

'Not surprising,' Emma says, spooning leftovers into Tupperware. 'Men get better with age.'

Dylan twists a tea towel and spanks Ines's bottom. 'Keep your knickers on, girls. I'm not gonna marry the guy; we're just having a bit of fun.'

'Are you ever going to take anyone seriously?' Noah's voice strangles. 'Or do you think you'll dry-hump strangers for the rest of your life?' He demonstratively applies Tupperware lids.

So, he had seen, the pervert, but she refuses this quake of embarrassment.

'My vote's option two,' is Kit's pathetic attempt to partake in the banter and Dylan narrows a scowl at him.

'Dry-hump – that's an old one.' Emma's clearly entertained.

Dylan is frustrated. She sees how badly her sister wants them to come together in her home, the discomfort of which also leads to her passive aggression.

Kit suggests they watch a film, another passive route for getting through a whole day with her family. He'd made it apparent he was inconvenienced by having them here today. Emma brightens at the idea, also wanting a get-out card. So, they go into one of the sitting rooms and sink into the large sofas, which are so deep they encase Sunny, who sits with her legs flat in front of her. And when someone suggests popcorn, it's Noah who gets up to make it. Dylan waits a few moments, takes a breath, then asks if anyone else wants a glass of water.

In the privacy of the kitchen, she rounds on him. 'Were you spying on me, you creep?'

'Hardly. I needed the toilet. I didn't know you pair would be in there, did I? Does Ollie know? They play golf together, don't they?'

They hiss back and forth at each other over the sound of popping corn.

'Oh, listen to yourself – grow up.'

'Why don't you take that advice and stop running away from any opportunity at a meaningful relationship?'

'It doesn't have to last two decades for it to be meaningful. And get Emma's words out of your mouth. Construct your own insults.'

'Okay, fine. Here's one. Bouncing from prick to prick certainly isn't meaningful, and if you're fooling yourself that it is, you're more screwed up than even I realised.'

She knows the wounding is visible, can see it in the twist of his mouth. He'd gone too far with the makeshift big-brotherly energy. She thrusts a glass under the tap and storms back into the living room. Noah follows, once the popcorn is done, and when he places the large bowls on the coffee table, he says he's not feeling great, has a headache, he's going to shoot.

Ines sits forward on the sofa. 'Oh . . . are you okay?' Her concern is tentative. 'Do you want me to get you some paracetamol?'

He says he's fine, just needs an early night, and when Ines says she'll go with him, he tells her to stay and enjoy the film in a way that's difficult to push back on. Dylan wonders what they're fighting about this time and offers her a lift back. Emma says she can stay the night if she likes, it's no trouble.

His headlights shine through the living-room window as the car wheels spin over the gravel. Dylan huddles closer to Lilah, pulling the blanket up around their waists. 'Can someone turn it up, please?'

2000

Three Years After They Moved to Laurel Road

Emma is thirteen, Edi is twelve, Dylan is eleven, Ines is eight

No one dared mention den-gate. After Ines got back from the hospital two weeks later it was as if the slap was still lightly imprinted on Dylan's face, like the fear of God taking its time to leave her. Mam had kept them all off school, wanted them where she could see them, where she could keep them safe. Ines loved the attention. Her class at school made her a card, and Glenys would bring her dog over to sit on the end of her bed and keep her company. Emma would bring chicken-paste sandwiches and warmed Welsh cakes to her room whenever she was hungry, and Ines would pick out the raisins. Initially Ines hadn't thought to blame Dylan for what had happened, though the idea congealed in her when she saw Mam did: making Dylan help with the laundry, collect prescriptions and pick things up from the shop.

After they had had three weeks off school, Noah knocked on their door and it was Ines who answered.

'Hello ...' She stood looking up at him, excitement nose-diving into the expanse of her affections.

'Hi, Ines.' He had a soft lisp, then gave her his signature half-smile, the one Dylan had written in her diary reminded her of Elvis. 'How are you feeling?'

She looked down at her feet as if to register what she might wrangle out of him with a response. Should she ham it up and widen his worry? Or perhaps it would make her more appealing, more grown-up if she played it all down.

'Funny how you all look so alike.' He pushed his weight into his feet.

'I'm feeling much better.' She chose bravery and drew his attention back to her accident.

'Good, that's good. You had your mam so worried. All of us were.' He ran the back of his hand across his mouth. 'We can all build a den together next time, if you like. That one's gone now. The police took it away.'

Her shoulders rose slightly. 'I'd like that.'

'Where's Dylan, then?' He looked straight over her head. 'She's not been to school in ages. I brought some stuff over for you.' He lifted a blue carrier bag.

'Things for me?' Ines play-acted surprise, trying on a humility that didn't belong to her, a small hand clasping the brass door lock as she pictured Dylan's face, sore from crying every day.

'Yeah, some sweets and candy cigarettes, stuff from Mr Salem's.' He gestured, widening the mouth of the bag. 'Are your sisters in?'

'Ines, who are you talking to?' Mam came to the door. 'Oh ... Noah, how nice to see you.' She placed a hand on Ines's head and Ines quickly shook it off.

'Is Dylan home?'

'She's gone out to run some errands for us.'

He looked disappointed. 'I just wanted to drop these off.' He handed over the bag and Ines snagged it. 'Just some sweets, and there's a comic for DW. She hasn't been to school ...' He trailed off.

'That's very thoughtful of you. Thank you.'

'See you, then.' He made his way back down the path towards the rusting gate.

'Noah,' Mam called after him, 'I don't think we can ever thank you enough for getting Ines out of there. The doctor's said if she'd been in the water any longer ... Well, it doesn't bear thinking about. She was incredibly lucky.' She looked down at Ines and pressed sternly, 'And she won't ever do anything like that again, will you?'

'No.' Ines blushed at being reprimanded in front of him.

'But we'd like to start by inviting you over for tea. Maybe Wednesday?'

He looked up at her and grinned. 'Okay, thank you. I'll come back Wednesday.'

'Six o'clock, then.'

When Mam closed the door, Ines ran upstairs to her bedroom and emptied the contents of the carrier bag onto the floor, enjoying the sweets and reading through the notes he'd left on the comic book as though they were written for her: the parts that reminded him of her and the characters he thought she'd like best. Small drawings of Cherry as a superhero. It's not that she didn't consider giving it to Dylan, but it was Ines who'd been in hospital and who was receiving all the get-well gifts. Handing it over would have cracked a delusion that was fast to form.

When Dylan got back from the shops, Mam told her Noah had come by. No mention of the carrier bag, though, so when Dylan never mentioned his handwritten notes, Noah had been too embarrassed to ask.

'You should give it back to Dylan,' Edi urged, as if it were of importance.

'I'm in love, Edi.' Ines lay back on the carpet as if to make a snow angel. 'I'm in love with Noah Ingelton.'

1986

Gwendoline is seventeen

When Gwendoline opened the front door she could hear the TV on in the living room. Asked Tommy to wait in the kitchen, said it would be better if she told them herself. She stood in the doorway between their kitchen and the living room. Her parents were sitting next to one another on the sofa, matching trays decorated with red and purple pansies resting on their laps, with soup bowls and crumbs from the buttered white bread Gwendoline had started trying not to eat. She supposed her weight was of little consequence now.

'Terrible,' her mam said. 'Bunch of scabs, the lot of 'em.'

'Ah, Edith, don't start. People are starving, love. They're struggling to feed their families.'

'The things they've done to you?' She turns to him, horrified. 'The injuries you've come home with? You should be lucky I'm not calling them something else. I could think of a lot worse.'

'Well, save it for that dragon Thatcher.'

Gwendoline looked at the screen and the scenes from the miners' strike, men in leather flat caps and thick winter jackets running, some falling to the ground in the riot as they pushed against rows of police officers. Then a young man in a flying jacket getting carried off, hands cuffed behind his back, jeans ripping against the pavement. Others in the background were hit at full force with truncheons, making Gwendoline wince.

'I've told you, I don't want you going down the men's club. It'll only be trouble. It's not you-er fault. It's your job to protect the law.'

He sighed dejectedly. 'All right, love, you've said – made your point, haven't you? I haven't been down there now in months, not since Christmas.'

'Making *cawl*, Dad? Gwendoline interjected, before it turned into a row.

'Aye, love. There's enough for you and Tommy 'n'all, if you like.'

'Great, thanks. I've got something I need to tell you both first.' She knew they weren't going to take it well, yet she still felt the excitement in her belly. 'Can you turn tha' off a sec?' She nodded towards the TV, her mam tutting as Dad lifted the remote from his tray to shut it off.

'Well,' there was no point in sugar-coating it, 'Tommy and I, we've decided to get married.'

'Don't be so bloody ridiculous,' her mam said, her frail body almost disappearing into the grey settee.

Gwendoline descended into the speech she'd planned, about how they loved one another, wanted to move in together and Tommy had his name down for a flat. It was what they both wanted. Her mam told her plainly it was out of the question.

'Please.' Gwendoline's hands were held out in front of her as if the desperation embroiled in her palms might draw some compassion. 'Just listen to me.'

'Oh, I've heard enough, *diolch yn fawr*.'

'Edith, calm down a minute, will ew?' her father tried.

'I will not calm down. She's seventeen.' Then towards her daughter, as if she were unaware of the fact: 'You're seventeen, Gwendoline.'

'And how old were you when you married Llewellyn's dad?'

'Don't you dare bring him into this.' Her mam's rage sharpened.

'Gwen, please. You're not helping yourself, love.'

'I love him and we want to get married. We've been together since year ten. Surely you saw this coming?'

'He's a waster,' her mam spat viciously, teeth yellowed.

'He can yer you. You know tha', don't you?' Her patience dilated. 'He's stood right in the next bloody room.'

'I couldn't care less. He may as well yer what I think of him.'

'You're too young. That's all it is, love.' Her dad leaned forward, put his tray on the coffee table. 'What do you need to get married now for? It can wait a bit, can't it?'

'It can, if you're happy for me to be pregnant out of wedlock.' She folded her arms.

Her mam gasped with outrage. 'Stupid, insolent girl.'

Her father's face folded in, dubious that his baby girl could be carrying one of her own. 'That can't be right. No, that can't be right.' Total disbelief as the situation grew more complex, pushing her further from his safekeeping.

'I'm three months. Won't be long before I start showing.' In that moment, she felt smug. She really had them. Had her mam backed against a wall just like she'd had her for so many years.

Edith started seizing on the sofa then. 'Arwen . . .' she took dramatic loud inhalations as if struggling to breathe '. . . Arwen, get me my inhaler.'

Gwendoline rolled her eyes, not buying a bar of it, as her dad dithered around in a panic, lifting cushions to look for the inhaler. She walked to the sewing box and opened it, lifted out the tartan medical bag. She unzipped it and reluctantly handed her the blue inhaler. 'You're acting like something apocalyptic has happened, not a new life, for Christ's sake.'

'You're a selfish girl, Gwendoline Wyn. And you've ruined you-er life, do you yer me?' She administered the inhaler.

'Because *I* ruined your life, is that it?' She was staggered. 'That's what children do.'

'It should have been you!' her mam cried, her pointed finger severing any connection that was left between them, a maternal thread turning to bloodied floss, disintegrating in the air between them.

'EDITH.' It was the angriest she'd ever seen him, but still he did nothing, her name in his mouth only bookending his spinelessness.

Then her mam collapsed back into the sofa, crying like she was the only one who felt it. 'It should have been you,' she wailed again, tears running down soft, wrinkled cheeks.

'Right, grab your coat,' Gwendoline shouted to Tommy, turning her back as she marched into the kitchen. 'We're going.'

He nodded at her, biting a fingernail as her father weakly followed them out to the car. 'Love, don't, please, she doesn't mean that. She's grieving, is all.'

'I know, Da.' She opened the door to the blue Peugeot and got in. 'We all are,' she said, slamming it behind her.

Wedding-Dress Shopping

May

Rooted in the cottage's self-making cabin fever, Ines had arranged to see an old school friend, which gave her a reason to get into the car and go somewhere. She'd woken alongside her angst, worrying about whether she'd forgotten to water Noah's vegetable garden and whether her own death would be painful, about Mam dying and never being able to ask another living soul what time she was born. She'd got stuck on Edi, feeling the longing pull her under. Her sister in her mind's eye, hair greasy like her own. Running Ines a bath as she cried out in resistance. Taking the bottle of bubble bath shaped like a sailor and unscrewing his hat to breathe in the familiar marzipan scent: *See, Inny, smells nice – you like it, don't you?* Her hands as small as Ines's as they shook about in the water, drumming up bubbles. Damp then as they lifted her top over her head, and for a few seconds she was caught in it all alone, face hot with tears, tangled in all her feelings as the neckline stretched and she popped out the other side. And there was Edi, again, always waiting for her at the end of a tantrum, long after the others lost patience.

She continues to feel claustrophobic on the drive over. There is only so much countryside she can take and all that's left after that are grey concrete roads joining up with endless roundabouts that lead to motorways set on taking her nowhere. She feels clasped in the in-betweens of a more exciting life deserving of her. But how to get there?

When she arrives at the café to meet Tamara, she looks up at its overhead sign. It has always been there, ever since she was a kid, and yet there is something eerily suspicious about it. She keeps experiencing this sensation. As if being at home everything looked as it should but the details were slightly off. She sees her friend through the window, waving enthusiastically.

Inside Ines offers a tight hug, before settling herself in the seat across from her.

'I texted to say I was running late and then I was bang on time,' Tamara marvels.

'Imagine that,' Ines says, releasing the underwhelm through her nose.

'We didn't get a lot of sleep last night. Honestly, we can't remember what life was like before the kids. Exhausting doesn't cut it.'

Ines shakes her head as if to offer pity, registering Tamara's thick Welsh accent, pertinent to this washed-out town they're both from. She'd learned to tone hers down at drama school and now she found it grated on her, as does Tamara's tendency to employ plural pronouns where singular ones ought to be. Drenched in perfume and a blusher too pink for her complexion, Tamara was also the same as she'd always been – wholly committed to the façade she'd constructed for herself as a sixteen-year-old girl – and yet there was something about her that wasn't quite right. She spoke in authoritative inflections on menial subjects as if she were being interviewed on a panel about the parochial. Ines sanctions the small talk, listening to her friend drone on about how excited she is to be pregnant again and how wonderful it will be to have another baby join her already-abundant clan. Instead she focuses on the skin fraying around each of Tamara's nails, resisting the urge to reach across the table and pull it off with her teeth.

'We should get our nails done,' she says pointedly.

'Oh, I don't really bother with them much, these days.' Tamara smiles. 'And you and Noah, then? Do you think a baby is on the cards once you're hitched?'

Still unable to talk about the miscarriage outside the therapy sessions Emma had insisted on paying for, Ines felt protective. She didn't want anyone to know. Tamara had never been a safe place to store delicate feelings, especially those that drew knives in the dark, gently pushing their way into her. She answers the question with a casual air: 'We've not really thought that far ahead. Organising a wedding is time-consuming enough.'

'Oh, it is – but, trust me, the honeymoon makes up for it. You want to make sure you shag the shit out of each other before kids anyway.' Tamara bites the tip of her tongue.

The highly sexualised part of her character had formed in their pubescent years and Ines knew feeling sexy was what Tamara, unfathomably, attached her identity to. As she contemplates her own tethering she seems only to circle back to Noah.

'Oh, Noah and I've never had a problem with that,' she lies.

'How is being back, then? Has it been a difficult adjustment? You must miss London.'

'He's happy here. I'm not so sure. It was nice at first, being home and seeing my sisters and Mam. But the honeymoon period's over. I don't really know what do to with myself.'

Noah had been working a lot and she was starting to feel a little pathetic, creaking the door of his studio open just a sliver, allowing narrow shadows to form on the hopeful part of her face. She could tell it was starting to annoy him.

'You're welcome round to ours anytime – we'll find you something to do.'

Ines forces a smile and sees Tamara acknowledging she's unlikely to take up that offer. She feels stifled now by the interaction. She'd been looking forward to seeing her but the truth is she can't wait to get out of there.

Everything took so long in Wales. They'd only ordered a sandwich and a coffee but forty-five minutes later Ines is still waiting for it, hungry, as she stares at Tamara's frayed cuticles. She suggests they order some wine and her friend says she'll only have a glass. Ines flags the waiter over, orders a bottle of the Merlot.

'I don't think you ever told me your proposal story?' Tamara continues to navigate her conversational comfort zone.

'There isn't much of a story, really. It happened at our place in London. I woke up to a mug of black coffee on the nightstand, like always – he wakes up before me. And he did it then, pushed the ring onto my finger while I was still sleeping, got down on one knee.' The memory softens her.

'What – while you were sleeping?' Tamara scoffs.

'Yeah, it was sweet. I don't know, intimate might be a more accurate word. Sort of like doing it in the place you feel safest.'

Tamara nods at her but the curl in her lip punctuates her disappointment. Not everyone wanted a grotesquely public proposal like hers, done at her parents' pearl wedding anniversary.

Ines drinks her first glass of wine as fast as is socially acceptable before pouring herself a second. When Noah had proposed, she had felt relief. She was happy he hadn't done it in a place infused with childhood nostalgia, but instead where they'd found their own footing. She knew their marriage would set them apart. If she was certain of one thing it was of his sustained presence in her life. He was already a Wyn, totally enmeshed in every childhood memory and folly. His height marked in pencil on Mam's wall, his scars from the bike rides they'd gone on together and his destiny cast in the mouths of her sisters, who'd decided on him. But marriage would mean they belonged to one another. They would be their own entity.

Once the sandwiches arrive, she is quick to demolish hers along with the rest of the bottle, then makes her excuses about needing to get back to Noah before Tamara can show her photos of the downstairs bathroom they've just renovated. But when she eventually escapes she doesn't feel ready to go back to the cottage. Instead she happens upon a wedding-dress shop, considers whether she should go in. She positions her head above the mannequin, trying to gauge from the reflection how she might look in something like that. Her hand smudges the window as she leans towards the beaded veils, cream satin shoes and tiaras glistening like sun on ice. *Go on*. She hears Edi whisper to her. *Why not?* Feelings of torment form like viral condensation on her internal organs.

'Ines?'

She hears her name and turns to see them crossing the road.

'What are you doing here, love?' Mam struts over, awash with surprise.

'I live here now. Remember?'

'I thought you said you didn't want to wear a wedding dress.' Dylan, confused, was looking up at the store.

She'd never felt the effect that brides in magazines seemed to experience, when happiness exploded from them like confetti. She just thought it would be more original to wear something less traditional.

'I'm . . . I don't, and I think you need an appointment, anyway.' She squints awkwardly, her hands tightening around her waist, elbows pushed forward.

'Well, you don't have to try anything on, but we can still have a look, can't we?' Mam straightens her palm and starts to peer through the door.

Dylan sighs. 'I thought we were picking out furniture for my studio.'

'Yes, we are.'

Mam sets off the bell, opening the door to the bridal shop. Ines and Dylan reluctantly follow to find a woman with a forced smile ready to receive them, her bun so tightly pulled as to give her face a slight lift. She asks if they have an appointment.

'No, we don't.' Ines is apologetic.

'We're still okay to have a look, though, aren't we?' Mam answers her own question by defiantly sifting through the dresses.

The woman demurs. She's had two cancellations today, they're in luck. The prosecco arrives quickly after that. They select dresses with the small wooden pegs they're given, some of which Dylan pegs as a joke. Ines is happy to indulge her. The one that gives them the most laughs is a beaded crop top, with a full mini skirt, paired with the longest veil in the shop. Mam tuts, pushing Ines to try on something with a mermaid cut. But Ines goes back into the changing room and tries on her favourite of the dresses, the one she can most see herself in. When she emerges from the changing room, she stands on the Lazy Susan in front of the mirrored wall, looking back at this version of herself, intrigued, wondering if she's more like Tamara than she'd ever admit. 'You look beautiful, Ines.'

'Do you think so?' She smiles as Mam fusses around the dress, allowing herself to linger in the image.

It wasn't that Ines didn't know who she was, it was just that she didn't like herself and tried to be something different. Her emotional disfigurement made her hell-bent on satisfying the emotional needs of others. What was wrong with that? She knew she was snide and sometimes corrosive, saying things that sounded like a compliment but salted others in insult. But she could be sweet too. Thoughtful. And, despite the family consensus, she knows exactly what she wants and that is whatever others crave. Because everything tastes sweeter with the dew of another's desire on it. And everyone's a bit like that really, if only they could admit it to themselves.

Mam starts asking her questions about what she might do with her hair, and she relishes the propelled excitement, imbibing it as her own while they consider a veil. When Ines turns to ask Dylan's opinion, she's frozen in a fawn-like state. Their eyes meet and her sister lifts an eyebrow slightly, some attempt to conceal the contortion of pain on her face. Ines watches realisation dawn on her that this *is* happening. Ines is getting married. This isn't an apparition, or some quick fix that will never materialise. She will go next and, in doing so, perhaps she is stealing something a younger sister should never take.

It's Dylan who breaks this tension. 'Noah would love it.'

Ines looks behind her then and out through the shop window to where this had started. Was she really this bored? To end up here?

She doesn't put a deposit on the dress, despite Mam's protestations. And later that evening Emma messages the Sisters group chat to say how disappointed she is at being excluded.

> Ines: *I told you. It wasn't a planned thing. I don't know why Mam sent you photos. We were just being silly.*
> Emma: *I'm just saying it would have been nice to be included.*
> Ines: *I don't know why you're making this about you, Em.*

She sees Dylan start typing and when nothing comes through she feels the sensation in her own mouth of her sister biting her tongue.

2000

Three Years After They Moved to Laurel Road

Emma is thirteen, Edi is twelve, Dylan is eleven, Ines is eight

Noah was nervous, but he reassured himself there was no need to be. Miss Wyn seemed sound and, besides, he had rescued their little sister – DW said she was the favourite, too – which would keep him in her good books, at least for a while. He had always wanted to go to their house for tea and had wondered what it was like upstairs, where they slept. He imagined them sloped over each other, a mass of hair and attitude. The Wyn girls had a lip on them, that was what people said, and he'd often heard them referred to as 'those trashy girls at number seven'. His mum would scowl at him warningly whenever he mentioned them. But all she cared about was her book deals and running off to London to have dinner with the people who made them. There was always some excuse for why she needed to go, leaving him behind with his nan. But that was okay. She was a lot nicer anyway.

He'd liked Miss Wyn from the off – Gwen. He needed to get that right tonight. From what DW said, she wasn't always around either: she got these sad spells. But she was some lioness, fierce as hell she was. He watched her before making friends with DW, observing from afar how she prowled around them on the pavements, ready to bite your head off if you went near them. Emma, she was the quiet one, stood back and watched it all kick off, then got a dustpan and brush for the damage. A fixer, that was what his mum would call her; he thought she'd quite like Emma. Wasn't so sure about DW: she was more gobby. And Ines, well, he hadn't spent much time with her, though he always had to listen to DW complain about what a brat she was. He felt guilty too. It was their den that had made her fall into the river that night.

The neighbours had talked about it for weeks, and he was relieved not to get into trouble. He had sworn to his mum that he wasn't involved in it. That was until some nosy journalist came along and wrote it up in the local paper: TEENAGE BOY HERO SAVES GIRL FROM THE RAPIDS. That dobbed him right in it. His nan said they could hide the paper. Then some dozy cow went and texted his mum anyway, and she came down on him like a tonne of bricks. *I don't want you hanging around with that sort.* Well, she wasn't around to say otherwise, was she? And, besides, everyone else seemed pleased with him about it.

Noah had thought himself all the way to their gate, which stuck when he tried to open it. He had to kick it. He knew to knock because the bell was broken. He waited and listened to the yowls of Kate Bush coming from inside. No one answered, so he stepped into the overgrown weeds and peered in through the front window. There they were, dancing around the table like a bunch of maniacs, Gwen too, a light-pink glow coming from fringed lampshades that he knew his mum would think were naff. The Wyn girls all had matching flowery scarves tied round their bodies as their shadows drew pictures across the kitchen walls. It was like watching happiness. He stepped back and knocked harder. It was DW who finally answered, with Ines peering over her shoulder at him – the spitting image. The loud music poured out onto the street.

'Hey.' DW looked at him like he was meant to do something, but he wasn't sure what.

'Hi,' he said, shifting awkwardly.

'Well, let the poor boy in, then. Don't stand there on ceremony,' Gwen's voice came cheerily, so DW pulled the door back.

He stepped into their small porch and could tell it had been tidied for his benefit, with scuffed-up shoes in a neat line where school bags and coats were usually thrown. That much he'd seen from the doorway when calling on DW. The side of the porch led onto the kitchen, which was small, with a table that felt too big for the space and had mismatched chairs around it, then a dark-orange armchair in the corner. Who has an armchair in their kitchen? No one offered to take his coat so he scrunched it into a ball and discarded it. They all seemed happy he was there. DW offered him a squash, which he got in a crystal wine glass with a crack in it that he was careful to drink around. Ines said they were only used for 'special visitors', and DW said that was tosh. Music was coming from a record player that Emma said was their Grampy's, and it was strange to him that the house was full of so much old-people stuff. He watched then as they took turns tasting the bolognese, throwing warm spaghetti at the kitchen tiles to see if it stuck.

'It's how you know if it's done or not.' Gwen told him he should give it a go, so he did.

It was way more fun than tea at his nan's. They would eat at five o'clock on the dot, and she'd be asleep in front of the television by six.

'These were our nan's,' Ines said to him proudly, showing him the floral scarf tied to her waist.

They were wearing denim pedal-pushers that hugged their legs.

'Neat, can I have one?' he asked.

But she liked that, rushing off upstairs on a mission. Gwen wore hers like a headscarf tied at the back of her neck, DW's was wrapped around her wrist like a bracelet, and Emma had hers tied around her neck, the way scarves were supposed to be worn. They all stank of old-lady perfume. Like the posh talc on his nan's dressing table.

'Here you go.' Ines had found him his own scarf. It was ugly, with orange and brown flowers on it, but he didn't care, tied it around his head like Rambo, and she laughed.

'Perfect. You're one of us now.'

He felt a rush. Then she took him by the hands and made him dance with her, DW watching, pouring more lemon squash into his broken glass. DW always took the piss, calling him a posh boy. But he wasn't, not really. His nan might have been. She had a big house and that, and he was meant to move in with his mum, but she never really got around to bringing her stuff. She had a flat in London too, and she kept most of her things there.

He helped lay the table, swooping the tablecloth into the air with Emma on the other side until it fell down, covered then with plates and knives and forks that weren't the same size, a small vase of dead flowers that had dust hanging from the leaves. Ines had a tantrum after that, about making a setting for Edi, which he could tell made Gwen embarrassed. He didn't mind, though: it felt like she was there anyway, the way they all talked to her, turning their heads to thin air at the exact same time, like they'd heard the same question. When they sat down to eat, Ines insisted on sitting next to him and kept asking him loads of questions. But he didn't mind.

'What d'you wanna be when you grow up, Noah?'

'That's such a boring question.' DW rolled her eyes at her. 'Who cares?'

'Dyl, don't start.' Gwen poured herself another glass of wine from the fridge. He noticed she seemed to like the stuff. The bolognese tasted a bit strange, but he didn't say so.

'It's good.' He smiled, scooping the spaghetti into his mouth.

'Well, I'm glad you're enjoying it.' That made her happy. 'Eat up, there's plenty more.'

'I'm going to be a famous actress.' Ines leaned forward.

'Cool. That would be a fun job, I reckon. You'll get loads of free stuff.'

'Exactly. And everyone will want to be my friend.'

'My girls are all pretty set on what they want to do, aren't you? Well, Em doesn't know yet, but she's bound to wind up doing something with people. She's very caring. Have you noticed that, Noah?'

He nodded.

'She's got a huge heart, that one. And then there's my Dyl.' She flung an arm around her. 'She's the creative one in the family, always making things with her hands.'

He felt for the red string under his T-shirt, the two jagged beads with a small leaf between them. She'd said it was because he liked nature.

'Mam, what did you wanna be when you were little?' Ines sucked the spaghetti over her chin, and Emma looked up keenly for the answer.

'Oh—' she seemed shy '—I had all sorts of dreams.'

After dinner, they went into their living room, which Noah thought was also small, but it was a lot cosier than his nan's, which had three living rooms, all with different rules about where you could or couldn't sit, what shoes you could wear, or whether friends were allowed in. Emma and Gwen cleared up while DW and Ines argued about whose turn it was to play snake on his phone. Ines said it wasn't fair because her go went so fast: she should be allowed two goes because it took Dylan ages to die.

'Shut up, Ines. You're so annoying. Just go away.'

'She's only so good at it because she's been playing on Liam's phone.' Ines took a spinning top and let it rip.

'Liam from form . . . ?' DW had told him she didn't like him much, thought he was a tell-tale after grassing her up for stealing supplies from the art room.

'I saw him on the weekend.' She doesn't pull her eyes away from the game. 'His dad bought him a new phone, said I could play on it.'

And then again, that strange feeling spinning around inside Noah, making him dizzy.

'You weren't here,' she says then, defensive like he was upset or something.

'I like Liam.' He puts her right. 'We should invite him to the cinema this weekend.'

'I love the cinema,' Ines says, delighted, leaning forward on the sofa. 'What are you gonna see?'

Dylan looks up from the phone at him. 'Do you really like him?'

'Yeah.' If she was going to be friends with him, then so would he.

The truth was, Noah didn't like any of the boys interested in the Wyns, wasn't sure exactly why either. Maybe because it felt like they could suddenly disappear from his life just as quickly as they'd entered it, leaving a much bigger hole. When it was time for him to go home, Gwen told the girls to walk him back. They raced him from their front door all the way to his nan's, Emma ahead, DW screaming out behind him, and Ines crying somewhere in the far distance because she was so slow.

'Bye, then,' Emma said, out of breath, smug that she'd won.

'Come on, Ines, hurry!' DW called to her, as she sulked slowly down the street, arms crossed.

They waved him in as he put his key in the door. He went straight into one of the living rooms, following his nan's snore, took a blanket, and gently pulled it over her, then rushed upstairs to her bedroom, which was at the front of the house, where he watched them hold Ines's hands as they raced back down the street. And he hoped he would be invited for tea again soon.

★★★

Dylan climbed into the cupboard under the stairs, wedging the phone line under the door for some privacy. She dialled Noah's number, just as she did every night, waiting until it was six p.m. and calls were cheaper. When he answered, they mostly spoke about Mam letting them go back to school. They'd had a letter in the post, though she didn't know what it said, but social services had come around and told them they had to go back. They were relieved: it was boring being at home all the time. Dylan asked Noah to relay his conversations with the rest of the class on MSN, what the girls were saying and if Liam wanted to come to the cinema.

'Ask him now,' she said impatiently.

'I am!'

'We need his dad for one of the lifts.'

'Why doesn't your mum have a car?'

'I don't know. She just doesn't. I'm gonna learn to drive, though, as soon as I'm seventeen.'

'Me too.'

'Yeah, but I'm older than you so I'll get my licence quicker, won't I?'

They sat in silence then, Dylan twirling her fingers around the cord, listening to his fast typing the other end.

'I really liked coming to yours for tea,' he admitted.

'Did you?'

'Yeah. Your mum is nice.'

Dylan didn't say anything to this.

'I could come again if you like.'

'Drop a hint, mind.' She knew that would embarrass him and felt a little cruel. 'It's just she's not always like that. I told you. She gets sad. But you can come again when she's feeling better. She likes you.'

'Yeah?' He sounded encouraged.

'Yeah, said you were well brought-up.'

She could practically hear him smiling down the phone, then Ines's breath followed through the receiver. She was listening in from Mam's bedroom.

'INES!' Dylan kicked open the cupboard door and screamed at the top of her voice: 'I CAN YER YOU, YA KNOW! PUT THE PHONE DOWN! NOW!'

★★★

Noah went to London with his mam for half of the summer holidays, and those three weeks dragged by slowly. Dylan missed him so much she couldn't breathe, but she refused to check the post while Ines looked ostentatiously each morning.

'Nope. No postcard today.'

'For God's sake,' she snapped, 'of course there's not. He's only been gone a few days.'

'Nothing will have happened for him to write about yet,' Edi comforted.

It was typical of people to make promises they wouldn't keep; he didn't text Mam's phone like he said he would either. Dylan resolved not to care and they distracted her as best they could, especially Edi, who encouraged her out for walks and came up with ideas for building their new den. Then one afternoon the phone rang. They spoke to him in turn, asking all about his trip, except Dylan, who stubbornly refused to go to the phone even after Emma relayed that his mam had forgotten to buy him credit.

'Come on, he wants to talk to you.' She held the receiver out to her and Dylan eventually took it, huffily telling Ines to get out of the way so she could wedge herself into the cupboard under the stairs.

'DW? Are you there?' Noah's voice came down the line.

'Yes,' she said absentmindedly, and then, 'Hello.'

'How's it going?'

'Fine.'

'I'm sorry I didn't text. I kept asking Mum to top up my phone. She's been so busy, promoting this new book and that.'

'How's London?'

'It's okay. Bit boring. Mum's taken me along to a few of her signings. It's weird. She's got, like, fans and stuff.'

'Mmm ...' She was unmoved.

'I'll be back soon anyway,' he reassured her, and she hated how much she needed him to. Didn't like the power he'd gained, hadn't been aware of it until he'd gone.

The Wyns had realised that Noah had the ability to leave, just like everyone else, and it wreaked intolerable havoc, especially in Dylan. They had let their guard down and it lingered between them, the unspoken mistake that was too far gone to undo. As the days drew by, each was laced with a more astringent melancholy, thick on the roofs of their mouths. The verges of green fields were heavy with creamy meadow blossom, the air fixed with a honeyed scent – a Welsh summer turning acrid as the manure was spread across farmland, back-to-school advertisements looming, Mam starting to stress about who had grown out of last year's school shoes.

★★★

When Noah eventually returned at the end of the summer, he brought gifts for all of them, even Edi. Dylan was outwardly unimpressed. Things seemed to change quickly after that. They stopped building dens, their interest turning to other things, like the *Karma Sutra* book they'd found under Mam's bed, giggling through this new encyclopaedia of human parts and where to put them. Years passed, and when they made their own Ouija board everyone insisted it was Edi who moved the glass around even though she grew less poignant. They grew up into teenagers, got part-time jobs, paper rounds, and waitressing gigs, earning some extra money, which was spent on real cigarettes. They spent Friday nights on the marshes or spinning in the graveyard, sticky cider running down their throats as they threw themselves into the rush of getting drunk for the first time. Soon they were old enough to meet Noah at the pub, and Ines would kick off because she wasn't allowed to go.

They followed one another down the corridors between girlhood and womanhood, becoming confident in the power their new bodies deployed. Dylan got picked up down the street so Mam wouldn't see the boy racers who'd come to collect her, chasing the current of freedom as they'd drive down the dual carriageway, her head out of the window, the bass vibrating through her cracks. Noah soon learned not to be fazed, waiting for her to drop these new friendships as soon as she grew listless, which, of course, she always did.

Eventually, they decided it was time to stow Edi away, to send her back to where they'd conjured her. Emma suggested a burial would be fitting, so they took her out into the garden, gathering under an agonizingly bright moon, with a cobweb-covered shovel, pushing hands into the dirt. Laughing at the absurdity of it, mud soaking into the edges of their pyjama bottoms, evidence of a farewell. A shoebox of those things she liked and those she didn't like: a consideration of the qualities they possessed as a unit, the ones they'd have to let go of, pulling in three different directions to stuff the hole. Not realizing the scar tissue would remain long after they let her go.

Engagement Parties

June

The engagement party had come around fast, with a tension neither of them had invited. Noah had tried to talk to Ines about what she'd said on the hike but she wasn't able to be straight with him again after that. She just kept saying, 'I'm sorry, I'm sorry,' telling him she'd come round to the idea of a baby, saying how much she wanted to be there all the while pushing her body into him, wanting like always to resolve things by fucking. But he knew the words printing off her tongue were a figment for his own ears. And he couldn't bring himself to fuck her anyway, couldn't find himself neutral on the subject of starting a family. And for some reason the image of DW grinding against Dan replayed itself over in his mind like a scene from a horror film that comes just as you're about to knock off to sleep.

Ines had thrown herself into planning the engagement party, which now only proffered evidence of her boredom, tightening the knot between them. He was suddenly off-put by her overcompensations, performatively watering the garden in her wellies and nightie, looking to him for instruction. Instructions for a life. Brewing coffee, bringing it back and forth to his studio, only to take a bath in the middle of the afternoon while watching reality TV, calling to him that she'd taken out the bins. He watched her wander around the cottage trying to find herself in it, sprawled across the sofa reading a play, repositioning herself with every page turn. He wanted to exonerate her because for Noah that was what love was. But he didn't recognise this new distaste.

This evening as they're getting ready for the party, he thinks she looks pretty, wearing a dress made of heavy lace with matching bows in her hair. He looks at their reflections in the mirror, does his tie up as she attaches the ribbons. They look good together, and she liked that. The flawless image they present. Childhood sweethearts who had never looked in other directions. But he's got this feeling that he's seeing the picture differently, and when she reaches to top up his glass she says, 'Let's take a picture,' positioning the champagne bottle in view, and he wants to say he doesn't feel like it. 'Smile then,' she says, and he follows suit.

They stay upstairs in the bedroom for a while, her chatting about the evening ahead, who's going to be there and so on. And he can only think of them back in this room at the end of it, sore feet and pesto on his shirt, a crumpled dress discarded, wondering which parts of them are real.

Their party is in a grade-two-listed hotel in a room he had agreed to. They had hired the orangery made almost entirely of glass with a kitchen at the back for the caterers. Noah drives them in his Saab and her hand curls around his, resting on the gear stick as they enter the long drive to a pink horizon, like a wide-open mouth, yawning over their future. There is a round of applause when they enter and she laughs, relishing the spotlight, then letting go of his hand, leaving him shy against the backdrop of the perfect party. He doesn't know where to look so he follows his eyes up to the birdcage-shaped roof, wondering how many engagements have been celebrated here. He feels someone shaking his hand then, starts greeting his uncle and other extended family she'd pressed him to invite. He goes over to his mum and kisses her cheek; she tells him he looks smart.

'Thanks for coming; we appreciate it.'

'I'm your mother.' He watches her stiffen. 'You don't need to thank me for the effort of attendance, Noah.'

'That's not what I meant. I just mean ...' he takes a deep breath '... I know you have a lot on, that's all.'

'That's right. I do.' She takes a sip of her champagne and squints as if she doesn't care for the taste.

'Are you staying with Uncle Ron?'

'Don't be ridiculous.' She looks over his shoulder, rifling the crowd for someone more interesting to talk to. 'A hotel.'

He readies himself then for what he knows she's going to ask.

'How's your work going?'

'It's going.'

'Gwendoline tells me you're doing very well for yourself, getting more work than you know what to do with. You should start hiring a team.' Then *he* starts looking for a way out. 'She tells me you're working on a book too. Is that right?'

He cringes, hadn't wanted her to know, didn't want her thinking he'd taken any inspiration from her own egocentrism. 'A few short stories, I wouldn't call it a novel. It's just a bit of fun.'

'You should send your mother some material.' She rouses. 'I could give you some constructive criticism, some pointers and—'

'Like I said, it's just for fun.'

She nods. 'Oh, yes, that's right. Wanting to make something of yourself is unsightly in this town. I'd forgotten that. You're meant to pretend you're satisfied. And are you satisfied, son? What you're yearning for shouldn't be a difficult question to answer, but it is, isn't it?'

He nods half-heartedly. 'It's good to see you,' he says, then points his finger to the left. 'I should start making my way around everyone; I don't want to be rude.' Then he kisses her cheek again but there's no warmth in it for either of them.

As the evening wears on, the light chit-chat doesn't get more interesting and the canapés are harder and harder to get hold of as more people press into the sweltering room. The white-suited three-piece jazz band starts up and people begin to dance and do drugs in the toilets. He watches Ines on the dance floor, laughing loudly, drinking prosecco now they've tapped out on champagne. The orangery's glass panels are black from the night sky as she reaches for Emma's hands through the crowd to mouth: *Where's Noah?* He moves on camouflaged in the black sea of suits.

'The man himself.' Kit is heading towards him, hands locked behind his back and hair wet with gel, which ages him.

'How's it going, fella?' Noah puts out a hand and he takes it.

'Now, are you absolutely set on marrying a Wyn? It's not a sport for the faint-hearted.'

Noah slaps his back firmly, feels the dampness of his shirt. 'Oh, I don't think I need any advice on that. Ines and I have been knocking about as long as you and Emma, haven't we? At this stage marriage is a formality.'

'You're a naive lad, if you believe that. Then again, I suppose we all told ourselves that lie to get ourselves down the aisle.' He puts a hand at the back of Noah's neck patronisingly. 'Marriage is a far cry from decorum, much less a box-ticking exercise. It changes everything. It hasn't hit yet, has it? You'll be dipping your pen in the same inkwell for the rest of your life. Let that sit. It doesn't get any easier, especially after kids ... never quite the same. The relationship or the—'

'Some might think you're incredibly ungrateful, mate,' he cuts him off. 'I think your arrogance distorts things for you – you wanna watch that, could fuck up your life.' Kit's amused expression spurs him on: 'You have two amazing daughters and an incredible wife, and I'm not sure you're even aware but you're really not that nice to her a lot of the time. Let that sit.'

Kit looks a little embarrassed as Noah brushes past him to walk back through the corridors, wanting to get away from it all. He sees a flash of cobalt blue in the corner of his eye and heads in her direction.

'Yeah, okay, sounds good. I've gotta go, but I'll call you when I'm home.' She hangs up, fiddling with the clasp on her clutch. They hadn't spoken since their fall-out at Emma's.

'You're always on that bloody thing. It makes us all feel so unimportant.' He tries teasing first but he can tell she's still pissed off with him. 'Come on, DW, let's not fight.' He reaches for her arms. 'It's my engagement party.' But she pushes him off and his weight falls against the oil painting behind him.

'Go and entertain your guests.'

'You're my guest, aren't you? Look, I'm sorry, okay? I don't want to fight with you, not tonight. Can't we just talk about it?'

'I don't really want to talk about it, no. Not here.'

He can see she isn't going to let this one go easily so he takes her by the wrist and walks further down the corridor, trying a few doors until one finally opens. They can't find the switch; he notices the patterned wallpaper lit by the lights from the car park and a large crystal chandelier, which hangs above a long table set for lunch. They sit against the table in the dark, listening to the washed-out music and the occasional laughter ripple from the orangery. It's not lost on him, this relief at being away from it all.

'I didn't mean what I said the other night; I was out of order.'

'You mean you don't think I'm totally fucked up?' She tilts her head and a muscle in her temple tenses.

'No. And your sex life is none of my business. I shouldn't have passed comment on it.'

She tells him he's got that much right but he can see there's more she wants from him; more he doesn't want to say. He isn't sure why Dan from the White Hart got to him this much. It's not like he didn't spend puberty and much of his teenage years seeing her with different people.

'I didn't mean to catch you two together.'

'You opened the bathroom door.'

'I didn't, I swear it! There was a crack; I only peered through. I was being a bit nosy I'll admit it, protective even, but I wasn't looking to see that.' He stares down at his shoes.

'Okay,' she says, as if she might be softening.

'I just can't get the image out of my head.' His face creases and she misinterprets the expression for judgement.

'You're jealous.' He can feel them slipping into dangerous territory. 'Jealous that you can't fuck whoever you want any more, and I can.'

He shrugs at her in agreement, puts his hands into his pockets and pulls a panicked face, which makes her laugh. 'I admire you, you know.' She tuts at this. 'No, I do. You're completely open about everything you want. I've always loved that about you. Ever since you ate all my sour laces on the swings.' He gives her his boyish half-smile. 'And I don't think you're screwed up.' He leans closer because he feels bad if he's made her second-guess herself. 'Only a screwed-up person would ever say that to someone. And I was pretty out of it that day, pissed off with Ines, and I took it out on you. I shouldn't have.'

Selfish Girls

'What were you two fighting about?' She leans back on her hands, and he takes a huge breath, filling his cheeks as he looks away from her. 'It's okay,' she says peaceably. 'It's okay to tell me.'

'Arggh.' He lifts his weight off the table, then sits down again. 'Okay, fuck it. She doesn't want a baby. Or she didn't want our baby when she was pregnant. I'm not sure yet if they're the same thing. That's why she's been beating herself up about it so badly. Thinks it's her fault. And she's been taking contraception, when this mug—' he points '—thought we were trying.'

'Ines,' she says, under her breath, as though she's disappointed in her, but not surprised.

'I don't know, DW. It's not just about a kid – I'm not even sure if she wants a life here with me.'

'And why do you want to be here so much? You could be anywhere with your job, New York, LA.'

'Those places aren't for raising kids, though, are they? Besides, my family are here.' He looks at her.

'Why are you so set on the family gig? You've got loads of time.'

He answers with a shrug because she already knows: he doesn't need to say it. He'd never met his father. Knew he was part of the publishing scene, someone his mum had worked with, but he hadn't been interested in having a relationship with Noah. He googled him sometimes, read reviews he'd written, turned over things he'd said in interviews as if he was trying to get to know him through comment pieces. He'd not forgiven his mum for abandoning him in Wales with his nan. Paying visits, buying gifts with her guilt.

'You need to communicate better. You're on completely different pages. And you know she won't be honest with you. Not if you don't push her to be. She can be incredibly selfish like that. She wants all versions of her future, but that's not how it works. Eventually she's got to pick a door and walk through it.'

They sit quietly in the darkness and he doesn't need to look at her to see she's removing an earring and is using it to get something out of her teeth, something she's always done. He waits in the silence for her to dislodge something that he can't seem to.

'What's your most heretical opinion?' He changes the subject and she obliges, tipping her head back in thought.

'It's probably that I don't think a partner should be the focal point of your life.'

'I knew you were going to say that.'

'Yeah, well, most people only do it because they're scared of being alone, and they pretend a lot of the time that their relationship is better than it really is. But if they were honest with themselves, maybe they would see it's not that great. A relationship is like a performance. You get stuck in the idea of what it was or could be, rather than facing the reality of what it actually is in the moment. And by the time most people realise, they decide it's too late to roll the dice again.' She waits for him to say something, and when he doesn't, she says, 'I know you all think I have attachment issues, but the truth is there isn't a relationship I've ever witnessed and wanted for myself.'

He takes this in slowly, wondering what part of the message is aimed at him.

'So, come on, then,' she asks. 'What's yours?'

'I prefer the bottom deck on buses.'

She laughs, knocking over a glass behind her, and he becomes serious. 'In terms of non-monogamy, though, sharing Ines in any emotional sense would be ruinous for me.'

She raises an eyebrow. 'I'm not sure it's that deep for me. I just like sex.'

But this is bitterly unsatisfying. 'Come on. It's always *just sex* with you.' He pulls a face. 'Don't you want to experience more? Be intimate with someone who loves you?'

'I've been intimate with you.'

He focuses on the strand of hair curving under her chin, framing her face perfectly. That's when he feels something shift. She's coquettish and it creates a different-shaped space for him in the dynamic. He gazes at her through the darkness, allowing himself to look down at her breasts, lifted by the corset sewn into her top. DW knows exactly who she is, and she'd never lied to him. He lets the back of his fingers brush against her soft cleavage as she takes a breath. He looks up at her, knows her well enough to see she's turned on. He draws his fingers up, tucking the loose strand behind her ear, then taking her chin and, as she's about to say something, make some protest, he puts his mouth on hers, pushing his tongue inside as she gives way to something he's always wanted.

2006

Nine Years After They Moved to Laurel Road

Emma is nineteen, Dylan is seventeen, Ines is fourteen

Noah never showed interest in other girls but Dylan became fixated on the shift between him and Ines. They all felt it. Emma told her not to read anything into it. Their feral little sister had given way to a flirtatious teenager, who had mastered the arch of her back and a thigh gap as wide as the one between her two front teeth, which they all had to acknowledge she'd grown into. Ines had always hung off his shoulder. Now Noah had morphed from a brotherly manner into indulging her, paying the occasional compliment, handling her more gently, as if she were some precious pearl in his pocket. But Dylan understood how pearls formed: it only took a tiny organism to invade the shell and co-opt its world, disrupting the peace in the mantle. It was an irritation, something the oyster couldn't shake, a defence mechanism that, over time, layered to form a so-called gem. And while it wasn't a predatory gaze that Noah had developed, they could see it was certainly a revelatory one. Ines was now a young woman with a new sheen. And Dylan didn't know how to stop it, only that she wanted it to stop.

That wasn't how Dylan realised she was in love with Noah, though: the irritation Ines represented was merely a by-product of her condition. She realised when they were mucking about and laughing: there would sometimes be this knowing pause between them, a suggestive glance. And she'd get all gawky and end up saying something disparaging or would excuse herself to use the loo even though she'd just been. She sensed on all levels that he liked her too, but something held her back, a want not to ruin something special, something that had stood the test of time. And then there was the familial pattern of guilt across her skin: it was the trauma that had made Ines so attached to Noah.

And that had been Dylan's fault. This was the family line: Ines could have died in the river that night. And even all these years later Mam still witnessed her presence like some sort of miracle.

But at their sixth-form leavers' party that evening, Noah and Dylan had got drunk. Her sisters knew how much she enjoyed these opportunities, which presented high walls behind which they were not invited. Where Noah and Dylan could dance all night with just each other. Much to the frustration of the girls in their year who were mad about him. The music pulsing, strobe lights and smoke machines, sweat dripping down backs until moves slowed and transmuted into something more seductive. The taste of vodka from a water bottle and the feeling of having your whole life ahead of you. Then a taxi back to Laurel Road, Noah realising he'd lost his key.

'Check again – she'll kill me if I need to get another cut. That's the second I've lost this month. I definitely gave it to you.'

'It's not in here.' She laughed. 'It's only tiny. I can just about fit mine with my lip gloss.'

He rubbed at his mouth anxiously. 'I'll have to wake her up.'

'You can't wake your nan because you're a drunken idiot. Just stay at mine.'

There was nothing new about Noah staying at the Wyns' house. He had done so a hundred times before, curled up on a bed of blankets on Dylan's floor. When they got in, giggling and stumbling to the fridge, she made ham and cheese toasties while he ran orange squash under the tap. Then they took them upstairs to eat on Dylan's bed.

'What do you think, then?' He pranced around in one of her nighties. 'Does it do it for you?'

'As if!' She threw a pillow at him. 'Shush, or you'll wake everyone up.'

He ripped the nightie back over his head and jumped onto her bed, topless in just his boxers. 'Can I sleep in here with you?'

Dylan scowled playfully.

'Oh, go on, don't make me sleep on the floor under this.' He pulled at her comforter. 'It's freezing.'

She rolled her eyes and lifted the quilt to signal he was welcome. And when he got under the cover, his skin was cold as he huddled closer to her. Then they were led by the feel of their feet pressing against one another. And it was Dylan who kissed him first, his eyes widening with surprise as she drew back, unsure.

'No.' He took her face and kissed her back. 'I want to.'

He had always smelt the same to her – like butter and detergent – except now there was something arousing about it. And they kissed like that for ages, discovering and touching parts of one another it seemed strange they'd never known, awoken by the breathlessness and moans, and by what they could do to one another.

★★★

The following week, Dylan was waiting for Noah outside his class. It was nearly the end of term and summer broke with hushed anticipation, the longer days like a comma in their story, Dylan could think only of all that was still to come. Emma had left already to go to college and Ines was thriving, spending all the time she could in drama class. They were all finally going to get what they wanted.

She hadn't seen Noah since the leavers' party, and although they'd spoken on the phone, they'd not discussed what had happened that night beyond a few gentle jokes. Dylan felt they hadn't needed to: it was all the evidence she needed that he was on the same page. She was nervous to tell him about the scholarship, but lots of their friends were planning on staying together even though they were going to different universities. He'd already said he'd come and visit all the time. London wasn't that far away, Mam reminded her, but it felt it. Other than for her interview at the British Academy of Jewellery, Dylan had been only once.

'There she is!'

She turned to see him swinging his bag around his side, nudging his friend's shoulder before making his way over, and Dylan could see it, was sure of it: he was happy to see her.

'Are you waiting for me?'

'Might be.' She turned her hair over on itself.

'Shall we go for a pint at the Lion tonight? A few of them are doing the quiz. I feel like it.' But he clearly sensed some unease. 'We don't have to. We could do something else?' He squinted at her through the sunlight. 'What's up, then?' She grinned at him. 'Oh, my God. You got the scholarship, didn't you?' Dylan nodded. 'Shit. DW!' He pulled at her shoulders. 'You got it! That's nuts. I'm so happy for you. They gave you the whole thing?'

'Full scholarship, and then I'm still eligible for a student loan. I can get a job while I'm there too, between classes and studio time. Can you believe it? I actually got in!'

'Yes,' he said. 'I can believe it. You're the most talented person I know. Screw the quiz then. We need to celebrate.' He wrapped his arm around her shoulders and led the way.

Dylan felt then that there was so much more to her story. She knew moments like this were fleeting, something you couldn't pin down but could always feel your way back to. So, she carved the memory into herself as something she could keep, their feet in school shoes for what might be the last time, treading through the grass and into their chapter after all these years.

'Look at where you're going to live!'

'It's amazing, Dyl!'

Back at Laurel Road, Emma and Ines gathered around her acceptance letter and the brochures that had come with it, flipping through the pages of Dylan's new life, assessing what it could all amount to.

'It won't be the same here without you.' Ines slumped, and Emma agreed.

Dylan looked at Noah, observed him watching them from the kitchen table. She wondered what it must feel like: to be so outside something you were somehow bound to. She insisted she'd come back and visit, but none of them was confident of that. She'd been vocal about wanting to get out of this crappy town, was climbing the walls, and they had all grown tired of having to coerce her down. And in that same kitchen where they'd once fought over clothes and swapped sausages for peas so Mam would finally let them leave the table, they'd also grown. Small feet dancing on the kitchen table now touched lightly underneath it as they realised they would have to learn to mine outside this unit. One they'd created of necessity to survive what had happened. Dylan wondered what the outcome of telling Noah she loved him might be. Everything would change and she felt too much was changing already. He was planning to study music at Cardiff University and perhaps having one foot in his new life and another in hers wasn't what he wanted. A part of her suspected some relief in finally being able to separate himself from them.

When Mam got back from the chemist, she screamed when Dylan handed her the letter. Threw her pinafore uniform over her head and went straight back out to the shops to get some fizz. Emma made dinner, music played, and they sat all night laughing and talking, Dylan and Noah finding one another's gaze across the kitchen table, and Ines monitoring this fumbling tête-à-tête. Wanting to ask pointedly: *You two have done it, haven't you?* Thwarted by the humiliation of her suspicion, of whether it might finalise things.

'And what about you, Noah?' Mam reached across for his hand. 'You're gonna miss her something terrible too, aren't you? You pair are joined at the hip.'

Noah stiffened at this as if some external force was tightening him. He felt himself pulling back from her. If Dylan was leaving, maybe it would be best to leave things as they were. It wasn't like he hadn't gone over it in his head a million times before – her going off to London and all the exciting things that would be waiting there. And if he told her, he was putting things at risk of ending badly. If he said nothing they could hold on to some sameness: he would remain in her life, wherever she was.

His long pause made Dylan uncomfortable so she stuffed it: 'Oh, it'll be fine, we'll quickly get used to it,' she said, shaking her sisters out of her thoughts.

'Yeah,' Noah agreed. 'Suppose we'll have to.'

Mam was the first to go to bed, and when Emma announced she was tired a few hours later, she encouraged Ines to follow her upstairs. The two of them sat in the kitchen for a few more moments, deciphering the new awkwardness until he said: 'I'd better be getting off, too. It's late.' He motioned as if to yawn but didn't follow through.

'Oh, okay.' She tried not to sound disappointed, knowing Ines and Emma would be sitting at the top of the stairs.

'Big day, eh?' He lifted his arms in a stretch.

Dylan showed him to the door, which was a strange thing to do. He'd always shown himself out. But something felt unfinished. She lifted her foot and pressed it gently on top of his, a small gesture of desire, too scared to reach out, her whole body calling for him.

'I'll see you tomorrow, then,' he said finally, picking up his rucksack, discarded earlier in the porch in the midst of so much excitement, and then for a moment she thought he was going to kiss her. 'Night, DW.'

He walked through the door. This punctum in the image of happiness as she visualised their feet in the wet grass on the school yard earlier, not treading as she'd thought onto a new path but rather walking as they always had, side by side, as friends and troublemakers, one of a pair. And the only thing that allowed her to catch her breath – standing in the porch, back pressed against the door, her eyes starting to well – was the vindication of finally being the one to walk through it herself. Which she did, a few months later.

Emma had chosen to study social work at a local college. Leaving the family had never been a consideration: she understood she was needed. She started working part-time at a nearby golf club, often serving medical undergraduates attending the local hospital. Most of them blurred into one another, except for a tall, dark-haired man they all called Kitten. There was something about him, a seriousness occasionally punctuated by a grin, but only when something was deserving of it. She was chatted up by a few, usually in a slur. But never him. So, it took Emma by surprise when one night, as he finished his pint and handed her the glass, he said he often found himself thinking about her. She looked down at the beer taps, glanced back up, unsure of what to say as he awarded her that grin. And all she could think afterwards was how she might inspire the next.

Their first date was at a white-tablecloth restaurant, not the sort the Wyns could afford. Ines and Mam insisted on helping her decide what to wear and, no, not those shoes. Mam said she could borrow her earrings before texting Dylan a photo. The imminence of change inciting a knowing absence, like a meal without salt. Their reflection in Emma's eyes loosened as they glazed over for this Kitten. An intuition that something was here to take her, that they'd become a whisper on the edge of the night sky, a backdrop for her new north star.

'You look beautiful, Emmie.'

The restaurant was dimly lit, romantic in a typical sort of way. Emma could feel Dylan's eyes rolling into the back of her head, the rush of Ines, gushing. She tried to detach herself from her sisters, pushing their opinions out of her own mind. Focusing instead on the candlelight that outlined Kit's jawline and the sort of nervous schoolboy energy that gave her access to some part of him she could tell he didn't feel comfortable sharing. He intrigued her, his charm mercurial in nature; she couldn't quite grasp what offset his energetic shifting. At first she enjoyed the sound of it: *Emmie*. This new version of herself crafted in his mouth. Who might this Emmie person be? The fragments of possibility lit up like fireflies. And when he ordered the wine, it struck her, not having to consider anyone else.

'It's a Barolo. Have you tried it before?' Not waiting for her to answer: 'You'll like it. The steak is the best thing on the menu here. I'm assuming you eat meat.' He closed his menu conclusively. 'Yes, good. How would you like it?'

She blushed, unsure of the answer. How did *Emmie* like it?

'Medium rare is how it's done best. Yes?' He raised his hand for the waiter's attention and she zoned out of their conversation, creating a blur around his outline. This man knew what she liked, what she wanted, how she wanted it. A real man, with large hands and a posh accent that sounded like stability. A man who called her beautiful and said he couldn't stop thinking about her. One who would lend her his poetry books, folding over the pages on those he said reminded him of her, just as Noah had done in his comics for Dylan. So, when Kit proposed just three months later, Emma said yes. Not long after, she moved out.

Ines was the last one left. Like always. Tirelessly waiting to follow her sisters through passageways she hadn't even decided she'd wanted. She had witnessed it, the selfish relief smudged across Dylan and Emma's escape. Once again, everyone else was able to do whatever they pleased while she was trapped at home, waiting for life to start. After Emma had packed up and gone, she lay on her bed, discovering the new grooves in this loneliness. Trapped in the silence of a house that had witnessed not just their childhood but Mam's too. Walls thick with stories, the remains of which seemed to be closing in on her. She'd tried calling Dylan but she never answered her phone, too busy being a fresher and going out with her new friends. Mam's depressions were less frequent, but when they came, they were a heavy dark cloud that covered only Ines. So, on a lonely Saturday afternoon, bored as the sun poured through net curtains and Mam refused to stir, she sat up on her bed. Quickly she went downstairs, taking the phone off the hall table and pulling it with her into the cupboard under the stairs. She dialled a number – one she knew by heart – and waited, her heart pounding until he picked up.

'Noah? Is that you? It's me, Ines.'

1987

Gwendoline is eighteen

She tried to let herself relax against the hospital pillow that the nurse had just positioned behind her, afraid to take her eyes off Emma for even a second. She latched on then, suckling like a *mochyn bach*, her skin blotched, nose pressed tightly, skin on skin.

'She's lovely.'

Gwendoline looked up and saw her mam standing at the end of the hospital bed. 'We weren't expecting you.' She stiffened her jaw.

'Tommy rang, said she'd come early.' She held her bag with both hands, wearing her Sunday best. Gwendoline wondered why.

She winced slightly at the pain then, drawing her eyes back down to her new daughter, curled in on herself, prawn-like.

'Where is he, then?'

'Down the pub, wetting the baby's head.'

'Can I see 'er?'

She pushed against her own instincts, motioning her over with a hand.

'She's precious, mind. Looks just like you when you were a *babi*.' Gwendoline smiled down at Emma, overcome, heart thrust open, expanding. This new love interfering with an old wound, that it was possible in the face of it to be so cruel to your own child. 'You don't know what it is to have a sick child. I pray to God that never comes for yew.' She locked her gaze. 'Listen now, I'm sick, Gwendoline.'

She shifted her eyes down to her mam's swollen feet, squashed into grey leather court shoes on hospital tiles. An image that would keep washing back when testing the temperature of milk on her wrist.

'I wanted you to know. I wanted you to yer it from me.' And then, after she'd said nothing in response, she added, 'At least our Llewellyn won't be alone any more.'

The twelve-year-old girl inside her was screaming, holding up a glass bottle, beseeching that the message inside could still save them. But Gwendoline, tightly twisting her into silence, distressed and fraught, stuck in her lower abdomen. She breathed a sigh of relief and said plainly, 'I'm sorry to yer tha', Mam.'

'Look after you-er father for me.'

And she nodded, wincing again at the suction and pinch at her nipple as Gwendoline reached over and kissed her forehead. 'Don't worry, it won't hurt like that for long, mind.'

But she was wrong, and it always did.

Therapy, II

'I mean what the hell does this mean *huuuse stufi*?' He holds up the phone for their therapist to see, swears he sees her wince.

'It means stuff for the house,' Emmie plateaux, 'polish, bleach, olive oil, things you don't ever have to think about.'

'I wonder if we're getting distracted here on the surface level of the disagreement,' Avril tries. 'Why don't we consider it from a slightly different angle?'

Kit puts his phone back into his inside jacket pocket, loosens his tie.

'Why do you think it's so important to you, Kit, that Emmie keeps a list of the things she buys on this, er, split now?'

'Split Wise.' He helps her out. 'I think it's important, for both of us, that we document our spending, watch what we're apportioning our money to each month. That's quite normal.'

She nods and he can see it's a pacifier: she's not convinced. He pictures the poor buggers who have sat on this couch before him, degraded to scrambling around for this woman's exoneration. Emmie thought everything was his fault and so did her family, it was likely only a matter of time before Avril took this stance.

'Emmie, try telling Kit how this process of documenting makes you feel.'

'How do I feel?' She acts as though the concept is a foreign idea. 'Like a child.' She clutches her water bottle and he notices her knuckles turning white.

'Say more.'

'I feel incompetent, as if he doesn't trust me to do anything other than look after the girls. He has control over the finances, which is difficult for me. We agreed I'd give up work when I had Sunny but I was always planning to go back and then ... before you know it, Lilah is on her way and it's like I feel ... compressed. Like I'm in a vice.'

He coughs, looking out of the window for a distraction from this nonsense.

'What did you hear in what Emmie just said, Kit?' Avril draws him back in.

'You're the expert. You tell me.'

She definitely flinched that time.

'Kit,' Emmie sounds like she's losing the will, 'how is that conducive? I don't need Avril to understand me. I need you to.'

And this was just another of her misconceptions. He understood Emmie perfectly. He understood she would rather die on the altar of her martyrdom than face any confrontation. That she wanted more than anything for her family to feel sorry for her, see how much she'd sacrificed for them. He also understood that not only was he financially responsible for looking after his own family, but remarkably she'd assumed he was financially obligated to hers. And now she had the audacity to complain to other people about their finances.

'It's quite simple,' he begins. 'We have different views on how things should be executed. I have a ... structured approach. I like things done logically, efficiently. Emmie, on the other hand, tends to be a bit disorganised. And while she spends most of our money, I am the one who has to earn it. So, I think it reasonable that we track our spending.'

'Can you give me an example,' Avril prompts, 'of Emmie being disorganised?'

Was this woman listening to a single thing he said? '*Huuuse stufi* is an example, is it not? Or being late for one of your sessions. Forgetting our daughter's costume the night before her dance recital. At the hospital such chaos would lead to fatalities. I'm not afforded disorganisation.' He senses he's losing the room. 'Look – I'm from a privileged background, I'll be the first to admit that, but my childhood was very much famine or feast. My father gambled in business and, while he won big in the end, money was always ... well, volatile. Let's put it that way. That's why I want to manage it properly in my own household.'

'Your desire for order makes sense and is clearly important to you, and it also seems to be impacting Emmie's sense of autonomy.'

'Well, her autonomy is impacting my sense of order. Especially when she uses us like a piggy bank to fix the leaks in her own extended family.'

'Nothing is ever good enough for you, is it?' Her eyes flash at him and he can see she's upset.

Then she's crying, turning on the waterworks to make him look like the bad guy. But he can't cry his way out of things. And this is so typical of her, never willing to recognise her part in things, only insistent on him taking accountability.

'Emmie, please don't cry.' He squeezes her knee.

'I'm more than just a mother,' she snaps. 'Can you not see me past my skin any more? Am I just a walking chaotic breast to you? What else, Kit? What else?'

He sits back, arms crossed, shrugging at Avril as if to say, What to make of it all? Knowing that whatever he says next will be wrong. Will only make it worse. Trumped again by the instability of her emotions in this peculiar forum where that's a good thing. And all he wants is to go home and be with his children before he has to go back to work and face the onslaught of anxious patients, stressed-out nursing staff and faces that fold in on him when he delivers news that is really worth crying over.

2007

Ten Years After They Moved to Laurel Road

Emma is twenty, Dylan is eighteen, Ines is fifteen

The family felt unearthed by Dylan's return from university. Mam was nervous, fussing about the house to ensure everything was immaculate, as if someone important was coming for tea. Ines viewed these efforts as futile. Dylan hadn't been home at all, except for a couple of days over Christmas. She had distanced herself from their tightly knit bond to blossom into a new person, one Ines didn't recognise any more. Dylan was always too busy to chat on the phone and often made excuses about why she couldn't come home – there were endless presentations, birthday parties for these new strangers she simply couldn't miss, and the risk of losing her bar job if she skipped a weekend shift. When Emma had called her to break the news, she'd slid down the wall of her tiny room in her halls of residence until she'd met the floor, waiting for the information to settle as she hung up the phone. Ines remarked that London and her new life were more important now. Emma tried to stay out of it while Mam vented. The rejection was an affliction they all felt.

Dylan returned late that night before Noah's nan's funeral, which was the following day. The National Express had been much cheaper than the train, especially with her last-minute booking. She was used to living lean, counting pennies, but it landed differently alongside the thoughtless wealth of her friends. When she handed her ticket to the bus driver, his warm Welsh-valleys accent instilled a pang of homesickness. A feeling she'd learned to numb herself to. She couldn't say whether she was looking forward to going home or not, was unsure why it had taken her so long.

As the taxi pulled up outside the house, she felt for the key in the zip-up pocket of her rucksack, where it had stayed since she'd left for

London. The driver helped with her bag, though it was only small, and she realised she'd missed the friendliness of strangers. She was only staying the weekend, needing to get back to London to work on her end-of-year assignment. The kitchen light was on, and before she could get to the door, Mam opened it, arms spread, offering a firm but brief hug, still smelling of the same old poppy perfume.

'You're home.'

Dylan sank into the familiar warmth of that word: home.

'I made chilli,' Mam announced, wiping both hands on her dressing gown. 'I thought you'd be back earlier.'

'I know.' Dylan contested the imposition as she dumped her bags in the porch, reminding Mam she had texted, that the traffic was terrible and she'd got the earliest bus she could. The judgement was evident, and Mam's silence suspended them into old sensations, both hanging with all those things they knew they owed it to each other to say.

'You look tired.'

She sighed. 'I'm just not wearing any makeup.'

'Mm . . .' Mam looked her up and down, feeling for the soft undercarriage of her bob, before gesturing towards the stove. 'Want a bowl of this, then?'

'I'm okay. I made a sandwich for the bus.'

'Right.' Mam pulled her dressing gown tighter, unsure of what to do with her hands.

Dylan wasn't sure what to make of the awkwardness pirouetting around them. An old picture of the family sat on the Welsh dresser, frame slightly cracked. 'Feels strange now, doesn't it, with Em moved out?' Dylan was undecided on whether to sit.

'Oh, I'm used to it now. Every mam has to adapt to being on her own eventually. You were always going to fly the nest.' She placed her hands on the back of a chair.

'I'm knackered,' Dylan said. 'The bus took seven hours – I might just go to bed. If that's okay?'

'Of course it is.' There was sadness in her mam's smile.

'And Noah,' Dylan asked hesitantly, 'how's he doing?'

'He's a mess,' Mam replied, squinting into the obviousness of this answer.

'I spoke to him the other day,' Dylan said defensively, 'but he was at the undertaker's sorting everything. It wasn't really a good time to chat.' Mam encouraged her to get some rest then, so Dylan collected her things from the hallway. As she was halfway up the stairs, she whispered, 'Ines is asleep already?'

'No.' Mam paused. 'She's at Noah's tonight.' The words were offered gently.

Dylan looked down at the foot poised over the next step in front of her. 'At Noah's?' Her perplexity was unshielded.

'Yes, love.'

★★★

The next morning, when Dylan came downstairs in an oversized black dress, with thick tights deliberately ripped, the first thing Mam said was: 'Do you have to wear those?'

Emma, who was sitting on the arm of their grandfather's chair with a cup of tea in hand, got up to hug her. Dylan could tell by the way Mam and Emma were holding themselves that they'd been talking about her. Kit stepped out from the living room behind her and she studied him carefully. He leaned in for two kisses, and when she gave Mam a curious look, she diverted her eyes and asked Emma for the time. Dylan put the kettle on only to be told they should start making their way over.

On the walk to the church, Emma carried Dylan's heaviness with her in silence and Kit tore Mam's ear off behind them. Dylan hadn't slept much: she couldn't stop thinking about Ines's empty bed. She imagined her sleeping next to Noah, but it seemed unrealistic. It was possible – no, likely – he just hadn't wanted to be alone the night before the funeral. There were four other bedrooms in that house: Ines could feasibly have spent the night in any one of them. Dylan was aware they'd been spending more time together. Mam had mentioned she was out at the cinema with Noah or looking at a car with him when Dylan called the house phone a few times. But that made sense, with her off at uni and Emma playing house with her new boyfriend.

The four of them joined the modest crowd of people standing outside the church in dark clothing.

'Why did Ines stay at Noah's last night?' Dylan asked finally, but Emma looked away.

'Shush, come now, love. Let's go and pay our respects.' Mam ushered them into the church.

Inside, Ines was already seated at the front next to Noah. Dylan felt an unprecedented desire to punch the back of her head. Mam found seats a few rows back, and when Ines finally turned around, sensing the live glare boring into her skull, she waved and mouthed, 'Hi,' before turning to face the altar. Emma handed her a packet of tissues when Noah got up to deliver the eulogy, which played out in slow motion like a bad car crash you saw coming a mile off. Dylan hadn't been there; she hadn't understood just how awful things had got for him. When the ceremony finished, they queued with Mam to exit the church. Dylan could see Noah upfront, Ines dutifully standing next to him, shaking hands, like a bereft wife. She tried not to look at her, didn't need more riling, struggled again to get Emma's attention, but Emma was absorbed in Kit and everything he had to say. They got distracted then by a commotion upfront, watching as people started to desert the queue and make their way outside. Dylan could see Elizabeth, Noah's mother, could hear Noah's voice getting louder.

'I don't know where you get off, issuing instructions and snide side comments. I didn't hear you offering to arrange it. I also don't remember you changing bedpans or reading her favourite books to distract her from the pain. In fact, we've barely seen you at all, have we?'

'Noah, calm down.' Ines placed a hand on his arm.

'I won't calm down.'

'I know you don't understand this, son, but the grandmother she was to you wasn't the mother she was to me.' Elizabeth was distressed.

'Yeah, well, she was a hell of a better mother than you've ever been.'

'Right – that's enough.' Mam interrupted the commotion. 'Nothing good will come from this, and it's not what she would have wanted neither.'

That was when Noah finally caught sight of Dylan. He looked angrier than she'd ever seen him, hands resting on his belt, rotating his body to pass through his agitation. He looked so handsome as he gave her a look she couldn't decipher.

'Elizabeth, why don't you come with me?' Mam took her by the arm. 'Come back to mine for a cup of tea. We can talk there. There's chilli too. I doubt you've eaten today, have you? I'll warm some up for the pair of us.'

Dylan watched the silent exchange between Elizabeth and Mam as she guided her away. She looked back at Noah, wanting to say something but Ines had already ushered him off: 'Come on, let's go home.'

And this time that word pricked against Dylan's skin.

The small congregation made their way to Laurel Road for the reception, which was at Noah's nan's house. Dylan walked silently behind Emma and Kit, who was banging on about Steve Jobs and the introduction of the iPhone, Dylan all the while trying to absorb something that refused to integrate. When they arrived at the house she said she needed the toilet, seizing the opportunity to go upstairs.

'Dyl!' Emma called, in a tone that verified her suspicions.

She went straight into Noah's bedroom, where the bed was left unmade, a nightie strewn across the pillows. She tore open the wardrobe to find some of Ines's things hanging there, as if to tease her, then stormed back across the landing into the bathroom where a yellow cup housed two toothbrushes, their bristled heads leaning against one another: caught in the act. She went back downstairs, feeling righteous. The betrayal confirmed in the broad light of day. Heat in her chest as she tried to breathe through a jealousy she'd never experienced.

'Are you okay?'

Emma reached out to her but Dylan shook her off, walking straight past and stopping in the kitchen doorway where she could see into the utility room. A place she had stood so many times before, waiting for his nan to magic another ice lolly from the bottom of her chest freezer. She stood motionless and watched. Watched as Ines stroked back Noah's hair. Watched as she soothed and comforted him. Watched still, as she jabbed playfully and he flinched, grabbing her arms and pulling them tight behind her back, their faces drawing closer, smiles meeting and twisting her stomach as they kissed. Ines's eyes opened then and she looked over his shoulder at Dylan, cheeks flushed with lust and shame. Their lives a shaken snow globe, the sediment settling where it was always going to. As Noah pulled Ines's attention back to him, unaware of what they had just exchanged, Dylan felt Emma's hand on her. 'Oh, Dyl.'

Her voice breaking, 'Why did no one tell me?'

Family Holidays, I

July

When Ines tried to make excuses and back out of the trip, Emma laid down the law. A family holiday had long been on the agenda but never seemed to materialise because no one wanted the responsibility of planning it. She had, of course, been the one to organise it and she was adamant everyone would have a great time. When she'd first suggested it, she'd been excited about having Noah and Ines back. It hadn't been easy to find a date for a long weekend, but when Kit also had some leave at the hospital she locked it in. She'd thought it would be good for them; now she's starting to wish she hadn't bothered. It was like herding desperate housewives through duty-free – no one appreciated her efforts; they'd much rather bicker and pick at one another. She'd been spending *a lot* of time with her sisters recently, more time than she had in years. She was realising the swathes of time apart had always made their intensity palatable: central nervous systems were adequately recalibrated, and passive-aggressive outbursts faded from memory rather than stacking up, like unwashed dishes. Their new proximity had created an unexamined expectation to see one another all the time and no one had quite figured out the boundaries for peace, least of all her.

So, as they're preparing to board the flight – Lilah screeching in her papoose, Noah with his head in a book, Dylan and Mam having a debate about sexism and whether it's worse now – she honestly isn't sure she wants to go.

'Did you book that restaurant I emailed you?' Kit pulls their passports and tickets out of a plastic folder, and for a moment there's this glimmer of what her sisters see.

'No. I told you already. It had like a two-month waiting list.' How is it possible that she's already feeling attacked? She scrabbles around for a dummy in her pockets. 'I did ask if there was somewhere else you wanted to go.'

'So you haven't booked *any* restaurants?'

'Yes, obviously I have.' He tuts at her, like she's incapable of doing anything, and she gives him this look, like: *Please don't start*. Dylan catches her eye: *He's such a dick. Why do you put up with it?* She'd asked him to make an effort, the same effort she always afforded his family. But he'd kept insisting her sisters didn't like him. And he had even gone off Noah, said he was rude to him at the engagement party, which of course was all her fault. He accused her of being obsessed with them needing her, said she wouldn't know who she was if she weren't wrapping herself like a blanket around her fucked-up little sisters.

They walk onto the plane and it's still excruciatingly early. She tries to get Lilah to stop arching her back, while he shoots off more questions about the 'itinerary' and where they're staying, mentioning that it's such a shame to go all that way and waste time on a beach instead of exploring any culture. She knows it's because he can't stand not having organised the damn trip himself.

'We're on the beach for two days, and we'll have the last night in Lisbon.' She fixes Sunny's seatbelt and hands Lilah her iPad.

Dylan interrupts: 'Unless you'd wanted to plan the entire trip yourself, Kitten, I guess you need to suck it up and do as you're told.'

Emma gives Dylan a grateful glance, and Kit reminds her again that he's asked them expressly not to call him that. Dylan orders two large vodka tonics from the flight attendant, who says she'll have to wait until they've taken off. Mam complains about her aisle seat so Ines swaps, and Emma notices that Noah is only pretending to read his book and has stayed on page fifty-four for over an hour. She sees how he steals glances at Dylan, which makes her stomach churn. Whatever it is, she doesn't want to know. It's off to a predictable start, no matter the effort put in from her side: they all pretended to put the interests of others before themselves but cared only about having their own needs met.

When they land, Kit is 'surprised' to find no transfers waiting to pick them up. Dylan storms off to the taxi queue with Mam, her irritation starkly obvious.

'If he's like this for the whole trip, I swear to God . . .' She grits her teeth and Emma hears Mam telling her not to rise to it.

They get into a cab with Ines and she gets one with Kit, Noah and the kids. She'd planned for them to get here early so they could make the most of today but she already feels drained. As they drive over the red suspension bridge, she points out that it's just like the Golden Gate Bridge, explaining it was built by the same architect. Noah nods absentmindedly and Kit doesn't say anything as Sunny asks for the seventeenth time if Bun-bun can swim in the sea. They pass some holiday homes tucked a little further off the beach, rows and rows of caravans under yellow awnings with no sea view. Kit remarks that they look like refugee camps and she pretends not to hear him, then hopes desperately the cabins she's booked are as nice as they looked online, or she'd become a drawing board for their selfish complaints.

Ten minutes later they pull up at the back of the beach cabins and the setting is perfect. Satisfaction undoes itself on her face. Costa da Caparica is an endless coastline of beaches with nothing but golden sand for miles. She looks down at the sprouting succulents, which crisp at their edges, turning amber in the sun. The old fishermen's cabins had been bought up and converted into luxury holiday homes for middle-class families and stag-dos. They are almost close enough to kiss the shoreline, spaced neatly apart. One is the colour of egg yolk with white stripes, the other a deep seaside blue as unbounded as the Atlantic Ocean that faces it. Emma's favourite is a worn white cabin with a red door and a yellow seam, with two surfboards outside. You can tell the ones that are occupied by the short curtains blowing through a window, white towels hanging from ocean-blue pegs on an old chipped washing line. She'd booked two: one for her lot and one for the rest of them.

Kit and Dylan pay for the taxis and Emma makes her way over the small sand dunes towards the owner, who is standing waiting for her. The woman introduces herself and shows them around, with relevant instructions. She's relieved by how nice they are inside, the washed-white wooden interiors and crumbling old lighthouse sculptures. Ceramic fish hang from rope as do light bulbs, which are wrapped around the white beams of a slanting ceiling. The bathroom has exposed grey concrete, which Kit nods at approvingly, as Sunny mounts a ladder up to a bed, which is in the nook of the ceiling. Downstairs there's another double bedroom, a bathroom with a huge walk-in shower and white sofas covered with throw cushions. Window panes battered by sea air frame the ocean where surfers are skimming waves. Emma thanks the owner, and Kit follows her sisters a few doors down to make sure theirs is, as Emma promised, the better cabin.

It's not long before he and Noah are topless and googling the best places to rent a surfboard, cutting the wings off her angst: she'd known Kit would get over it, both of them needing an ally in this family. Mam suggests they pop to the shop to get some supplies but Emma assures her she's already made an order. A delivery should be with them in the next hour. 'There's nothing here for you to do but relax, Mam.' She smiles. 'Do you think you can handle that?'

Mam responds by using her index finger to push her sunglasses further up her face.

'I want to go swimming!' Sunny shouts loudly.

'We should buy you a dinghy boat,' says Ines. 'You'll love that. Mummy and I had one when we were little.'

'I don't think so, no.' Emma frowns at her from the floor where she's sitting, plaiting Sunny's hair.

'What's a dinghy?'

'Nothing,' Emma says, pulling her head back to twist the bobble as tightly as it will go. 'They're dangerous and you don't need one.'

'They're hardly dangerous.' Mam cackles.

'You've got your new armbands, haven't you? Here, go and fetch them from the suitcase and I'll blow them up for you.'

'She can blow them up herself,' Kit remarks, from the doorway, and she nods as if that's new information.

She slathers Sunny and Lilah with sunscreen, thinking about the time Mam had forgotten to make them wear any, how they'd all burned so badly and, with the jellyfish stings, they'd cried themselves to sleep, stuck in a painful pink casing.

Ines and Mam go down to the water and offer to take the girls for a swim to give Emma a break. Finally, Kit finds a suitable establishment, which he assures Noah isn't going to rip them off, and they return in wetsuits, the arms hanging at their waists, carrying surfboards. Kit says they'll be back in an hour or so, and Emma tells Dylan that Kit will spend more time prancing around with that thing under his arm than he'll ever spend on it in the sea. Dylan doesn't comment, as if slagging Kit off is a sport Emma can't play. Instead, she reads her book in a hammock and it grinds on Emma that she hasn't asked once if there's anything she can do to help.

Emma lies back on a sunbed on the washed-out decking, enjoying the quiet, awaiting the food delivery. She closes her eyes as the wind rushes over her face and fantasises about what would make her happy.

★★★

'Oh! You're back already?' Ines says, surprised.

'The waves weren't very good.'

'Okay, great – we've got a Zoom with the caterers now.'

'Do I have to?' Noah says, and Ines looks disappointed. 'No, I will,' Noah corrects himself by standing up. 'I'll join you.'

'It's fine. The sun is gorgeous. I'll only be twenty minutes, if that.' She takes her laptop under her arm. 'You sorted the lights guy out anyway.'

Her calm reasoning unsettles him, but he nods anyway. 'Right you are. I'm off to sunbathe then. See you out there.' He avoids her gaze, which invites a kiss, distracting himself from it with efforts to find a towel.

When he steps outside the cabin he hears Dylan cursing and follows the sound down the beach where she's springing off the edge of a stranger's towel, spreading her apologies liberally. He slides on his shoes and follows her towards the water. She's laying out a towel, then lying down, eyes closed, absorbing the sun's warmth with her own gravitational pull. Her skin is glistening with sunscreen as he watches the slow rise and fall of her chest. Her fingers occasionally twitch against the rhythm of the waves but there is something intensely intimate about her stillness, how relaxed she looks.

'Hey.' He has to stop himself bending to touch her.

'Oh, it's you.' She props herself on her elbows as she leans back, legs stretched out, the sun lavishing its attention on her.

'Oh, it's you,' he mimics. 'It's nice to know I still exist in your world, then.'

'And that means?'

He shakes his towel at her, the energy a quiet intensity.

'Noah! You're getting sand all over me.'

He shakes it again, deliberately this time, and she snubs the immaturity. She lies down, shading her eyes from the situation. He can't stand how much he wants her. Can't help staring at her limbs, arranged so inelegantly on the yellow towel. How was it possible for her to be like this? A faraway star and the ground beneath his feet.

'You've been avoiding me since the engagement party. I feel like I'm going mad.'

'I don't know what you want me to do about that.' She rises up sharply, looks at him like she's about to reach out and grab him. 'You need to stop looking at me like that, Noah.'

'Like what? I'm not even looking at you.' He turns his head, watches some surfers on the shoreline.

'Even Emma's starting to pick up on it, your gawping – staring at me on the plane and following me around the cabin like a wet dog.'

The words make him wince. They seem unnecessarily cruel. 'I've just been trying to get your attention. Trying to understand what's going on in your head. You haven't answered my calls. What am I supposed to do, DW, seriously?'

She reaches for her bag and pulls out a crumpled paperback. He takes it from her and throws it down the beach.

'Your childishness never ceases to amaze me.' She gets up to fetch it, but he sees she's enjoying the flirtation.

'I'm sorry if you don't want to talk about it but you have to – we need to sort this out.'

'There's nothing to sort out. Nothing happened. We just need to forget about it.'

'Nothing happened . . .' he jeers, as if sharing the news with passers-by. 'We had sex, DW. Last I heard you're not meant to fuck your in-laws.'

She looks around as if to catch the paranoia sitting on her shoulder. 'Nobody needs to get hurt here. And it's not like we haven't had sex before, is it? You didn't need to talk about it then.'

'You what?' He looks at her disbelievingly as she ruffles in her bag again, distracting herself from him. 'We talked about it last time.'

'No. We didn't.'

'Well, that was different; we were just kids and you were going off to uni. The scholarship was a huge opportunity.'

'But was it one or the other?' She presses on something uncomfortable. 'I could only have you *or* the scholarship? Or was it that you were waiting for me to leave so you could pounce on my baby sister?'

'Don't sully it; that wasn't how it was. I thought I was going to be in Cardiff, not stuck on Laurel Road nursing my nan.' His sneer is weathered by an old resentment. 'There was no one else.'

'Did you imagine what it was like for me? I leave, I barely hear from you, and when I come back, I find you shacked up with Ines.'

'Come on! That's not fair. She was there for me when I was going through it, that's all.'

'Oh, I bet she was.' She comes close up to his face.

He doesn't know what to do, doesn't trust himself with her, searches for the right collection of words that might save him. 'I can't live in it. I can't wake up to her every morning, knowing what I've done. I have to make vows to her, DW. Vows. You don't.'

'She's my sister and we were born into our vows.'

He can't believe what he's about to say. 'I love you. I am madly in love with you and that was tolerable when we were living in different cities, but it isn't any more.'

'So move.' She looks aroused but then her expression turns to sadness. 'Don't you just want to carry on with your life, like normal? With someone who loves you the way you want to be loved?'

'Why have you always been so convinced that isn't you?' His voice sounds pathetic to him but he can't stop imagining his hand sliding up her thigh and under those lavender bikini bottoms.

'God, it's boiling.' Ines's voice comes from behind him. 'Aren't you guys boiling?' She plants herself on the end of his towel. 'Did you bring sunscreen? I feel like I'm burning already.'

'I've got some.' Dylan rummages in her bag and hands it to her.
'Will you do my back?' She hands it to him.

'I'm going for a swim.' Dylan's tone flatlines and he watches her walk into the sea, light years away from him now as Ines drones on against the waves, something about a revised seating plan and charitable party favours.

★★★

She feels panic, the realisation that he might say something even as she walks away, leaving them together on the sand. She's surprised by how cold the water is at first, splashing up against her thighs and darkening her bikini bottoms. She walks slowly into the waves and lowers herself into the swirling white foam. Way out of her depth, dipping her head back into the salty water, the sea filling her ears as the effect of the vodka tonics wears off. The anxiety starts to cloud her body, smoking out any sense of herself. All that's left: a glistening despair that waits for her in drawn-out moments of silence.

Noah had been coming to her now in her dreams, his half-smile, sometimes as a warning and at others to signal the jeopardy of missing it. A moment between them, a fleeting opening that would quickly close: her last chance at being happy. She wanted him so much. Found herself thinking about him whenever she was alone in bed, promising herself she wouldn't, only to roll into her final moan, skin hot and the longing cutting into who she was. Knowing she would do it again. That, no matter what, she would find a way to have him, to taste him and feel him, make him lose control in a way he never had with Ines. And she hated herself for thinking such awful things but her thought patterns were circular now: the self-loathing always tiptoed into lust, which swirled and won, the whole cycle starting over again until her mind wandered to when she might be alone with him.

She tries to feel for the ocean floor but it's not there. Lies on her back and lets the water take her, motioning her arms like a sea angel, the high waves pushing her further into the abyss of her crime. And then there's Ines, a deafening contradiction, a person who travelled through the same aperture to the same world, yet was so different she'd never make sense of her decisions. Hands that looked just like hers but weren't. Her baby sister, the scaffolding of her and an incisor in her heart. Even if she could never forgive, she would keep loving her. Her limbs scrabble underneath the water, hands frantic, nails digging into her skin, ripping at the lilac bikini top she'd picked out with Ines in the warmth of a good mood. She might never have that again. But the thought of giving him up felt like missing out on her life. That if she didn't seize this moment, he'd slip out of her fingers and she'd be numb, stuck on the outskirts of who she was meant to be. The panic screams with her under the surface, the salt stinging her eyes as she grips her skin tightly, roughly pinching. Reminiscent of the childhood games where they'd twist each other's arms until it burned. A test of who could withstand the pain the longest. Imagining the vastness of the entire ocean filling her, washing away the corridors of her lungs. She needs to stop it. She has to stop. And when she splutters to the surface it's Ines calling her name from the shoreline. Making her way into the water, happy and smiling, wanting to be near her, like always.

***

'What were you arguing about with Noah earlier?' Ines's legs dangle from the countertop where she's sitting with a cup of coffee in her palm, a beach towel wrapped around her waist, hair still wet from their swim.

Mam looks up from loading the dishwasher. 'You were arguing?'

'We weren't.' Dylan dismisses the conversation, handing her more glasses.

'You looked like you were having words,' Ines prods.

Emma appears in the doorway of the cabin, erasing the patterns of light on the wooden panelling. She looks drained. Dylan disappears into one of the bedrooms and the three are left looking at one another. Ines senses the tension though she's unsure who the carrier is. When Dylan reappears, Ines is taken aback by her vulnerability, visibly soaked in, like the edges of her large T-shirt dampened by bikini bottoms. What's going on with her?

'Where are the girls?' Mam asks.

Emma slumps on the sofa. 'Gone for a walk with their dad. I've told them he can deal with them for a few hours. It's my holiday too, in case no one noticed.'

Ines welcomes her irritation: 'He probably needs a break from *us* anyway.'

'Did you hear about their falling-out?' She looks at Emma quizzically.

'Kit said Noah was rude to him at the engagement party. Seems they've resolved it. Men and surfboards, it's like they're wandering around the beach with giant dicks in their hands trying to fuck the sea.'

'No, not there,' Mam complains, handing Dylan a towel before she's allowed to sit on a chair.

'He's really not been himself.' Ines feels Dylan's eyes on her. 'I think I might have upset him.'

'Have you finished with that?' Mam takes the coffee cup out of her hand before she answers.

'We fell out.' She ingratiates herself. 'Nothing serious, he just won't let it go.'

Dylan's sudden exhalation is loaded.

'I see he's brought you up to speed then.' Ines can't retain her snarl.

'I'd say taking contraception while he thinks you're trying for a baby isn't *not* serious. It's a bit of a betrayal.'

'That's not really any of your business, though, is it?'

Dylan lifts her hands in submission. And Ines is furious at being caught out again. Dylan was always so worthy, puffing her own chest out with all of Ines's shortcomings.

'If you're not ready for children you shouldn't rush.' Mam squeezes her knee, coming to her defence.

'Wise words from a woman who didn't want them in the first place.' Emma picks up a tangerine, starts peeling it.

'I wanted you.' Mam continues to wipe the counter. 'I wanted all of you.'

Ines can tell Mam's not used to having them all in her space, sees she's finding it difficult, just as she always had.

'Not *all* of us.' Emma picks up an old book on Portugal and flips through it torpidly.

'Em, don't say things like that.' Ines finally gets the hint from Mam, pushes herself down off the surface so she can finish cleaning it.

'I'm just saying losing the baby had a real effect on you, that's all. And I don't think you're ready for children. You're still so young. I don't think that's what you really want, but you're incapable of separating your wants from his. That's the real issue.'

'Why don't you tell them what you told me?' Emma scorches the air and Mam stares at her, mouth drawn.

'I don't know what you're on about, Em.' Mam seems confused by the attack, which Ines also thinks is unprovoked.

'That you didn't have a miscarriage when we were kids,' Emma states plainly. 'You had an abortion.'

'Emma.' Mam's protest fills what's left of the space. She throws the towel into the sink, shaking her head.

Ines looks to Dylan to see if she has any inkling and they make a silent exchange: *We've never really had the conversation.*

'But wasn't losing the baby why you left?' Ines is confused.

Dylan gets up, takes the towel she's been sitting on and starts drying herself. Ines zones in on her, perfectly framed by the ocean in the windows behind, and watches as this feeling takes over someone else's body. It was as though she shared part of her nervous system with her sisters, their fear: it had the same palette, shared hues and shades. This feeling had been stowed away inside all of them and she watches now as it pushes open Dylan's mouth. 'Where did you go, then?'

'I don't want to talk about this.' Mam stands, looking embarrassed and clearly outnumbered as she readies herself with her cigarettes.

Ines is panting because it seems odd now that they've never talked about this. How could they never have had this conversation? But family trauma is like that, held in your cells, an intelligence constantly communicating beneath the surface, given its power by being unspeakable.

'I don't care about the termination, Mam, obviously. I just care that you lied and pretended to have a miscarriage, as some justification, which is pretty messed up, isn't it?' Emma throws down the book she's pretending to read. 'You've never wanted to talk about it. Why not?'

Ines tries to warn her off but Emma pushes back: 'Don't you think she owes us an explanation?'

Mam starts boiling the kettle, still devoted to the cup of tea as adequate resolution for crisis. 'This certainly isn't the right way to broach things.'

Emma goes for her: 'Oh, my apologies. I'd forgotten for a moment you bequeathed *your* maternal duties to me. How dare I slip out of character for a moment and—' her voice sharpens '—be a whole fucking person? You left us. When are you going to hold yourself accountable for that? We were just babies. I was just a baby.' Her hand finds her chest. 'And all this time I thought it was because you were mourning, that you were protecting us from your grief.'

Mam refrains from eye contact and this disconnection tightens the rope around Emma's anger but Ines still wants to protect her: 'I think we should stop. She's said she doesn't want to talk about this. Just stop.'

'No, Emma's right.' Dylan joins in. 'You've never said. What was more important than us?'

Mam wipes her face with her hands and, for a moment, it's as though they've successfully dented her armour, found a new way in. 'If we're going to do this, let's go outside.' She flicks the kettle off, pours herself a glass of wine from the bottle the owner left as a welcome gift and walks out of the cabin onto the decking. Then, for the first time in their lives, they talk about what happened.

1997

Two Months After They Moved to Laurel Road

Emma is ten, Dylan is eight, Ines is five

They asked if they were ever going home and their Grampy said: *This is you-er home now because you-er father is a waste of space.* Ines insisted this wasn't their home and Emma agreed. It was Grampy's, and also it had been Mam's when she was a little girl. They couldn't accept they would never be going back to their council flat, the only home they'd ever known and the last place they'd seen their dad, Tommy. Would he think to look for them here?

Mam was in the hallway, fussing like always before leaving the house, opening her purse then closing it, wedging something behind the receipts. Checking her reflection in the mirror, her navy court shoes on the vinyl mosaic tiles in the porch.

She spoke to herself, 'Right, is that everything?' and 'Did I remember to pack my hairbrush?' Felt again in the coat pocket for a letter that was written that morning; it couldn't have been for them.

'Are you sure you want to do this, love?'

They looked up at their Grampy. He wasn't happy about wherever it was she was going, as if there were a ticking time bomb, one he didn't know how to shut off.

Mam told him not to fuss, insisted again on getting the bus. The brown leather suitcase's lining still smelt of her own mam, of all these journeys she hadn't been on and yet carried inside her. Opened and closed her purse again, then pushed it into the handbag hanging off her shoulder. 'Right, that's me.' She looked down, smiling reassuringly. They were trapped in the liminality of an equinox, standing on the threshold, about to watch their sun cross over and out of their lives. They asked Mam not to go with numbed stares, Ines's finger in her mouth, Dylan biting into the side of hers and Emma trying to make out the anger mutating inside her.

'I'll pick you up tomorrow, then. Give me a call, whenever you're ready, I can come and get you,' their Grampy reprieved, finally giving in.

Mam said nothing. Ines suggested they might all go. But where exactly? Dylan reminded everyone again what day it was. Emma sat at the table, watching from the kitchen, her hair slept in, last night's toothpaste stuck to her, obscuring the Care Bear's expression on her nightie.

'I'll see you tomorrow then,' Mam said, then kissed Ines's head and ran a hand over the top of Dylan's, 'Bye, Dad. Look after the girls, Em,' and, with a half-smile, closed the door on them.

They watched as the dust offset by the slam found the sunlight and gathered around it. Grampy complained about the milk being left out. Emma moved first. They were quick to follow her up the stairs and into Mam's bedroom. The faded sheets were pulled back on the unmade bed. Poppy perfume faded into the muskiness of a room slept in without a window opened. The sheets were still warm; the floral bedspread was stained with the remnants and bodily fluids it took to rear daughters. All those sacrifices they couldn't yet hold in their small hands. They sat on the window seat then, watching from behind net curtains as Mam made her way down the street. It was like a scene from a film they'd feel differently about when they rewatched it in their adult lives.

They waited in the window for almost a year for Mam to come back.

Family Holidays, II

By the time Kit arrives back at their cabin with the girls the sun is almost starting to set. They'd already been interrupted by the grocery delivery, the scene of a difficult conversation dispersed, the remnants of which are lumpy, hard to swallow.

'On the wine are we, ladies?' Kit smoothes his wet hair as Emma reaches for Sunny who is crying hysterically, saying she'd had a baddie in the sea. Dylan can see she's furious.

'I told you she needed to wear her armbands. She's eight, not a strong enough swimmer to contend with the Atlantic, for fuck's sake – there's riptides.'

'Emma, language please.' Gwen pulls her up and Kit apologises reluctantly, sitting on the sofa, loathsomely using his nasal spray. Emma tries to calm Sunny and Gwen picks up Lilah who's also kicking off, crying and arching her back, feeding off her sister's angst. A condition Dylan can relate to – poor kid.

'What happened, darling? Tell Mummy.'

'She's fine, Emmie. There's no need to make a fuss.'

Sunny grizzles breathlessly, hot-faced and snotty, something about not being able to swim and being scared. Emma wraps the towel tightly around her, rocking her in her arms, and Dylan is flooded with tenderness. Feels the longing to put right the distance she has felt between her and Gwen after all these years.

Noah had been downstairs napping after such an early flight but he appears right on cue, sleepy and unbelievably cute, his hair sticking up, as he helps Gwen try to calm Lilah. Dylan observes them from the sofa with a glass of wine. Ines looks drunk already, ruminating on what their mother has just told them, and Dylan feels torn by the urge to comfort her. But how can she play the comforting big sister now?

She remembers the day their mother left like a series of Polaroid snapshots: a still of her applying pink lipstick in a mirror in the porch;

a hand-written letter sticking out of a trench-coat pocket; the image of court shoes on vinyl mosaic tiles so familiar it resurfaces like a memory of the present. One that washes back when testing the ripeness of fruit in a supermarket aisle or waiting for the kettle to scream. But now she's having to incorporate new imagery. She tries to imagine Gwen all those years ago boarding the train, sitting staring out of the window, sore and alone. Not with it – that's what she'd just said. Still drugged up on meds after the abortion, knowing if she'd gone home, she'd have a breakdown. So, instead the alternative, violent and irreparable, leaving different parts of them broken. And Dylan's own conflating feelings are written on the same balls of paper that were crunched up tightly in Gwen's head – that was how she'd described it: like stuffing. She hadn't been with it and neither had Dylan. She wasn't able to think straight, just as she wasn't thinking straight at the engagement party. Couldn't seem to get to herself.

Funny, they'd been right about her being pregnant with a girl. Or perhaps that made it sadder. She remembers them giggling behind their hands and getting told off for constantly touching her tummy. Their childish exhilaration soon to be met with a familiar wound; another thing that would leave and not return without explanation. Their construction of Edi then so real, so vital. A passage to what might have been, a new past running like a river through all of them.

Their mother insisted she hadn't had a plan, hadn't organised herself to leave Wales after the procedure. Instead she talked to them about Princess Diana. And Dylan still remembered that morning she died, the news running along the bottom of every television channel, even the cartoons. Going upstairs then to wake her. How Gwen had sat in her dressing gown for days afterwards, crying in front of the TV as they'd brought her cup after cup of sugary tea, watching the endless news cycle, wondering what to say, what might make it better. Three black dogs sat on her feet. It was the worst her depression had ever been. When Dylan was older, she'd perhaps understood the significance, a remarkable woman who had taken her power back, on the cusp of freedom crashing to a sudden end in the Pont de l'Alma tunnel in Paris. So, was it really that strange that Gwen had wanted to pay her respects?

She said that after the abortion she'd left the hospital and picked up a bunch of white tulips having read somewhere they were Diana's favourite. She claims she didn't remember getting to the station, startled by the Tannoy announcing they would shortly be arriving at their final destination: London Paddington. Went and laid the flowers at Buckingham Palace with some note, she'd tried to remember what it said; something was tugging at her, a thing that had nagged her for as long as she could remember, and Dylan feels this tug inside herself now.

'All okay, Dyl?' Gwen asks then, and she nods, smiles at her reassuringly. 'Right, it's getting late. I'll make a start on dinner.' She wraps an apron round her and ties it at the waist.

Noah plays sous-chef, sifting through the ingredients, handing her the butter and chives as she calls for them.

'Anyone for more wine?' Ines asks, opening another bottle.

'I think you've probably had enough.' Kit starts on her.

'Why don't you just fuck off?'

'Oi!' Gwen intercedes. 'Enough.'

Ines mutters something spiteful so Emma joins in, telling them to knock it off.

When it's ready they sit out on the decking, the table lit by candles. There is the scraping awkwardness of metal knives on plates. Dylan mostly avoids eye contact, listens instead to the conversation holders thrown out.

'The sole is fresh.'

'Mm ... lovely.'

'Can someone pass the potatoes down?'

Finding the whole thing excruciating, she can't wait to get away from them. When Emma says they're going to make a move because she needs to get the girls to bed, she is murderously jealous of the get-out ploy. Lilah is already sleeping, a chin resting on Kit's shoulder, and it's hard to believe something so perfect shares his gene pool.

'I'm going for a walk.' Dylan stretches her arms up with a casual air and prepares herself to leave with them.

'I'll come.' Noah gestures to her. 'I could use some fresh air.'

'We're literally on the beach,' Ines slurs from her chair. 'All there is is fresh air.'

'You're not going with them?' Gwen encourages her, but she doesn't want to.

As they tread down the steps and their feet meet the sand, they walk in the opposite direction to Emma and Kit, who call, with sleeping babies in their arms, that they'll see them in the morning. They wander along the beach, the sky dark, nothing but the washing up of waves to distil the mood as both of them try to crack the code, figure out how to get out of this one. Perhaps Ines would eventually recover from it. Or perhaps they would have a chat about how silly it had all been, and things would eventually go back to normal. A decade-long aggravation, something she'd secretly wanted to see upturned. But not of her doing. Now she needed to put everything back in its place. Dylan isn't destructive, knows it's not in her nature: she's a mender, a maker. Yet, no matter what, her next act would strike her in two. She can't help but compare the situation to Gwen's all those years ago: the decision she had to make was a dead end, the alternative an impasse.

'I wanted to come and visit you,' Noah says then, and she's brought back to the sensation of sand between her toes.

'In London, I mean. When you went, that was obviously my plan. And then Nan got sick. I don't think you realised how poorly she was, and I dunno . . . I didn't exactly have the fresher's experience, did I?' He sinks his hands into his back pockets. 'Spent most of my time on the M4 trudging back and forth to see her. I knew she wasn't going to get better, and after all she'd done for me, I didn't want to be enjoying freshers, getting drunk with strangers, pulling random girls. I wanted to be there. With her.'

'I know.' She sighs. 'You should have told me to come back, been honest about how ill she was. I could have helped.'

'I didn't want to ruin your year as well, did I? I wanted you to have a great time. All you wanted was to escape. And then it was complicated, with Ines. She grew up fast and I was lonely, grieving and that.

She was there. I couldn't help it, it just happened. We did ...' He pauses then, waits for his hesitation to dissolve. 'We did fall in love, just in a very different way. She's fragile, you get that. And I know it sounds strange, but ever since that night in the river, I don't know, I've felt this responsibility for her. This need to take care of her. And, let's be honest, you've never needed anyone.'

She shields herself from the wind. How could the making of a person also be their unmaking?

'The best way I could love you was to facilitate your ability to walk away, DW. That was the thing that would make you feel safest. It's why I never said anything after we slept together. I didn't know what you wanted. I was already losing you. You were moving away and I was out of my head about that.'

She pictures her mother's expression in her mind's eye, wrenched in guilt: *Each of you had needed me more than the last. And then when I got back, you were different, each of you affected differently by my absence. I didn't know what to do, how to fix it.*

It was Ines who'd struggled most, at least at first: she was the most dependent, needed feeding and help getting dressed in the morning. All they'd wanted to talk about afterwards was Edi. Gwen said she'd spent a fortune on taking them to see a psychologist – Dylan had forgotten about that: the memory had unfurled itself earlier on the decking. Separated from one another, endless questions from a woman in a grey suit in that strange room full of toys, which smelt of other children. And Edi taunting her all the while, giggling from the corner: *They think you're all mad because of me.*

'Dylan, say something, please,' Noah stops walking and takes her by the shoulders.

'I don't know what to do.' She starts to cry. 'I want to make this right but we've messed it all up because the only thing I love more than you, Noah, more than myself, is Ines.'

She will never be whole: either way she loses someone she can't live without. And she sees the tears forming in his eyes now as he whispers to her, stroking her face, saying that it's going to be okay, that he knows, he already knows. And she grabs at his shirt, kissing him desperately, a head-splitting desire overriding logic, the current inevitable, something neither of them can control. As she lets herself go down onto the sand, trembling, the weight of him on top of her. The broken pieces of her life falling away, the sand rough against her skin, leaving only this – this burning, beautiful now.

1997

Nine Months After They Moved to Laurel Road

Emma is ten, Dylan is eight, Ines is five

It was Mam's smell Ines missed most. Like the smell of warm toast or clean hair, a smell of safety, some essential reminder of who she was. She had been wandering around the house for months in Mam's jumpers, the sleeves almost dragging across the floorboards. Miserable, she would ask Grampy when Mam would be coming back, to which he would tell them all the same thing: *She might not ever come back, and if that's the case good riddance to 'er.* He said it was unnatural for a mam to leave her *babis* and when they became overbearing, pouring honey and flour over the kitchen surfaces, singeing their school skirts, he'd scold them and say, *No wonder she left. It's because you're so bloody naughty.*

Their Grampy, Arwen, was a serious man who wore so much gel in his hair that it always looked wet. He smoked so much that his fingernails were tinged yellow. He'd learned discipline early at the end of his own father's belt: he was the son of a coal miner whose consternation surrounding Catholicism led him to disturbing punishments, which he inflicted on both his naughty son and whore for a wife. So, Arwen had left home at sixteen and joined the police force a couple of years later. He lodged with a young widow who lived near the station. She had a son called Llewellyn and he grew incredibly fond of the boy. The two bonded over their mutual interest in trains and he'd regularly take him out on long walks on his day off. He respected Llewellyn's grit, born with a condition that meant people pitied and underestimated him, and that was something Arwen, too, could relate to. Now he expected that same grit from his granddaughters.

When he rang the hospital and they told him Mam had already checked out, he came home expecting to find her at the house. When he got back, he asked: *Where's you-er mam, then?* Their drawn blank faces gazed back at him, lips slightly parted. That was when he told them Mam had lost the baby. And it was hard to get their heads around that, how something so precious could be lost, like their homework or a lunchbox. And weeks later, after no word, he seemed more furious that Mam had abandoned him, barely noticing his granddaughters' interest in death growing as the days went by. Asking him questions about where the baby had gone exactly: *To an incinerator, I expect.* And whether their baby sister would go to heaven: *That's what the big book says, aye.*

His patience started to wear thin, so that morning, when Ines entered the living room drowned in yet another cardigan that belonged to Mam, he lost it. She was being ridiculous and he shouted at her for making them late for school again. Ines's response was to burst into tears and run upstairs. Emma let out a heavy sigh and followed her to Mam's bedroom where she knew she'd find Ines sitting at the bottom of the wardrobe. The mirrored doors were closed and in front of them there were piles of shoes to make space for her grieving nest. Emma looked at her reflection in the wall of mirrors and wiped away her own tears, listened to Ines sobbing inside. Their insides ached, some soreness — a recurring pattern imprinting itself, a humiliation they wanted to conceal. The one person who was meant to love them unconditionally couldn't, had chosen not to, revealing something obvious: there was something wrong with them. Emma took a deep breath and opened one of the sliding doors to reveal Ines, her small girlish legs huddled up to her chest, a fist in her mouth to control the crying.

'It's okay, Inny. I promise it's going to be okay. She'll come back. She's just sad about the baby, that's all. She'll be back as soon as she can, I know she will.'

Ines's face was red and covered with strands of snot. 'No, she doesn't like us.'

'We can't send her to school like this,' Dylan said, from the doorway, looking down at her foot as she ran it across the smooth pink carpet, making a dent and smoothing it again and again.

Emma went down to see Grampy. 'We're not going to school today. Ines is crying and Dylan's sad. I don't want to pretend that—'

'Fine,' he said, without turning his head away from the screen. 'What?'

'Don't go to school. I'll call them later and say we've got a sick bug, tell them you won't be in till next week, all right?'

She ran to him, wrapped her arms around his shoulders to which he told her to mind his coffee. Then she left before he changed his mind and went back upstairs to tell the others.

★★★

'Now that our sister is dead shall we make another?'

It had been Dylan's idea to begin with, but they were all equally comforted by it. Each of them in their own minds knew who their new sister should be.

'I'm still the baby of the family,' Ines insisted, brushing the hair of her dolly.

'I quite like having an older sister.' Dylan smiled at Emma, as she snatched white bristles from the toothbrush.

They created her in Mam's image. By now she had been gone for months, her bedroom kept like a shrine: the discarded toothpick on the dressing table, the cup of tea with lip stains pressed against the bone china; a dressing gown still filled with the imprint of Mam's body as it was discarded on the floor.

They collected the things Mam liked best, those things she didn't like at all, and then sat to think up a list of the qualities a sister should possess. They placed the items on Mam's bed: bristles from the neglected toothbrush, their favourite fluffy cardigan, Nan's charm bracelet, which they were never allowed to play with, they sprinkled it with white pepper, poured over the remnants of the cold tea, tried not to sting themselves as they counted out stingy nettle leaves. Emma took a sewing needle and dug it into each of their fingers; they winced as she pushed a droplet of blood onto the mound of maternal treasures. Then they held hands as each of them said a few things about this new sister.

'She will never ever be sad, only silly, and she'll always want to play.'

'She will always want cuddles and kisses and she'll make us laugh every day.'

'She'll be very, very brave and won't be afraid of the things we're afraid of.'

The one thing they all agreed on, the thing they hoped for most, was another sister, who would never leave. But the thing they couldn't agree on was what to call her.

'I like Ariel best, like a mermaid.'

'No, let's call her Julie.'

'That's a silly name.'

Emma grew tired of their bickering and suggested they take the first initial from each of their own names: Emma, Dylan, Ines. They called her Edi.

When Grampy didn't find them in their beds the following morning he went straight to Mam's room, where they were all enmeshed on top of the covers.

He didn't pay much attention when they got excited about their new sister, racing around the house, asking if he could see her. At first, he'd tell them off for getting a fourth plate from the kitchen, dividing up their food to make an extra portion, until eventually he gave in and started laying an extra setting without them having to ask.

Edi Wyn

1. Emma, Dylan and Ines are the sun, the moon and the stars, and Edi is the dark night sky where everything horrible lives.

2. Emma, Dylan and Ines are the Graeae. Edi is the eye they see the world through and the tooth that eats through the rot.

3. Edi is mycelium, a mass of branching, thread-like thriving, which connects them at their black roots.

4. Edi is semantics, each and every way they talk without saying a single word: she is maternal lineage and tongue.

5. Edi is the fear rambling through the woods of their minds when a door gets closed or someone forgets to say goodbye.

6. Edi smells like poppies, helps them grieve, jumps into the water with them, holds back their hair and says, *Ssh, love, everything is going to be okay.*

7. Edi *yw'r groth*, a grandmother inside a mother inside a child inside a future.

8. Edi is Edith.

9. Edi will go into the bedroom first.

Family Holidays, III

'Come on, let's get ready for bed,' Gwen sighs, and it's pitying.

'Do you think he'll always do this?' Ines feels the warmth of the wine in her body.

'Do what?' She picks up the glass from the coffee table and starts to tidy around her.

'Reconfigure his anger with me in their friendship.' She looks dopily towards the cabin's closed door and the longing leads her to self-loathing.

Gwen sighs at her impatiently. 'There were always going to be ramifications.'

'Ramifications?'

'For what happened.'

Gwen starts shutting off the lights around her, and Ines feels panicked realising there isn't more wine left to drink. She isn't ready for bed yet. 'Do you mean taking contraception, or him?'

'You're not a stupid girl.' She reaches for the brush on the table, pulls it through her thick hair brusquely. A ritual she had always conducted before bed. It mattered how she looked even then. That was where Ines had learned the value.

She tries to picture Gwen in London then, standing in a red telephone booth, subsumed by her own longing for a life taken, ambivalent in her motherhood, soaked through to the bone with loss. Could they really believe her plan had been to get the last train home? She imagines Angharad, her old school friend, on the line, repeating the address back to her several times before she'd let her hang up. She had said she was in a right state. Sodden from the rain, floppy from the painkillers, hailing a black cab, knowing her friend would sort the fare when she got there.

'Would you have come back, if it hadn't happened?'

'Ines, please.'

'Do you still talk to Angharad?'

'I'm tired.' She puts down the wooden hairbrush. 'I just want to go to bed. We can talk about it another day.'

But Ines can't help it. 'Have you ever considered that my shortcomings are wrapped up in the ramifications of *your* actions?' She knows she's pushing at her like some irritable toddler. 'You know, it's never done me any favours, your favouritism. It's only made them resent me.'

'I don't have favourites—' Gwen's sigh is listless '—and that's a reach, even for you. Not everything is someone else's fault. Eventually you'll have to grow up and cut your own path, learn the discovery of such things lies in sacrifice.'

'I don't know what that means.' She's playing with the cap of the wine bottle.

'It means your need to be loved overwhelms you, Ines.' She tucks her hair behind her ear. 'Overwhelms you and your life and prevents you from living. You want to be loved by everyone so much it makes you deceptive, even to yourself.' She shuts off the last light, only leaving on the lamp next to Ines as she tells her she'll see her in the morning.

Left alone she tries to visualise Gwen ringing the doorbell and waiting for Angharad to answer, nerves track-cycling through her stomach, like they are in Ines's now. There were these deliberate comments as she'd sat and told the three of them about where she'd gone. How light her luggage had been, the mess she was in: *I hadn't packed more than a night's stay for the hospital, but when Angharad saw the state of me she said I needed to get myself better before I could even think about taking care of anyone else.* Sage advice from a woman with no children. Ines had witnessed Gwen coming alive again as she relayed this version of events. Angharad had managed it, had got out and pursued her dream of becoming a dancer. Gwen had described the house like it was some sort of palace: Ines pictured a long hallway with tall sculptures and expensive art hanging on the walls. And then she had inserted Gwen's sheepishness upon arrival, awkward to realise Angharad was hosting, coy and unarmed in a room full of strangers with contrived haircuts. Being introduced to her partner Josh for the first time, liking him from the off. And it's hard to untangle Gwen's loss from her own now as

Ines watches her wet clothes blowing in the wind on the line outside the cabin, imagining Gwen's soaked-through jeans on Angharad's radiator as she ran her a bath.

Ines looks between her thighs then, feels for the blood that isn't there. Sees Gwen's instead, darker blood that's dried to her skin as Angharad helped her into the tub, washing her hair, setting aside a sanitary pad and clean pyjamas before they curled up in bed together. She claimed those first few days had been a struggle, that she kept trying to leave. Angharad and Josh insisted she was in no fit state. The days then blending into weeks, soon months until time grew too surreal to keep hold of.

The cabin door creaks open. Noah and Dylan finally make an appearance.

'How was the walk?' She tries not to sound needy.

'Yeah, nice,' he says, smiling at her. 'It's beautiful out there.'

She nods and Dylan says she's going to bed. 'Today was a lot.'

Ines's look is worn and disbelieving, and it's Noah who's in the dark now.

'Shall we go down too?' He gestures to her.

'You go. I'll be down in a minute.'

She waits for the fussing to stop, the trips to the bathroom, hushed whispers and lights coming from the stairwell flicking on and off again. And when the cabin is finally still, she sinks back into herself. She hadn't stolen Noah, he had chosen her willingly, yet the competition with Dylan dwelled. But it was Ines who loved him. And they needed each other, were good together. She knew he'd come round and eventually she'd get him back to London. She just needed to bide her time. The wedding would bring them closer.

She understood what it felt like when your own life started to evade you, stuck in Wales, bored and lifeless with nothing to do. Gwen's life would have started to evade her, the longer she stayed at Angharad's, bleeding into her and Josh's reality. She'd said she never saw the wet clothes she'd shown up in again: they were generously replaced with Angharad's things. Ines could see her now, strutting around their fancy house in low-cut dresses, sipping martinis, remembering how a certain arch of the neck or flick of her hair could extort something from men

– from Josh specifically. Angharad all the while telling her she didn't mind, that she wasn't jealous – they were open to loving whoever they wanted.

And for Ines this is true: you can't control who someone loves any more than you can control how the river finds the sea. Noah would always have Dylan on a pedestal but it was her he wanted to marry. Her he came to each night. She imagined Angharad's growing resentments, felt the jealousy tickling at the back of her own throat. The open deceit, like honey in her hands, this longing for a man desired by them both. And the lavish, wild parties Gwen was having while Ines and her sisters sat at home, pining, all hollowed out.

She gets up then, pours herself a glass of water and leans against the work surface, sipping it slowly, deciding to believe what Gwen had told them: *I don't remember wanting to leave you. I don't ever remember wanting that. I only remember that I left.*

1998

One Year After They Moved into Laurel Road

Emma is eleven, Edi is ten, Dylan is nine, Ines is six

It was a wintry morning and ice was stuck to the windows. Waking was only to relive the horror all over again: the realisation that Mam was gone would hit them as if for the first time. Like a fever dream, raising their heart rates, a pain over their bodies that was impossible to show others, no physical evidence just a weakening. The dark mornings made it even harder but they would still wake early and go into Mam's room where Edi would be waiting for them, wearing the floral dressing gown, trying on Mam's lipstick. They refused to believe Mam had left them for ever, convincing one another she would be home any day now. For how long she'd been away was inconceivable: a stretch of time too far-reaching for them to hold in their minds.

They lay on Mam's bed for a few hours that morning until the sun rose, waiting for Grampy to wake them. Usually he would come in around eight o'clock in a fluster and they would race about, taking it in turns to use the bathroom. But he didn't come in with his glasses of milk that morning, didn't shout at them, opening the curtains and pulling off the covers.

'Emma,' Dylan whispered eventually, 'are we late for school?'

'I think so.'

Ines, who was spinning her teddy bear around by its arms, asked, 'Should we go and wake him?'

It was cold downstairs. The heating had gone off. They'd usually be in school by then. When they went back up to his bedroom, the door was shut. But the door was always shut. He'd said he needed one room in the house where he could get some peace and quiet and he'd been cross when he'd found them in there playing with Llewellyn's things.

They knocked and called his name, but there was no answer. They stood outside the door looking at one another, sensing the strangeness of it all.

'You go first.'

'No, you.'

'Let Edi go.'

Edi reached for the silver knob and twisted it. At first, they were relieved to find he was still in bed, sleeping. They trickled into the room, stood in a line alongside the bed.

But when Emma reached out and touched his hand, she withdrew quickly. It was cold. She told Ines to go and wait outside but she refused, standing on tiptoe to get a better look, her bear hanging limply as she peered up at the yellowing face.

They tried to wake him then, pulling at his arms, gently shaking his head from side to side. But he didn't stir. When the initial shock wore off Edi started to cry and the rest of them joined in. Lifting themselves onto the bed next to him, holding on as tightly as they could, his stiffened body covered with tears and strands of hair. They lay with him like that for hours.

Later, Emma and Edi got up and walked next door to Glenys' house where they told her on the doorstep what had happened. She called an ambulance. Grampy's sister, Aunty May, arrived soon after, asking them who would be best to call and they directed her to Mam's old phonebook where there was a list of emergency contacts on the first page. They were put in front of the TV while men in all-in-one suits took away their Grampy, numb to what had just been said to them: 'He died in his sleep, girls. He went peacefully; he wasn't in any pain.' And then: 'Do you know where you-er mam is?'

They wouldn't be allowed to attend his funeral.

The rest of the day was a blur; they didn't leave the living room and people ferried food and drinks back and forth, whispered loudly from the kitchen about the state of the place and how 'now I come to think of it, I've not seen her in months'. They started on the pile of dirty dishes in the sink, asked where their laundry was, and whether it was okay if they changed the sheets on their beds. Edi nodded, so Emma said it was. They sat on the sofa in silence, staring at the TV screen, but filled instead with the image of his sunken-in mouth and strange-coloured skin.

It was Ines who woke first, roused by the sound of Mam's voice. She thought she was dreaming and, realising she was awake, cried out to her and ran straight into the kitchen.

They found Mam there, right where they'd last seen her, in the hallway, shoes on vinyl mosaic tiles, holding that suitcase with a tentative smile. Ines hit against Mam's legs and Dylan ran and planted herself in her arms. Even Emma was in tears.

'I missed you so much,' Ines wept.

'I missed you too.' Mam looked down at her, and it was as though she was relieved, quickly reassuming her position in the house like nothing had changed.

'How long have you been gone?' Glenys asked, and they listened to Mam lie.

'Just a month or two. I've been looking after a friend. She's not been very well.'

They didn't want to get Mam into trouble and focused instead on following her around the house as if she might suddenly vanish. Then Mam politely asked Glenys, Aunty May and the others to leave, told them they could manage, that she would call them tomorrow. They were all in shock and needed some time alone together. As soon as everyone was gone, Emma confronted her, arms crossed against her chest. 'Where have you been?' Her stare stripped Mam off the wall, like paint.

'I needed some time to recover from everything,' she said, touching her stomach, and Emma nodded, giving in to a shared understanding between them.

'It's been a difficult time for us all. But I'm back now, I promise. I won't be going anywhere again, ever. I swear it.'

'Good,' said Emma, 'we didn't like it.'

Family Holidays, IV

She pulls the baby wipe out of her mouth, can feel the bitter perfumed taste against her tongue. The wet wipe is attached to another and then another, her gullet the turquoise plastic container. She keeps pulling more, cotton emerging, neatly snaking itself up her oesophagus. They tickle the ridge of her tonsils. She's in the kitchen, a high chair and a baby. Music playing again. What is that song? The scent of the wipes makes her stomach wince. There are other people in the kitchen, busying themselves, stirring pots. She can't breathe. Someone needs to feed the baby. She pulls up a stool, the static from the wet cotton in her mouth. And then the baby is choking. The baby is heaving. She picks her up, puts her fingers into her mouth, but she can't get at it. She looks around for help but everyone has gone, just the sound of the spluttering infant now, reddening in the face. The look of panic in its eyes.

Waking up in a cold sweat, Emma abandons her plan for a lie-in and gets up to analyse herself in the bathroom mirror, searching her pores, an instinct to purge rousing as she pushes at the blackheads in her nose. She looks at her legs extending from striped shorts, and her arms, sinewy, losing their original shape. Puts her hands around her thigh and tests the circumference, then pulls the skin on her face back to smile at the child hiding there. When they were kids it was almost as if their bodies were porous, not always easy to tell where one began and the other ended. As if their mother's absence had somehow fused parts of them together. Now she is alone in this body. She can see she's failed to take care of it, has turned her efforts outward to accommodate everyone else. She loves her daughters, she reminds her reflection, and it nods back at her, nothing could be truer than that. Surely it was the point, had always been the point. She could never leave them.

She understands Gwen's devastation at being pregnant again all those years ago. Sitting in the greasy spoon where she'd stopped off to do the test after dropping them off at school. Afraid their dad would find it. She said in the end she'd told Tommy straight away: *I threw the match into the wastepaper bin.* He hadn't said anything at first, not until he'd got drunk that same night. And then it was how could she? They couldn't afford another. They could barely afford the ones they had. And the council weren't going to give them a bigger place. He'd accused her of wanting to see him suffer, wanting him to feel ashamed for not being able to support his family. Men can be so self-centred, never legible to themselves, only blinded by ego. She remembered times when Gwen would beg him not to drink any more, always telling him she was sorry when she hadn't done anything wrong. That haunting memory had roused quickly yesterday as they'd sat on the decking listening to Gwen give her side of things. Him kicking her in the stomach while she lay helplessly on the kitchen floor, Emma standing in the doorway in her pyjamas. Her dad screaming, and Gwen lying timorously as he opened a can of beer and poured it over her. She had been dazed, like maybe she was dreaming, a wet finger loose in her mouth. Strange, Emma had felt a release when Gwen brought it up – because it hadn't been a dream. A voice from the past finds her, tries to reassure her: *Go back to bed. Mammy will come up and see you in a minute.* Before he slammed the door so she could only hear the contemptible things going on behind it.

The arrival of fear in her body prompts her to check on Lilah, whom she finds sleeping soundly. She wanders up the stairs of the cabin to the kitchen and makes some coffee. Sunny is up already, sitting on the sofa reading her book quietly. She takes her little index finger and places it to her lips, smiles at her knowingly as if it's their little secret. Emma doesn't know why her eyes fill with tears, doesn't understand the emotions clutching at her. While the coffee brews, she sits on the sofa, arm around her eldest. The view of the empty beach and the blue water in front of them fills a realisation. Sunny remarks that Bun-bun likes it here and would like to come again, and Emma kisses the top of her head.

Their dad had left two days after Gwen had told him about the new baby. Ashamed of what he'd done, a coward. There had always been violence but he'd taken it too far that night. Even as a child she'd understood that. Gwen said he went to work that morning: *Took the car and left sixty quid on the kitchen counter next to the kettle – I knew then he wasn't coming back. Needless to say, the money didn't last us long.* And she remembers all this now, Gwen panicked, flitting around the house like a caged bird. The freezer starting to empty and soon she didn't have enough to take them to school. Thank God for Grampy. She can hear his gentle voice down the phone, tries to imagine the conversation that was sparsely relayed to them yesterday.

'Gwen? Is that you, love?'

'Yeah. It's me, Dad.'

'Are you all right?'

'I think so, why?'

'Is there something wrong with you-er car? Is Tommy getting it fixed? That's the perk of having a mechanic for a husband, surely.'

'The car?'

'Aye. Mindy tells me she's seen you getting the bus to school with the girls.'

'Oh. No, there's nothing wrong with the car, Dad. It's just gone, that's all.'

'Gone?'

'Yeah.'

'Been stolen, has it?'

'No, Tommy's taken it. Tommy's gone.'

'I see. Is he coming back, then?'

'I don't imagine so, no.'

'Right. Okay, love. I'll pop round in the next half-hour. We can have a chat, all right? Don't you worry about it, *blodyn tatws*. Everything will be fine.'

She can't imagine what it had felt like for Gwen to move back to Laurel Road. Back into all those memories from her own childhood as she struggled to steer theirs to safe waters. The baby had been a mistake and there had still been time to rectify it. It was never the abortion that bothered her, only the lie. When Gwen had scheduled the procedure, she hadn't registered what day it was, that it had been Mother's Day. She would have wanted to get it over with. Emma had listened as she carefully described how parts of her had been too dispersed to bear, puzzle pieces strewn so far it seemed impossible ever to fit herself back together. She recognised the sensation, wanting to bring everyone together now to resolve the self-neglect. She can't imagine what it must have been like, getting the call at Angharad and Josh's, hearing the news that Grampy was dead. Realising her time was up, that she had to come home: *I was never not coming back to you girls. It was a fantasy life that's all, some attempt at reliving a stolen youth. I wasn't even eighteen when I got pregnant with you, Em.*

And then there was Llewellyn, Gwen's older brother. The real pain she saw her carry inside her. It had broken the family's heart the day he went into cardiac arrest, dying like that right in front of them on the living-room floor. He had been dead before the ambulance arrived, and knowing his condition had made him susceptible hadn't prepared them for the despair, for how deep it could go. Gwen had only described the scene to her once: her own mother catatonic as she rocked his dead body. She wouldn't let the paramedics take him, not until their Grampy got home. Emma had no clue what it was to lose a sibling, a child, a husband. Perhaps her resolve was stronger than she'd realised. Perhaps, like the women who had come before her, she would cope.

She's the only one of her sisters with children, which means she's alone in not trusting Gwen's reasons for coming back. Perhaps if Grampy had lived longer and they'd been older, things would have turned out differently. She understands the desperate feeling that burrows inside a mother, the harrowing loneliness, the loss of sanity in a new love. How sickening it must have been for Gwen to come home and find them like changelings: *You were so out of reach when I came back, so untouchable, like an entire ecosystem that had learned to survive without me. I wish I'd gone about things differently. I wish I'd been there when it happened. I should have been there.*

Last night when they'd gone back to their own cabin, Kit had rubbed Emma's back as she'd cried, telling him about the violence that had formed part of her childhood as the scenes started finding their way back to her. He'd tried to reassure her by stating she was a much better mother. But that wasn't true. Your mother would never hurt you, yet every mother is guilty of that. So, what more did she want from her? From herself? Gwen had done the only thing she could: try her best with the cards she'd been dealt.

Soon Lilah cries out for her. She goes down to her, hears Kit start crashing around in the kitchen. When she walks back upstairs, he can't wait to start on her for making a scene last night. She'd forgotten the narrowness of his compassion.

'You made a right show of things over Sunny. They stick their oars in enough. Why do you want to make it worse? It's like you take some sick pleasure in it.'

She doesn't want to argue, resigns herself instead to start making breakfast. Asks if he'd like bacon, a simple direct question, which he blindly ignores. Sunny's eyes are on her, waiting to see what his punishing silence will provoke this time, if she'll say sorry. But Emma just smiles.

They all sit at the long white table outside on the decking and Kit buckles Lilah into the high chair while correcting Sunny on how she's holding her spoon. She ferries orange juice and bacon sandwiches from the cabin before finally sitting and helping herself to something. Before her, the infinite white sand and blue sky, her healthy and happy daughters chewing apple slices as her handsome surgeon for a husband hooks into her with the belligerence of silence. The sky isn't bright blue, though. It's just reflecting the mood of the sea, and now she sees the colour of her situation. Her life is more like the sand, only making sense when thousands of grains come together, yet always slipping through her fingers.

She excuses herself, goes inside and back downstairs to their large bedroom and into the bathroom, her bare feet on the cold white floor. She pushes the toilet seat up, takes her tongue to the enamel erosion on her teeth as she sinks her fingertips into the softness at the back of her throat and arcs her body to get the result she wants. Slows her breath to relax her diaphragm. The acid from her stomach some evidence of another part of herself she wants to trace. The feeling of what should go down instead coming up. Black coffee and bacon watery in a bowl. She stays sitting on the floor, her legs curving around the toilet. Then the door opens, their eyes meet, hers wet from the strain of heaving and his fastened with grains of cruelty. 'Emmie, is that really necessary?' Substantiating that she can stop it somehow, the corroboration she needs: she can halt it all if she wants. Change the direction she's going in, just like Gwen did.

Gwendoline Wyn

1. Gwendoline Wyn has three daughters. She keeps secrets from them all and uses silence and pregnant pauses, like a warmonger.

2. She works at the chemist and carries Gravy Bones in her coat pocket for dogs she meets along the way in life.

3. Gwendoline never fulfilled her dream of becoming a professional dancer – which was why she pushed Ines into such advances. Going for dance lessons at the town hall on a Thursday is her favourite part of the week.

4. She doesn't have a favourite daughter: she loves Emma best for her weaknesses, which she only shows to her; Dylan the most for her uncompromising appetite for more; and Ines always for her constant need for love.

5. She worries about her daughters, all the time, even the one she chose to let go, and she understands their rage is predicated on her wilful withholding of something she is at liberty to give – but she's given them all she can think of.

6. Gwendoline always grew up thinking she would be a mam but it wasn't all she wanted.

7. She met Eric at a dog-training show in Cardiff. They've been for several meals. She feels younger than she is when they kiss, but she's nervous to tell her daughters about him.

8. She's not at all religious but her favourite Christmas song is 'Mary, Did You Know?' because it captures the essence of her experience as a mam: that any child you deliver is really here to deliver you.

9. People think the greatest tragedy of her life was losing Llewellyn, but heavy grief is built on the foundation of love; her greatest tragedy was falling out of love with her own mam, a sensation that sometimes feels suffocating as she lies awake in the dark.

1992

Gwendoline is twenty-three

'What's she like, then? Does she look like you?' Angharad's voice came excitedly down the line.

Gwendoline looked at the new baby cradled in her arms, still amazed she's hers. 'I guess so. She has my nose.'

'That's good news. We don't want her having Tommy's.'

Gwendoline laughed and Tommy shushed her, angling his body closer to the television where he was watching the football. She got up, supporting the baby with one arm as she reached down for the base of the phone, turning inwardly to try to unravel herself from the cord, which was spiralled around her nightie.

'Are you still there?'

'Yes,' she whispered.

'How are you feeling, then? Do you think you'll be able to come up to London and visit me soon?'

Gwendoline sighed as she sat down at the bottom of the stairs, repositioning Ines so that her head was resting on her knees, holding the handset in place with her chin. 'I hope so. Maybe. When Ines is a bit older. How's it all going anyway? Tell me everything! Are you still knocking about with that Josh fella?'

'Yes.'

'He's lasted a while.' She grinned.

'Oh, don't be such a prude. It's not like that, I told you. Have you read that copy of *The Ethical Slut* I sent you?'

'No!' Gwendoline whispered down the line, 'I've asked you to stop sending me stuff like that. I've got kids, Ang. How am I supposed to explain to them what "slut" means?'

'Tell them it's a woman who values pleasure in her life, the same way they value toys and ice cream. Did I tell you the show got extended for another season? I'm just in the *corps de ballet*, but still.'

'Ah, listen to yourself, will you? You're dancing for a leading company at the Royal Opera House! What more could you want?'

'A principal role. I'll never get a principal role now. Too old. Do you know what *corps de ballet* means?'

Ines started to whinge and Gwendoline pushed a knuckle into her mouth to soothe her. Angharad didn't wait for a response: 'It means "the body of the little dance".'

'See, that's important. You're the central body of the production, the backbone, really.'

'Oh, listen to me rambling on about my tireless ambition when you have real-life stuff going on.'

'Gwen!' Tommy called from the living room. 'I'm hungry. What time's tea?'

'Just a second,' she shouted back, pressing the receiver into her neck. 'Real life is overrated. I'd rather talk about you. It's not the same here without you, hasn't ever been. Do you think you'll ever come back?'

Angharad's laughter was shrill. 'Move back? Oh, my goodness, never! No. London's my home now. Josh is.'

'Are you still living in his big fancy house having all those fabulous parties with famous people? Oh, you promised you'd send pictures, Ang. You never do.'

'Well, I'm too busy being the backbone of a leading ballet company to send pictures, aren't I? Besides, I don't need to send photos because you're to come down and visit, see it with your own eyes. We'll throw a huge party and you can meet them all, our friends.'

'Gwen? Are you gonna put tea on or what?' Tommy called again, and she sighed.

'How's it going with him?' Angharad asked flatly.

'With Tommy? Oh, you know what he's like ... he's, well, *Tommy*. Things here don't really change, do they?'

'You've changed. You've made three entirely new humans since I left. That's a humongous change. Especially for your fanny.'

Gwendoline let out a girlish giggle. 'Oooh, please don't make me laugh, I've still got stitches.'

'Gwen!' Tommy shouted again.

'Did you see the announcement last week?' Gwendoline knew exactly what she was referring to. 'Charles and Di, separating? Who'd have thunk it? Good for her, I say. Perhaps now more women will be inspired to leave their miserable, cheating husbands.'

'Perhaps.' An uncomfortable silence dwindled between them and Gwendoline scrabbled for something to say, not wanting her to go yet.

'Right. I'd better leave you to it, then. I've sent something for the little 'en in the post so keep an eye out for it, all right?'

'All right, ta.'

'It's not pink, so it'll probably be the only not-pink thing she has, right?'

'Let's speak again soon, okay?'

'I love you.'

'Love you too.' As she was about to tell her she missed her the line went dead and Emma and Dylan came from behind, scrambling over her down the stairs, kissing their new baby sister on the head as she started to cry.

'Mam,' one of them said, 'I'm hungry.'

Family Holidays, V

The second night on the beach was quieter, uneventful. No one unpacked at the cabins so it didn't take long the next morning to get ready and order taxis to take them back across the suspension bridge with its sweeping red cables. Jesus is behind her now, arms outstretched, as they turned into the city of Lisbon to an address Emma has provided for their Airbnb. Did they think reservations magicked themselves out of thin air? Evidently. She'd booked an old Portuguese house that was close to the city's estuary, with tight-fitted balconies just wide enough for the plant pots stacked across them. When they arrive, Ines notes that the view of the water would be beautiful were it not blocked by an enormous cruise ship.

'Is that honestly the first thing you can think to say?' Emma is flummoxed.

'What?'

The inference is lost. She personally thinks she's done a great job. It's the enormous attitude of this family that's ruining the vibe. The Airbnb also has a large courtyard, which is ambrosial and smells of jasmine. She wanders onto it, looking at the old stone statues placed around eclectic garden furniture. She assigns them their rooms and is surprised when no one passive-aggressively tuts or complains about their lot.

'Thanks for sorting all this out, Em.' Gwen tries to meet her.

Dylan flaccidly agrees. 'Yes,' she says, rummaging around in her handbag.

'The place is fab.' Gwen takes the reins again. 'We know you've worked hard to arrange all this for us, don't we, girls?' She nudges Ines who is biting her nail while on her phone and she lets out a whine.

'Yes,' Dylan says again, monosyllabic, applying her lip balm.

'Right. Go and get changed.' Emma pushes her shoulders. 'I could use a break from you lot. Come on, everyone to their rooms, please. You too, Mam. Ines, out of my sight.'

They are amused by her and in truth she's entertaining herself. After their tense chat at the cabin, Emma was realising they had always been having that conversation, talking about it ever since Gwen had come back, in the way they did, and didn't approach her. And there is a sense of relief now, and it barely even grates that Kit is stonewalling her unless he's in earshot of the others. The wide-winged angst feels like it's gone, replaced by flutterings of something seemingly new and invincible.

★★★

Ines had bought some more wine on the way over to the Airbnb and Dylan had grabbed a bottle from the kitchen and taken it to her room with her. What the hell was going on? This feeling was monstrous, like the sensation of re-remembering that someone you love has died when you wake up each morning. Because whatever happens she is going to lose someone and she has already started grieving – she just isn't sure for who. She slaps herself across the face. The betrayal wasn't a one-off, and she wasn't an accessory in this crime: she was the perpetrator.

She opens the wine with her penknife and drinks straight from the bottle. Lies back on the bed, head craning towards the ceiling, watching the fan go around and around, hoping it might fall and desiccate her. She's never been so hot in her life, fresh on the coals, asking for sanctuary from herself and what she has done. What she keeps doing. And the heat is everywhere, acidic, dissolving her constitution, hissing loudly to give her away. She takes another swig from the bottle. There's a knock on the door and it sure as hell better not be him. Can't he just leave her alone for one fucking second?

'Dylan,' Gwen's voice calls to her, 'can I come in?'

'Uh, yeah, sure.' She sits up and the handle lifts.

Gwen raises an eyebrow. 'Do I have to worry about your drinking problem now 'n' all?'

'No.'

'Do you only give one-word answers, these days?'

She wipes the sweat from her top lip. 'Maybe.'

Gwen nods, her presence contributing to the unbearable heat.

'Can you open a window or something? Isn't there any air-conditioning in here? I'm burning alive.'

'Don't be dramatic. You sound ungrateful and you'll set Emma off.'

'There is no number of adjectives that will satiate that woman's need for affirmation.' Dylan takes another swig of the bottle and holds it up to her.

Gwen sits down on the bed and takes a large swig. 'God, that's awful. It's warm.'

'It's not warm. It's broiled.'

She brushes a hand across Dylan's forehead. 'Do you want to talk about it, love?' And for a moment she's fourteen again, too afraid to tell her how she feels because she already knows she'll take Ines's side.

'*It* is complicated.'

'It always is.' Gwen hands the bottle back to her and moves further up the bed so she's sitting beside her. 'How about this? I'll tell you a secret of mine and then maybe you can consider telling me what's going on with you.'

'A fair trade.' Dylan puts the bottle between her thighs and gathers her hair, wrapping it around itself to free her neck from the suffocation.

'Well, I've got a gentleman friend. No, wait, that makes me sound ancient, doesn't it? I'm *seeing someone*, as you lot would say. It's not serious or anything, not really. But he's a nice man, loves his dogs 'n' that. I don't know, I like him.'

'Eric, the dog trainer.'

Gwen is appalled.

'Yeah, that's not a secret, Mam. Kit saw you together at the Phoenix Garden a few weeks back when he was picking up a takeaway.'

Gwen helps herself to the bottle held between Dylan's thighs.

'He told Emma, who told me, who obviously had to tell Ines. I didn't make the rules. That's just how the chain goes.'

'Fine.'

'You can't have secrets from us – you're our mam.'

'Only when you have your own kid will you know how bloody inaccurate that is.'

'*Kid* as opposed to kids?'

Gwen sat back against the headboard. 'For some reason I only see you having one.'

'Probably all my poor ovaries will have the vim for by the time I get round to it.'

It's quiet then, except for the fan turning above them.

'Are you okay? You know, after yesterday?' Gwen asks finally.

'I'm fine.' Dylan can't curb her default to reassure. 'We appreciate you being honest with us. We know it can't have been easy for you, being a single mum.'

Gwen hesitates, as if she's unsure about what she's going to say. 'Sometimes we feel we want to protect everyone, but loving another person that much means it's almost impossible to avoid pain, to avoid hurting them. The two sort of go together.'

'Like wine and ice.' She tries to lighten the mood.

'No, like life, Dyl.'

And it's as if she's just told Gwen about the explosion that's about to go off underneath them all. Has warned her in some way and, just this once, her mother's chosen to take her side.

'What are you pair doing in here?' Emma appears in the doorway, brows arched with accusation. 'Drinking the secret wine.'

'I thought you wanted us out of your sight.' Gwen folds her arms, marvelling at her predictability.

'I'm bored now. Come on.' She gestures to them. 'Don't drink that in bed, it's depressing. I've got olives and snacks plated up out here.'

★★★

'Come on, baby, it's been so long since we've done it.'

In the next room Ines is restlessly trying to seduce Noah. The more she tries the more he can't get it up, or doesn't want to get it up. Jesus, he was sick. There was something seriously wrong with him. But he's amazed at how much she can push through the pain barrier of rejection. It must be an actor thing.

'I told you, I'm just not in the mood, Ines.' He pushes away her hand again and sits on the bed to put his trainers back on.

But she's unyielding. Comes towards him again, starts kissing his neck in the spot that usually gets him, spreading herself over him.

'Ines, please, everyone's in the next room. It's hardly a turn-on.'

'That's never bothered you before,' she whispers, grinding on him, and the thought of DW the other side makes him revolting to himself. She mistakes the redness in his cheeks for something else. 'You know you want to.'

'Please. Just stop it, will you? I said no.'

She rolls off, scorned if not a little embarrassed. He feels bad but also relief.

'Boring,' she gripes childishly, picking up her phone to avoid the static between them.

'Fine, I'm boring. I'll take it, all right?'

He can see he's testing her patience and he doesn't know why. He's such a prick, a class-A jerk. He struggles to unlace the damn trainer and she stares at him, trying to read his thoughts.

'How long are we going to go on like this?'

He performs this look, like he doesn't know what she's on about.

'When are you going to stop punishing me?'

He loses his temper, throws the shoe across the room and it hits the door. 'I'm not punishing you, all right?'

She goes and gets it, starts unlacing it for him, like he's some child. When she hands it to him, he swipes it off her.

'Feels like you are.' He puts her hands on her waist.

'Believe it or not, your feelings don't dictate reality, Ines.'

She withdraws then, finally backs the fuck off. It isn't just his fault: she's constantly pushing him. She sits down at the dressing table next to the bed and opens her makeup bag, then sits perfectly still, staring at her reflection without blinking, sinking into her darkness. He can't suffer another of her meltdowns, not before the wedding. Not before he has a chance to tell her at least some version of the truth.

It was a drunken kiss; it hadn't meant anything. He would brandish a lie. Tone it all down. Yes, he'd kissed her sister, but he hadn't meant to, wasn't sure if she could even remember. If he'd kissed Emma, it would have been bizarre, hilarious even. Something they could joke about over Christmas crackers. But DW was a different detonation and he didn't know if they'd retrieve themselves from the explosion. Didn't know if he wanted to.

'Look—' he gets up and walks behind her, squeezing her shoulders '—why don't we go for a drink later, yeah? Just the two of us. It'll be nice to spend some time together. It's intense being around the family all the time. And it sounds like that chat with your mum last night was really heavy. We could both do with a break from it all.'

She smiles then, and he can feel her coming back as she raises her hand to his. 'You're right, it's been a lot. For all of us. Then again, Emma already seemed to know so much of it, and, well, Dyl, you know what she's like – made of metal.'

The mention of her sucks out his chest. Ines carries on and he zones out, wondering how he's found himself here. Lost in this family, a whale with a wide-open mouth that had swallowed him whole when he was just a kid. He was like petty krill stuck in their teeth. Of little consequence to the bigger story. The Wyn sisters, his lifelong obsession. Gwen, the mother he'd always wanted, constantly edging forward only to be batted away. They were unforgiving, he'd witnessed this many times, and he was putting himself at risk of the same fate.

There's a knock.

'Come in,' Ines says airily.

Emma throws her head around. 'Come on, lovebirds, we're having a glass of wine on the terrace before we head out and explore.'

And he wants that so badly, the terrace and the jokes, the dysfunction and the safety of knowing what someone really means when they say something entirely different. He isn't ready to give it up. And that's what's at stake. Perhaps DW was right: the best thing to do is say nothing, move back to London, maybe get Ines some more therapy – couple's therapy could be good – and pretend this shit show never happened.

★★★

They spend the rest of the afternoon as a family, wandering the city, pointing fingers at the neoclassical architecture and the *azulejo* tiles, ticking off tourist clichés: sardines, *vinho verde*, *pastel de natas*, which Ines is surprised Dylan passes up.

'Are you all right?' she probes.

'I'm not feeling well,' Dylan calls ahead to Emma, 'I'm worried I might be coming down with something.'

'No.' Emma turns back and waits for them to catch up. 'You can't be. I've booked this *really* cute restaurant. One of the dishes is an entire truckle of Camembert completely soaked in honey.'

'That sounds amazing but, honestly, I feel shitty. I think I need to go back and chill out for a bit. We've been walking around in this heat all day. Look, why don't I take the girls with me? They're knackered and you can let your hair down a bit and enjoy dinner.'

Emma considers this. 'I'd rather you were here, though.'

'Are you okay?' Noah lingers, waiting for them, and Ines watches carefully. Dylan reassures them all she's fine.

'It's probably just a bug, something I've eaten maybe.'

'Are you sure you're well enough to take them with you?' Emma says, already loading her with Bun-bun and the baby bag.

'I'm sure.'

'Right then.' She beams. 'Let's book you a cab.'

When they arrive at Praça das Flores, the bustling, self-satisfied atmosphere in the square chimes with Emma's mood. 'This is great, isn't it?'

'It's lovely.' Ines had promised Gwen she'd make more of an effort to appreciate the trouble Emma had gone to. She looks around at the people sitting about on benches, drinking wine and smoking, eating takeout pizza and breezily walking their dogs. They look happy. The restaurant Emma's booked is on the corner. It has glass-fronted panelled windows painted dark green and ivy running up trestles that meet with burnt-orange *azulejo* tiles. While she speaks to the waiter the noise of the restaurant spills out onto the street where their table is, and there's a subtle deciphering of who will sit next to whom before they order drinks. Emma looks pleased with herself, which Ines thinks is the closest thing she has to a hobby. But it's weird because Kit is in one of his stinkers, which usually makes her more neurotic.

And, in truth, it's nice to see her so relaxed for once, happy – glowing, even. As though she's finally learned to let the world swim over her. Perhaps the weight of early motherhood is starting to lift now Lilah is chewing a bottle instead of her nipple. She banters with the waiter and employs some creaky Portuguese, which she'd learned on a Brazilian app, but the staff are polite. She tells jokes around the table then, focusing her attention on making Gwen laugh and reminiscing about the few holidays they'd taken as a family when they were growing up. Gwen throws her head back, wiping the tears from her eyes as Emma tops up her glass, signalling confidently to the waiter for another bottle. Noah's mood lightens too, and she feels relief as he helps himself to some Camembert, putting the first slice on her plate in that way he does.

'It's nice to see you two getting on,' Kit's voice comes from the end of the table, 'after the terrible barney the other night.' He sits back in his chair.

The prick just couldn't stand to see her having fun.

'It wasn't a barney,' Ines neutralises.

'Well, Emma was so upset.' He keeps his eyes on her.

'I'm sorry if I upset you.' Gwen holds her chin.

'You didn't—'

'Oh, she was in tears all night.' He circles whisky in a glass. Emma tells him not to exaggerate, but he persists like some roach that won't die. 'What was it all over?'

'It doesn't really concern you,' Ines swipes back.

He scoffs. 'If it concerns my wife it concerns me.'

Emma repositions herself at him, taking a confident gulp of her wine. 'Why have you always got to be such a dick?'

He looks back at her, stunned, and it's too late for Ines to recover her snigger.

'That's an interesting question.' Gwen backs her up and he raises his hands as if to say he'll leave it.

'No, go on,' Emma challenges, 'if you've got something to say.'

'I haven't.' He backs down. 'I was simply asking a question.'

'It wasn't just *a* question, though, was it? You were poking at something you know all too well about, trying to make us feel uncomfortable. Is that it? Do you want me to feel ashamed?'

There's an almost-smirk on his reddened face. He shakes his head, dismissing the question as preposterous.

'Because I don't feel embarrassed. People are complicated. Surely you understand that, Kit?' Emma's lips pinch. 'You and I are complicated, aren't we? This relationship, our marriage.'

'Let's not do this here, Emmie.' He looks around the table for someone to edge onside, but Ines doesn't meet his gaze.

Emma keeps staring at him with a wild liberation Ines hasn't seen in her for a long time. Gwen lights a cigarette and inhales deeply.

'Let's get the bill, then.'

'That was fucking awkward,' Ines says, as they follow the jacaranda trees, fragrant and fernlike, lining the streets and reflecting shades of lilac onto the creamy sky. They are both relieved not to have to suffer the cab back with everyone. 'Do you think she'll be okay with that pair?'

'Gwen doesn't take any shit from him,' Noah says.

'I've never seen Emma stand up to him like that.'

'Mm . . .'

He's distant and distracted, and it's irritating. He was the one who suggested this drink. They wander down a cobbled side street.

'This looks like a nice bar.' She shows willing. 'Shall we try it?'

She follows him in and it's not nice at all, a little tacky with red strobe lights and the music is too loud for how early it is. The place is pretty empty, a guy in his fifties smoking at the bar with a shot in front of him. And when they sit down a waiter hands them two laminated cocktail menus, tells them it's happy hour.

'Nice and sticky.' She doesn't mean it as a complaint but sees he's taken it that way.

He shouts to her over the music that he's going to the toilet. She orders two pisco sours and two shots of tequila. Some booze should loosen things up. She should text Dylan to see if she's feeling okay. She reaches for her phone from her bag but the battery is dead, so takes Noah's instead. Types in his six-digit code. She goes into his messages and scrolls down. It's mostly work stuff, a message from Gwen asking him to get cigarettes, and then she sees DW's name.

'What are you doing on my phone?' He returns from the bathroom, reaching to snatch it from her but she pulls back.

'It's a little late for that,' she says, watching the panic crease into his face.

★★★

After checking on the girls, and Dylan, who are all in bed fast asleep, Emma sits on the edge of the sofa and stares out at the courtyard where they'd been eating olives and drinking wine. Talking about the time Dylan laughed so hard on a date she'd wet herself. She'd had to call Noah from the pub toilets to come and get her before the guy noticed and told everyone at school. The vibrations of their laughter are still captured in the atmosphere, the energy of them all still here. A version of her family that might not be that way again.

'Are they all asleep?' Gwen whispers, bringing over a bottle of wine and a corkscrew.

'Yeah, all three curled up together.'

Gwen smiles, then reconsiders, looking down at the bottle. 'Something a little stronger then?'

Emma stares out over the estuary as she listens to her rattle around the cupboards, checking the fridge drawers.

'There's vodka. Found this in the freezer.' Gwen pours a modest quantity into her own glass and hands Emma the other. 'What are we drinking to?'

'To numb the pain.'

Gwen laughs, and when the door opens they look up. Emma can see Ines has been crying but Gwen gets to her first. For fuck's sake, could she not have one single evening – not even for the public breakdown of her marriage? She asks what's wrong, but Ines is too beside herself to answer, rambling on, something about texts on Noah's phone. Cheating? No, not Noah. He never would. Emma tells her to slow down.

Gwen leads her to the sofa, sitting on the coffee table opposite, taking her hands calmly. Emma goes to the open-plan kitchen and sets down another small tumbler of vodka. When she hands it to her, Ines downs it in one. Her breathing slows and she starts from the beginning again: texts to Dylan, she says. He'd admitted it, said it happened at the engagement party. What?

'All right, it's all right,' Gwen soothes, unflustered. 'It's going to be okay. Just breathe, Ines, concentrate on breathing.'

'She's a selfish bitch.' Her face relishes her anger.

Dylan appears then in a short, faded nightie, half asleep. 'What's going on?'

Emma feels the expression of horror constructing itself on her face as she tries to compute what Ines has just told them.

'Dylan,' Gwen commands firmly, 'it's not a good idea that you're here right now. Go back to bed, please.'

'No. Let her show her face,' Ines spits. 'Let's hear what she's got to say for herself.'

'Ines, please,' Gwen warns again. 'It won't help.'

'She wouldn't.' Emma shakes her head at her, disbelieving. 'She just wouldn't.' She states this as a fact. 'Tell her, Dyl. This is a misunderstanding. That's what happens with texts. There's no context.'

Dylan just offers her a pained look.

'It's not just texts, Emma,' Ines rages. 'He slept with her.'

Dylan walks towards Ines, tries to reach for her.

'Don't touch me.' She pulls back violently. 'Don't you dare touch me ever again. I know you've always wanted him. Since the moment you met him. We've all known that. You've hardly been subtle about it.'

'Ines, listen,' Dylan pleads.

'There is no defending what you've done,' she hisses at her. 'Don't degrade yourself by trying.'

'I . . . We were going to tell you. He always wanted to tell you. I'm sorry.' She starts to cry and Gwen looks at the floor. Emma holds back on the instinct to comfort her.

'You weren't there for him when it came down to it, though, were you?' Ines points at herself. 'I was.'

'We were children.' Dylan starts ravaging her bottom lip. 'We hadn't figured things out yet. I didn't fight for him because I love you. I don't think I considered back then that you'd spend your lives together.'

'Is that a justification?' Ines gets up from the sofa and Emma stands between them. 'You fucked my fiancé at my engagement party, and you're trying to vindicate yourself.'

'It was an accident, I swear. I never meant to.' Her head shakes back and forth as if disbelieving of the information.

'I've had a life with him without you.' Ines looks at Emma. 'Without any of you. We were going to have a baby together.' She wipes at her tears.

'Just try to calm down, Ines,' Gwen squeezes her upper arms.

'You're right,' Dylan says limply. 'There's no defence, but I do love him. I can't help it. I've tried, I really have. But I love you both.'

And Ines runs at her, grabs for her hair and pushes her down to the floor, screaming, and all Emma can feel are hands and arms whipping at her face as she and Gwen grab at them, trying to pull Ines up. She can hear Lilah crying. Then Kit is towering over them. 'What on God's earth are you lot doing now?'

Dylan steps back, a hand pressed to a split lip, flustered and out of breath, her thick hair pulled out of its ponytail.

'Go to your room, Dylan,' Gwen shouts, still holding Ines by her forearms as she starts to break down.

And Emma asks herself if she's really surprised. Considers whether she saw it coming, if she'd sensed it. She knew something was up between them: did that make her culpable? She knew Dylan was in love with Noah, everyone did, and perhaps that's why no one had ever felt the need to confront her. It was part of their fabric, stitched into every dynamic and foul play. Her two sisters had wanted the same person for as long as she could remember, the silly, floppy-haired boy from up the road – that's who Noah would always be to her. And she loved him like a brother. Like Edi, he'd been some small fix, perhaps even a replacement for her as they grew up and out of their imaginary friend. As if somehow transferring that same trust to Noah.

Sunny is at her side, asking why Aunty Ines is crying, and she doesn't know what to say. Emma can hear Dylan repeating over and over again, 'I'm sorry, Ines, I'm so sorry. I'm sorry,' as she walks back down the corridor to her room. She tells Kit to fetch Lilah and put her in their bed, which he does, taking Sunny with him. Ines stumbles off to her own room and Emma follows her.

'I told him to find a hotel,' Ines says, getting into bed fully clothed.

Emma nods, helping her take off her cowboy boots, then pulls up the covers and tucks her in, like she had when she was small. Noah's clothes are discarded across the floor, his aftershave still in the air, and she plays for a moment with erasure. Replays all the scenes from her childhood, deleting him frame by frame, like she'd often tried to do with Edi. But it was too far-fetched, that their life could feasibly have happened without them both there. Then she realises that this version of her family is lost now anyway, regardless of what she decides to do.

1997

Gwendoline is twenty-eight

Gwendoline felt the pink linen sheets damp beneath her. Her hair was stuck to the back of her neck, her legs were wrapped with Angharad's and Josh's arm was thrown across her waist. She came to, remembering where she was. The night she'd first arrived she'd been taken aback by this house. It had multiple bedrooms across several floors, all with their own bathrooms and big enough to have sofas in them too. They were more like studio apartments. Angharad hadn't been bragging on her calls home. Even worse, she'd been underplaying it. Gwendoline knew Josh worked at a record company; what she hadn't known until she'd arrived in London was that it was responsible for breaking out one of the UK's leading indie boy bands. He knew everyone, of course, and there were always musicians hanging around. A lead singer sat on the Union Jack chair in the downstairs bathroom, offering her coke or starting a fight in the kitchen for no reason, until Josh had to ask the innocent bystander to leave. Gwendoline should have felt out of her depth and she knew the only reason she didn't was because of how she'd connected with Josh. Saying hello for the first time had rendered her in a yellow haze that felt like dawn, the emergence of this new person who already seemed to know her. There was an ease in conversation not normal for strangers. It suffused into excitement, then a friction that created a heat that singed her skin, the kind of desire that leaves its mark. She and Josh were drawn to one another, the flying sparks a by-product of something unexpected and inconvenient. They were always ending up in the same small circle in the corner of a party, finding ways to touch one another that would go unnoticed. The graze of her against him, the weight of such a gesture, now immeasurable in pleasure. She'd started to avoid being on her own with him, afraid of what might happen and the consequences it might set rolling.

She looked down at the soft-shell curve of her roseate bra, Angharad's bra. She hadn't arrived with any clothes, apart from those she was wearing. Hadn't realised she'd be staying. But London had expanded Gwendoline's lungs and she didn't know how to exist without the oxygen. She'd found a new way to breathe, yet woke each morning with a tightness in her chest that she was still there. Even more so that morning, finding herself in their bed. Angharad occasionally went to their friend Derek's house for sleepovers, but Gwendoline still couldn't bring herself to be intimate with Josh. Would say she was tired, finding an excuse to go to bed early or she'd spend ages in the bath until he eventually knocked on the door to say goodnight, leaving her wrinkled, like a raisin. Even after Angharad had encouraged her, looking at her through the dressing-table mirror as she brushed her own hair: *We're free to love who we like and I can tell he likes you.*

But Gwendoline didn't buy it. She knew her friend, really knew her. Not just this version she'd conceived in the city, and she understood the trouble sleeping with Josh would offset. But that didn't mean she could stop thinking about him, with his floppy hair and aloe-vera green eyes, trespassing into who she was, exposing an alternative life there. It wasn't how it had felt with Tommy: he had been steady, good in bed but, most importantly, a pass to escape Laurel Road. But Josh was more like a bridge that, if crossed, she might never get back to herself. Her want for him drew her awake at night. A whole new love just sleeping in the next room. The trajectory of another path running parallel with reality, calling for her down the corridors of his house, flirting with her on the landing. She'd lie still, her imagination reconstructing this fantasy life. Still again, when he stood outside her door as if wondering about coming in. He was all she could think of and her infatuation thickened, like a new layer of skin, making it harder and harder to leave.

She got out of Josh and Angharad's bed, reached for a dressing gown and left the room, closing the door quietly behind her. Went downstairs to the mess, ash overflowing in crystal ashtrays, champagne glasses and beer bottles discarded on every surface, and a mirror taken down from the wall, still speckled with white powder. Tony Blair's face was on the muted TV left on from last night, showcasing a better

Britain with that glint in his eye after winning a landslide victory. She straightened a painting, an attempt at levelling herself out, opened the fridge, found some leftover birthday cake, pulled open the drawer for a fork and ate it straight from the box.

'You know, I'd give up anything to know what goes on in that head of yours. I wouldn't need to see it all – I'm not an unreasonable man. Just some slight understanding of what's tormenting you.' Josh joined her in the kitchen in his boxer shorts, hands discovering her under the silk robe.

'We didn't, last night?' She tensed.

'No.' He shook his head and frowned at the insinuation. 'We were just pissed and larking about. We must have fallen asleep together.'

She nodded at what she already knew.

'We've talked about this. It's not about you, me and Ari . . . it's about you and me.'

How to tell him that she'd hated the sensation of another person touching her for her entire life. Until then. His hand teasing out the makings of who she could have been. Sliding a door open to a version that didn't feel new, more like a perforation into the way she'd always seen herself. Someone raw and full of feeling, not fashioned from values and archaic expectations.

They sat and watched each other, spooning cake into their mouths, wiping chocolate icing from the corners of lips as they made quiet noises of gratification. Tension pulling taut, she got up, wandered into the pantry and wondered what she might be looking for. Heard the pipes churning: Angharad in the shower. And then he was behind her, hands on hip bones turning her. A leg wrapped around him, a foot clutching a shelf to steady them. Then his hand against the front of her pants, which she pushed away until she couldn't any more.

'Please let me. Just let me make you come. I want to, so fucking much.'

She closed her eyes, feeling his hand warm against her. Pushing her head back against a row of tins as she cried out, his hand then over her mouth. Soon Angharad's footsteps were coming down the stairs and Josh went back in the kitchen, started pouring coffee as she wiped her mouth and tried to compose herself.

'God, I feel awful. Are there any painkillers in there?'

She called back that she was just looking, the heat in her face hell-bent on giving her away. It wasn't just her love for her friend that was holding her back. Who was she kidding? Gwendoline could never sleep with him because of the lie in the bed between them. Her three little secrets. She'd asked Angharad not to tell anyone about the girls, worried what people might say. It hadn't helped. They still expelled themselves through her as if the constellations of her daughter's births were glowing through her skin. Learning slowly that she couldn't un-mother herself, even through leaving. That every day would feel significant because of a birthday, or just a feeling, or seeing something that would make one of them laugh.

She handed her friend a blue box of pills, sat in the kitchen watching the rain through a window that seemed only to have bars on it for her. And she let how desperately she missed them come for her, let it tear through her lust and uproot a fresh disgust for herself. She knew if she told Josh it would change how he looked at her and that wasn't something she would readily give up. Stuck at the impasse of this lie, knowing she would break something between them with the three things she loved most in this world.

When the telephone rang a few weeks later, it was Josh who answered. He came into the living room, the cable trailing behind him, his index finger hooked under the phone. She knew then that it was over, saw it in the curvature of his confusion.

'It's for you, a lady called Audrey May.' He held out the receiver. 'She said it's about your father and your ...' His eyes looked grey then, as if they had hardened into something unfeeling, each blink a kaleidoscope lens re-forming her, an optical illusion, a person he'd made up. He coughed as if to bring himself back to the situation with a different perspective. 'She said it's about your father and ... your daughters?' His mouth curling inwards, waiting for her to say something – that this was some prank call, or a mistake, there must be another Gwendoline Wyn. It was then she decided on what she'd always known she would do.

Break-Ups

August

In the history of low-budget airlines there has never been a flight so awkward. Ines knows the only reason everyone's managed to keep their shit together is for the sake of Sunny and Lilah. And then this pathetic panic from Dylan as she rescinds, scrambling to swap her seat with Gwen to avoid sitting next to Ines. It draws a new rage into her heart. Emma has begged Ines not to make a scene in front of the girls, which somehow makes her culpable. She isn't the victim in their eyes, just a person caught up in this mess. Like a mouse, she'd scurried right into the trap. It's bitter on the tip of her tongue. She feels sick, spits into her empty cup. Stares out of the window at the clouds, which are like a seabed of foam. What was up is now down, her life inverted on itself. She doesn't speak or make eye contact with anyone, knowing that if she does, she'll lose it. Flashes of them making love on the beach keep coming as she winces at the image of herself in the cabin, drinking herself into oblivion, pitifully searching for the peaceful place inside her. The bile in her tummy churns as she considers what's best for her now, realising for the first time since she was a child that it might not be him.

When they land at Bristol airport, they all stand silently around the carousel. Ines watches everyone lift off their luggage as if each of them is claiming responsibility for their part in it. The parting is awkward; she stands back as the family stumbles over itself – cracked now – no one quite knowing how to say goodbye. Emma, all sympathetic smiles, and if Gwen asks her one more time if she's okay she'll flip a table. Obviously, she isn't okay. She knows she looks horrendous and it has value. Sees how she must look to him now, frail and childlike, as Gwen clutches her tightly in her arms.

They drive back to the cottage in silence. Noah tries to say something but Ines just stares blankly out of the window. She wants to feel her way slowly over the ice because she knows they're about to drop into dangerous waters, which they've been avoiding for so long. And yet at times like these – when the last thing you ever expect to happen to you happens – there is a washback of inevitability. As if the thing was always there, once deep in her unconscious, now a rapid ascent, like nitrogen bubbles in the blood, rising to the surface of her life, the pain excruciating and everywhere.

When they pull up outside their home, she doesn't collect her own bags from the boot, instead opens the front door and goes straight to the kitchen. He follows her after he's unloaded, watches her ravaging the teabags before they have a chance to brew. *Let's get this over with.* She doesn't hand him his mug, wraps her hands tightly around hers, both thumbs touching, bloodied and bitten down. How could this be happening to her?

'Do you want me to go first?' he says then, and she pauses to consider how things should be conducted.

'No,' she makes sure to say this assertively. 'I'll start.'

He pushes his tongue into the side of his cheek.

'It wasn't ever about me, was it? I was just tracing paper, the closest thing to an outline of her.'

He breathes out heavily, wipes two small tears away with the back of his arm.

'All you cared about was maintaining proximity to her. She's the real marrow you want to suck out of the bones of this family.'

'That's not true.' He folds his arms into himself, and in the window behind him she notices their garden, how parched it is, ruined from the cruel embrace of a heat wave with no one there to water it. The flowers are brittle and crumbling, the earth gasping – so much was dying.

'Are you going to say anything, Noah?' She looks at him, sees he's distraught but shuns her compassion.

'It's not that simple, is it?' he says. 'You've lied to me too. We've both been lying to each other.'

She's stunned he'd offer a retort, wasn't expecting any pushback. The scene begins to blur then as he recites a text she'd sent to a friend, making a joke about taking the pill, him none the wiser. Blathering on about auditions and emails from her agent. Her loss pushes everything else out of the way. She wasn't just losing him; she was also losing her baby – the child she sometimes longs for to fill the wretched hole of grief, and at other times can't stand the thought of. What choices did she have left? Her mother hadn't had many. Women of her generation didn't get to consider whether children were something they'd be good at, something they were well enough to do. If she could finally face herself, stop drinking, go back to therapy, she might shake this inviolable feeling, this knowledge that she'll be an ambivalent mother.

'Ines,' he calls for her attention. 'Look, I'm not claiming innocence here or making excuses. I know what I've done is unforgivable but let's be real for a second. I've also fallen prey to your shape-shifting. All this time you've just been reflecting myself back at me. What I did was wrong but I also think it was an extreme measure to figure out what was real.'

She places her mug down and looks at him pityingly, realising she doesn't have to do this. She'd already played out the different ways in which this conversation could go and they all ended the same way: with what she knew would hurt him most. So she removes the pin, throws the grenade.

'You lose, Noah. Don't you get that yet?' She leans back. 'You've lost. You don't get either of us now, none of us, in fact.' She laughs at him then, just like she'd practised. 'Water isn't as thick as blood and they'll let you go down the drain. Dylan will choose me. They're *my* family. And you'll be someone mentioned in passing, a character from our past, some faded memory.' She shrugs. 'It's over.'

When he punches the wall next to her she doesn't even flinch.

★★★

Emma hears Kit arriving, his car cautiously making its way down their drive. When they'd got back from the airport he'd been called into the hospital due to understaffing so they hadn't had a moment to talk. This had left her alone with her thoughts and with nowhere to put all this anger. She could feel the madness building within her, but honestly didn't give a fuck. Standing on their tall stepladder, she uses a sledgehammer to strike pieces off the lion statues that are either side of the gate of their home. The noise of the stone as it crumbles is so satisfying. As he pulls in, she can see his mouth wide open through the windscreen as pieces of the statue fall to the ground. His children are standing nearby, enveloped in the arms of Beata, who's got the expression of someone who's lost control of the situation.

'Emmie! What the hell are you doing?' He opens the car door with the engine still running. 'What on God's earth? Stop that! You're scaring the girls – come down.'

But she doesn't want to come down. She takes another wild blow and smashes into the lion's face. More of it collapses and hits a little too close to his Mercedes. He gets in, reverses the car, then starts trying to bargain with her. God, she hates the lions! How had she not seen how smug they were?

'Please, stop this. Come down and we can talk.'

It's her body that begins to tire, not her appetite for destruction. Her pale lipstick smudged across her cheek, hair blowing righteously around her, she's never felt so reckless. She was so Goddamn mad. At all of them. At Noah and Dylan for what they'd done, carelessly ripping apart the family she had spent her whole life trying to hold together. At Gwen and her stupid freedom story, at what it had exhumed. And most of all at Kit, for never bothering to save this marriage, and to herself for allowing them to fester in it.

'Beata, would you mind taking the girls inside, please?' His embarrassment fortifies her resolve. 'What's going on, Emmie? Come on, I can't do this now. I'm exhausted. I haven't slept. I've been at the hospital all night.'

She reverses breathlessly down the ladder. 'I'm leaving you,' she says. And when her feet touch the ground, her feelings transmute into a new story. 'I want a divorce.'

'Can you just put the hammer down, please?'

She drops it by her side. 'I realised something on our trip. Something about my nightmares, those dreams about babies. All this time I thought it was about the girls, that the baby was Lilah or Sunny, some post-partum derangement. But it isn't them, Kit.' She loses her footing. 'The baby in the dream, it's me.'

'Emmie, look—'

'My name is Emma and I don't want to do this with you any more.' She walks closer to him. 'You make me miserable, and I make you miserable. We can't stand one another, not really, not if we're honest about it. We've somehow accepted this as what marriage is. But it isn't, Kit. It doesn't have to be.'

He looks down at his leg, which fidgets with agitation, and she wonders if he will fight her on this. If on some level she wants him to.

'We don't want to teach our daughters that this is what love is. We owe them so much more. We've been sitting ducks in our own unhappiness. And I want you to know that I'd never pour poison into the girls' ears, stop you seeing them or anything like that. You're a much better dad than I ever had, but you're a shitty husband.'

And when there's no rebuttal she waits downstairs, shaking while he goes to pack a bag, the reality of what she's just said alive and manic inside her.

★★★

When Gwen texts Dylan to say Ines has moved in and that it's perhaps a good idea to give her some space, she thanks her for the heads-up. Feels the stitches pull on this old wound, a lesion of exclusion. Then, a few days later, without really thinking too much about it, she gets into her car and makes the short drive to the cottage. Sees his Saab parked on the driveway, confirmation that he's in. It makes her feel sicker than she already is. She makes her way straight to the outhouse, assuming he'll be in the studio.

'Noah?' she calls, pushing against the heavy soundproofed door.

And there he is, sitting on the couch in grey tracksuit bottoms, the surrounding area littered with empty takeaway boxes. She fans a hand over her nose. 'It stinks in here.'

'Doesn't it,' he says morosely.

'I'm sorry to interrupt your pity party.' She walks over to inspect her findings, drops a half-empty box of chow mein back onto the mixing desk and picks up a heavy folder on the table, which she starts flicking through.

He gets up. 'That's private.'

But she turns her back to him, see what's inside: magazine and newspaper cuttings. 'Local girl gets scholarship' in an old paper with a school photo Gwen had submitted. She's always hated that picture. She moves through the covers of the *Vogue* magazines her jewellery had appeared in, shoots that reference her name in the bottom-right corner in small white sans serif. The silly blog interviews she'd done online printed out and painstakingly held in place with tape or small paperclips. She turns and looks at him, using chopsticks to put cold noodles into his mouth.

'What is this?'

'What does it look like?' He chews with his mouth open.

'But why would you—'

'Because I knew you wouldn't. You're too busy moving on to the next thing you're doing to stop and realise anything you've already achieved.' He shrugs. 'I dunno, suppose I thought maybe it would make a nice gift one day.'

She feels relief then, that they might be able to manage this. 'Can we go outside?'

He follows her into the garden and squints at the bright light, as if he's not been outside since they've been back. She keeps going, walks to the large tree further down the garden that has two rope swings hanging from it. She sits on one and leans back, using her foot to push herself lightly as he sits beside her, letting the rope push against his shoulders, slumping, his hands reaching for the wooden seat.

'So . . .' she begins.

'I'm not sure I've got any talk left in me.' He gives a lopsided smile.

'I know.' She shakes her head. 'I wish we could go back and do it differently.'

'Me too, but it's a lot more complicated than us both being awful people.'

He had no idea just how much more awful they were about to become; she takes a deep breath.

'There isn't really an easy way to say this, so I'll just go ahead and say it. I'm pregnant.'

He looks at her, eyes wide.

'And before you make an unwelcome joke, yes, it's obviously yours.'

He sits there staring down at the grass, his mind computing everything that that meant: surprise softening to joy, then morphing back to the pain this would further inflict. They sit in silence and Dylan relies on the noise of birds and the occasional buzzing of flying insects. Over the tall bushes, the neighbours are pottering in their garden, having a light and normal conversation instead of learning how to equilibrate their trepidation with hope.

'How long have you known?'

'I realised when we were in Lisbon, at least on some level. I wouldn't let it be real. Did a test when I got home. Well, I did several. Part of me hoped it might change the result.'

'You're not happy about this, then?' He looks disappointed and her shoulders fold.

'I don't know how to answer that.' She uses her feet to stop the sway of the swing. 'What are we going to do?'

His hand reaches for the back of his head. 'I honestly have no idea. The only thing I'm certain of is that you're my best friend, DW, always have been, and I love making things with you.'

She looks straight at him. 'And it's important to say, I need to say, that it wasn't that I didn't love you. It's never been that. I don't remember ever not loving you.'

And he gives her this look then, one she's seen a hundred times before but for the first time in years she feels the wrench of possibility in a face she thought she was done studying.

1998

Gwendoline is twenty-nine

When Gwendoline got back from her shift at the chemist, she noticed the washing machine was on. Odd. She'd secured herself three shifts a week with overtime on offer, if things went well. She felt braver now. She'd got that from her children, that and scabies after a sudden outburst on her return. Emma was to sort their tea and watch the girls on those evenings she worked late. She heard the TV on in the living room, wandered to the sound.

'You're back!' Ines ran at her, wrapped her arms tightly at her thighs, as Gwendoline felt for the softness of the back of her head.

But she hated this performance, a fanatical standing ovation whenever she returned to her own home or they arrived back from school. As if they were surprised to see her there.

'I told you I'd be in by eight,' she said curtly. 'How was school?' Her tone then surprised: 'You put a wash on?'

'Big deal!' Emma's eyes didn't move from the television screen. 'How else do you think we cleaned our clothes while you were gone?' This was issued more as a statement.

The three of them turned to the same empty space on the sofa and laughed into it.

Gwendoline stifled her awkwardness. 'What's so funny?'

'Edi's joking about how useless Grampy was with the washing.' Dylan grinned at her, two front teeth missing. She'd informed her that the tooth fairy had forgotten to come for them. 'He turned all our knickers and school socks red!'

'Are you sure you can't see her?' Ines frowned as if confused, signalling her head towards the vacant space.

'You've eaten, then?' Gwendoline changed the subject.

'Yeah. We also learned how to feed ourselves while you were gone.'

Emma dared to glare at her. Her antagonism was ramping up as the days went by.

But Gwendoline had known Emma's forgiveness would be the hardest won. She couldn't stay mad at her for ever, she was her mam: that was the bane of any daughter.

'What are we watching, then?' she tried, lingering by the door.

'Where did you go?' Dylan knelt up on the sofa.

She took her handbag off her shoulder and straightened her dress, then sat down on the chair. It was strange how it didn't quite feel like hers any more, as if she was a visitor in this house that had been the backdrop for her own childhood. They had taken over the castle and made it theirs. There were different ways of doing things now: they were unanimous and she was damned to the peripheries of their Fort Knox bond.

'To the chemist, love. I told you, I've got a new job, haven't I?'

'No, she means where did you *go*?' Emma wears her new condescension well.

'Edi said we should ask you.' Dylan trod more carefully.

'Did she now.'

Before she'd left, each of them had been more attached to her than the last and she'd known she wasn't capable of mothering another. But now they were each contorted so differently by what had happened and she didn't know how to turn them back into the children she'd left. All they wanted to talk about was Edi. It was all 'Edi doesn't like carrots' and 'Edi said we should ask you why we weren't allowed to go to the funeral.' An instrument to taunt her with. The psychologist told her it was their way of processing death, that they'd grow out of it, and she was counting the days.

'Were you sad about the baby?' Ines, incapable of ever leaving her side now, pushed a small hand into hers and Gwendoline felt her stomach seize.

'Yes, I suppose I was.' She withdraws her hand, stands up and starts gathering the glasses discarded on the table.

'Sometimes,' Dylan stops her, offering a lifeline, 'when you have lots of children, you can't always look after them all, can you? You have to just look after one of them. Only sometimes.'

'I suppose that's right.' She was undeserving of this grace.

'Did you need to give her to the angels?' Ines hung off her arm and she repositioned to account for her weight, swallowing the sting in her throat.

'Yes, I did, I needed to give her back to the angels. I'm sorry I couldn't take you with me.'

'That's okay.' Emma shrugged at her. She couldn't stand to see her upset.

'Right – it's bedtime, then, girls.' Gwendoline tried to gather herself.

'No, it's not.' Dylan sat on the sofa defiantly, as if she were untouchable.

They had become their own ecosystem, entirely dependent on one another, speaking in a secret language for which she didn't have the alphabet.

'We actually go to bed later now. We told you this,' Ines said.

But Gwendoline could still see the roots of her daughters, the things she'd trodden on and those attributes she had over-pruned in each of her girls. Their foibles and misdemeanours were born out of her own misgivings. Their dark hairy strands, which reached down and connected them to one another so strongly. But she had been their creator. Whether they liked it or not, she was the soil. And when a finger got trapped in a door or a dead mouse was found in its cage, she would be there to wipe the tears.

'Bed. Now.' Her word would be gospel again. She reached for the TV and shut it off as they made protestations and moaned while she fluffed the cushions after them, gathering the abandoned socks and discarded school books.

They plodded up the stairs, wearing their reluctance like a shawl, one after the other as she hollered at them, dropping cups into the sink, calling after them not to forget to brush their teeth, waiting for Emma's retort – they had also had to do that without her. Then when she walked into the living room to turn off the lamps, she lingered for a moment. 'I've got them now,' she offered to the darkness tentatively. 'I'm back and I'm not going anywhere. It's okay, Mam, you can go now.'

Then she laughed at herself, at the ridiculousness of the idea, following her daughters upstairs to bed.

Therapy, III

'Oh. She's not coming,' Kit says to Avril eventually, having sat there for a moment or two gazing out of the window, waiting for the session to begin.

'She's not,' Avril confirms.

'No.' He shakes his head, the aftertaste of his failures rich in his mouth. 'We're getting a divorce.'

Avril lowers her chin and Kit waits to see if she's going to write that down. 'And was that a joint decision, or something you or Emmie decided on?'

'Her name is Emma,' he corrects her, with a soft grin. 'Apparently.' He claps his hands into his lap, the hands that had seemingly saved so many lives but couldn't work out how to hold down his marriage. 'I was the only one who ever called her Emmie. A sort of pet name, I suppose. She never mentioned she wasn't fond of the idea.' He could have emailed, yet he'd felt the need to drive this news to her. 'It was her call. In the end. I thought we were working through it. Now I wonder if, well . . . if her push for all this therapy was just some ploy to edge her way out of the relationship.'

Avril goes to say something but stops, opts instead to validate something with a pause. 'And how does that make you feel?'

'Sad for the girls. There are lots of studies on the traumatising effects of divorce on children.' He turns his head to review her shelves. 'I bet you've got a few of those on there.' She doesn't respond to this. 'No? Any on there that say divorce is marvellous then?'

Avril fiddles with her sleeve as if considering what might be helpful to say as Kit strokes the upholstery on the other side of the sofa, embarrassed now as he draws in the evidence: she isn't coming.

'You haven't told me how *you* feel about it, Kit.' She emphasises his name. 'Only that you feel sad on your daughters' behalf.'

'How do I feel?' He wipes the sweat from his palms, realising his hands are shaking. 'She says we haven't been in love for a long time. You may have seen that. It completely bypassed me.'

She blinks, confirming neither way, and Kit looks around the strange little room with its paling yellow walls, the gauche box of tissues some further evidence of a failed expectation of him. His pending divorce, like a heart attack. A stiffening in the sternum, unexpected, a hand pressing down, trying to contain the chaos underneath. The fragile veneer of your surroundings – the reality you'd always known suddenly undoing itself in your chest, and a new truth pulsates: the fragility of life. Your heart wages a desperate war until the darkness sets in and you know that you're all alone. That, really, you have always been so.

He had reinserted himself into the pocket of their marriage one last time to make sure there was nothing left to find in it. He looks down at his watch and says, 'I've got surgery at two. Thank you for your time.' He shakes Avril's hand as she stands with him. 'Best of luck with your future patients. You can't resuscitate them all.'

2020

Gwendoline is fifty-one

'Sort it out between yourselves'; 'I'm not getting involved'; 'Don't bring me into it.' These were the trusted fallbacks when one of Gwendoline's daughters was gunning for another, yelling at her for borrowing a top without asking, disdain leaping out of their mouths. It left a gnawing ache, that she could forgive her children anything, but as sisters, perhaps they didn't have the same dispensation. Perhaps their love had conditions, stipulations, unspoken rules that if broken would upend all the love borne inside one another. She couldn't stop spinning. She was whiplashed by the tempest of Ines's rage, caught in the echo of Emma's most significant ending and struck by the hopefulness in Dylan's new chapter.

Gwendoline didn't know how to play at referee. More than that, she didn't want to. And was that even a mam's role? She'd felt helpless, lost in a labyrinth of circumstance, wondering again which parts of the mess she could claim from the debris and agree to be blamed for. She couldn't condone what Dylan and Noah had done. It was a horrible thing; she felt ashamed of them. And yet she also couldn't turn a blind eye to the consequences of wrapping Ines in cotton wool all those years, never truly forgiving Dylan for almost losing her in the river that night. But it hadn't been her fault. She was just a child. And in the cold light of day the angst crushed like ice on her chest as she faced her maternal limitations: arms full of so many blunders and mistakes that she'd ruefully handed one to Dylan. Some small ease from the guilt that came with having children as it made its way under the bedroom door and curled up next to her; it would never go away.

Dylan had chosen to put Ines first because she loved her. Because as a big sister she had felt that was her duty. And this responsibility had been accentuated by the pulverising dislocation caused by Gwendoline leaving. All this lived inside her now, a thistle of anxiety that pricked at her conscience anytime her mind had the audacity to wander somewhere else. Which it did, to the hum of the refrigerator beside her, a distant, indifferent observer.

'Do you want a hand with that, Mam?'

Emma came up behind her and she crushed the teabag into the side of the mug, trying to compress it all. 'I'm quite capable, thank you.'

She'd needed a lot more from her since separating from Kit. It felt completely validating. Like everything she'd been waiting for: to be the fallback, the shoulder to cry on, the strong one for once, needed. But she felt Ines's distance away on set, living a fantasy life with a pending wrap date. When Ines had taken the call, not long after they'd got back from Lisbon, her agent saying she'd landed a role in a new drama series, they'd all breathed out a sigh of relief. That she'd have somewhere to go, some distraction from it all. But what about after? That was what kept Gwendoline awake at night.

Dylan had also withdrawn, which was why she'd been surprised to get a text that morning asking if she and Noah could pop in. She failed to mention this to Emma.

'So, how is it all going with Kit now, then?'

'I suppose divorces play out one way: disharmony, painful negotiation and a cesspit of money. But we're getting there. He's trying to do the right thing.' Emma considered this. 'I think.'

Gwendoline tugged at her again, trying to decipher how she was really feeling, and for once Emma opened up, allowed her to trample through it with her. When they eventually ran out of yarn, Emma diverted through platitudes so she directed their attention to the other disaster at hand.

'Have you spoken to your sister?'

'The heartbroken one or the mentally deranged one?'

Gwendoline heard accusation in her tone as she placed the cups on the kitchen table, wondered again what she could have done to prevent all this. She knew Emma was carrying it too: one daughter's pain always led itself inside all three of them.

'I've spoken to Ines a few times. She's busy with the new show but it's the best thing for her. Working all hours. She has something to focus on. And Dyl? Not really. We've spoken over text, she checks in to see how the girls are doing, but she's a little off. She's ashamed, I think, embarrassed. The whole thing, I can't get over it – it doesn't even feel real.'

She saw Emma kneading into herself, wondering, asking ... if on some level she'd known.

'They're close. They have always been close.'

Gwendoline wanted to reach across the table and grab her, say this isn't your fault, this is my fault. She knew she was neither a good mother nor a bad one. Nothing in life was that binary and the frame of reference to which she'd held herself needed dismantling. She would have to undergo the same realisations, rehash the same scrutiny in herself over and over until she accepted that such revisits constituted being a mam.

'What do your sisters make of the divorce then?'

Emma avoided her gaze, blew on her tea.

'Oh, Em.' She arched forward. 'You've not told them, 'ave you? Why the bloody hell not?'

'Ines doesn't need it on her plate. And I told you, Dylan is being ... I don't know ...' She tailed off.

'Well, you can tell her this afternoon. She's coming over.'

'Dyl?'

Gwendoline confirmed it with a valiant nod. Emma's eyes looked dark and swollen from the late nights turning over her own problems.

The doorbell went and they looked at one another, mirroring their confusion: why not use her key?

'See – cagey,' Emma sanctioned, rubbing her hands together, warming her angst.

Gwendoline laughed at Dylan when she answered the door. She was instantly defensive, claiming she didn't have her keys on her.

'Hi, Noah, how are you doing, love?'

She tried to give Emma a moment's heads-up. Imagined her body stiffening, ill-prepared for the awkwardness licking its lips in the kitchen where so many of their disagreements had been straightened out. It was predictably uncomfortable. Emma stern, visibly conflicted in her loyalty, and Noah, as sheepish as the first day he'd come round to the house. If she'd had known then that it would unravel this way would she have discouraged the friendship? Would she have paid more attention to the silly little love triangle she'd watched form in this very kitchen? But there was a sense that whichever way she'd moved her pawns they would still be locked in this checkmate.

Dylan put the kettle on, making up for ringing the doorbell, and Noah took a seat at the table, mindful not to sit too close to Emma. They made small talk and all Gwendoline could think was how much she wanted a cigarette. Felt this feeling at the pit of her stomach, an intuition that something else was coming.

'Have you spoken to Ines?' Emma drew her sword at Noah.

'She's asked me to stop calling. She doesn't want to speak to me.'

Emma gestured that this was reasonable.

'She's going to need time to process it. We all are.' Gwendoline tried to unearth what was coming.

'So what?' Emma jabbed inelegantly. 'You're like together now?'

'Sit down, Mam.' Dylan had only made a coffee for Noah. 'We've got something we need to tell you.'

'What could you possibly have to tell us now?' Emma looked at her with amazement, then back at Gwendoline, who nodded calmly, insinuating she would need to keep her cool for this one. Because somehow she already knew. Had seen it in Dylan's eyes when she'd opened the door, some new information, a sixth sense, a feeling given away. And her own contradictions wrung her out: 'How could you?'; 'Congratulations, love, that's wonderful news.'

'It's ...' Dylan stumbled over what she didn't want to say. 'Well, it's difficult to say really because ...' The tears welled and Noah's hand reached for hers, Emma's eyes following it.

'You're pregnant.' Sometimes Gwendoline could do the hard bits for them. Dylan looked up at her asking how she knew and she shook her head because she didn't know how. Perhaps it was that she'd experienced a life draining the energy out of you only so it could grow.

'You're what?' Emma looked at Noah, assaulted by the new fold in this calamity, appalled, as if wanting them to take it back. 'You can't be.'

'Three months,' Noah said, more defensive now.

'No.' Emma turned to Gwendoline. 'No. They can't be. That would mean ... and she can't ... she just can't, she wouldn't cope.' Then, as the information embedded itself: 'It will break her. Do you want to destroy her? Is that your plan?' She was upset, unpredictable in her movements, launching up from the table and looking for her bag, scrabbling for her phone charging next to the kettle.

She stormed out through the front door, and as Dylan went to stand, Noah squeezed her arm, reaching for his jacket on the back of the chair. 'I'll go.'

Dylan cried and Gwendoline let her for a while. Knew what it was to feel the confusion brought on by a new life. A sprout of fear and possibility, then a whirling chaos that never ends, only spirals further out of grasp.

'I don't suppose you remember much about my mam, do you?'

Dylan swiped her nose and shook her head, and Gwendoline felt her sadness at the front of her own heart.

'She was a strong woman. It wasn't easy in those days, raising a son with a disability, and alone, at first at least. Until Grampy came along that is. And it was strange because it was almost as if she resented in me the health that Llewellyn would never have. Some people, when they have a sick child, they long for a healthy one. But for mam ... well, I don't think she realised it would only intensify her anger, especially at the way people treated me compared to him. You see, she never really liked me that much—'

'I'm sure that's not true.'

'No.' Her tone was definite. 'Let me say this, all right? Because she loved me, of course she did. She was my mam. But she never liked me. I unsettled her. All my opportunity, how the world was to me, all those things I got given that he never did. And that was hard for her. I see that now. Took me having my own to realise it, but still. And that's why I knew I couldn't have a fourth. I wanted each and every one of you but I wouldn't take the risk of going through with a pregnancy I didn't want, a child I was in danger of resenting.' Dylan was still searching her face for the answer to the remarkable nightmare she'd found herself in. 'You let her 'ave him, that was you-er biggest mistake, love.

That you knowingly gave him away. That was you-er part in it. You should have stayed after the funeral, been honest about how you felt. She could have coped with it – she would have hated you but that wouldn't have been the first time, eh? Or the last. Huh. And he would have chosen you. You knew that on some level, and that was what kept you matted in all this for so bloody long. This is a lesson, my girl. Now, look at me.' She reached across the table and took her forcefully by the chin. 'You must never sacrifice like that again. You're gonna be a mother now. You need to learn to tolerate not being liked. Do you yer me? It wasn't you-er fault. Me leaving, having to look after Ines while I was gone, the river that night, that was on me, right? Not you.' She felt her daughter's tears running down her hand before she let go.

'I'm not going to be a mother.'

'No?' Gwendoline pushed the hair off her face, tucked it behind her ear.

'No. I'm going to be a mam, just like you.'

Restitution

September

When Emma gets back to the house, Beata has already done the handover with Kit's mother. That was where he was living temporarily and they'd agreed he'd take the girls for the weekend. She'd rarely have to suffer his family now. She goes into the kitchen, longing for the sweet scents found at her daughters' napes, the house deathly quiet without them all in it. She couldn't remember the last time she'd had an entire weekend to herself. She instructs Google to play 'Leader Of The Pack'.

'Okay.' Google's monotone voice comes through the speaker. 'Playing the Shangri-Las "Leader Of The Pack" on Spotify whole house.'

She opens the fridge for a beer, pops the lid and swigs at it, the cold liquid in her mouth offering a new sensation. She moves her hips, saying the lyrics to no one, turning her waist and then her arms, slowly reaching up over her head.

'Hey, Google, turn volume up to eight.'

The music rages from every speaker in the house as she dances across the kitchen, rolling against the island, then making her way into the hall, finding a new dance partner in the stairs as the emotion disbands like it's starting to leave her body.

'Emma!'

Dylan has let herself in.

Emma nods at her like she learned a new trick.

'Why the hell didn't you tell me?' She scowls and it's the same look of discomfort she's been giving Emma since she was a child. Emma shrugs, carries on dancing, acting out the dialogue from the song. 'Can you turn that down?' she shouts over the music. 'I'm sorry. About the divorce. I wish you'd said something, I feel like such a self-involved cow.'

'Thank you—' Emma dances down the stairs towards her '—but you're not a cow.'

'I should have checked in on you both when we got back from Portugal. I don't know why I didn't. It's just with the baby and everything that's been going on ...' She observes herself tumbling back into her own problems. 'I could see you two were having issues and I should have been there for you.'

Emma dances past her, playing silly, prancing down the hallway to the song, encouraging Dylan's amusement. Then, reaching for her hand, she starts to move her body to the music too, slowly at first.

'Emma?' The front door slams and Ines appears in the kitchen, an overnight bag thrown over her arm. 'You're an idiot, why didn't you tell me?'

'What are you doing here?' she calls. 'You're meant to be on set.'

'Mam rang. She told me about the divorce.' She shakes her head ingratiatingly, not acknowledging Dylan, whom Emma sees shielding her small bump. 'I'm not shooting tomorrow so I got a car.'

Emma dances over to the fridge, mindful not to make any sudden suggestions but wanting so badly to bridge the divide between them, and now this baby, another unexpected storm she didn't know if they could weather. She gets out another beer, hands it to her.

'I'm so sorry.' Ines takes it, and she tells her: *Don't be.* 'Do the girls know?'

But then the soft strains of another Shangri-Las' song fills the space, like a melodic invitation from the past, a suggestion of surrender in the face of all these unspeakable feelings. Ines looks at Dylan, unsure of her next play, and Emma can see she's conflicted, so angry still but heavy with the angst that's anchored in any argument with her sisters. It had been a strange year and the intense closeness had rendered them tangled like vines, encroaching upon the other, their roots interwoven as they'd fought for space, strained for the light. It is clear to her now that this togetherness isn't sustainable for any of them.

Ines unhooks her arm and drops her bag to the floor, sips her beer again before reaching out falteringly, graceful in her movements. The wisps of what's still left unsaid are so delicate they move through the air like smoke. They dance around Emma's island then as they once had around a table on Laurel Road, still passing between them what they couldn't stand to hold as something once relied upon casts a different pattern bearing more space.

Epilogue

The taxi drives her slowly up the gravel path. The scathing crunch against the tyres is so familiar to her, yet she feels as though she's arriving at a stranger's house: contemplating whether she'd worn the right thing, if the present was too fussily wrapped, has she an excuse smoothed out for an exit? As she pays the driver she can hear all the kids playing behind the fence. She takes a deep breath, brings her shoulders in closer, wishes she'd brought a jacket; it's a little early in the year for a garden party. Gwen had offered to come and get her from the station, said they could go together, but that in and of itself had made her feel ridiculous. She doesn't need hand-holding. It's better she shows up alone.

She pushes the fence open to reveal Emma's garden; it's filled with kids running around with ketchup on their faces, paper plates everywhere with discarded food.

'Inny!' Emma is the first to spot her, she rushes over. 'It's so great that you're here. I'm so happy.'

Ines gives her sister a stiff hug that's begging her not to make a fuss when Sunny comes bounding over. She can't quite believe how grown-up she is, how much her mannerisms mirror Emma's now. Behind her, Lilah lingers, newly shy about how to greet her estranged aunt.

'Say hello, Lilah,' Emma coaxes. 'Give your aunty Ines a hug.'

Giving her niece an awkward cuddle, she feels bad that she hasn't been around much. But she's been shooting abroad and getting time off is impossible when you're in the middle of a production: Ines has been happy to hide behind these excuses.

'You look really well.'

'Everyone looks well when they have hair and makeup.'

'Right.' Emma turns to the blonde woman who is now at her side. 'And this is Aimee, of course, who I've told you all about.'

'It's a pleasure to meet you.' Ines kisses her cheek. She's more elfin and muscular than she looked in the photos Emma showed her.

'This is Mummy's girlfriend,' Sunny says, as if giving away a secret.

'I know.' Ines strokes her head, looks across the garden and spots Gwen, who gives her a fortifying smile with a nod that confirms: *You've got this, love.*

But she's not sure she has. Because then she sees him, Noah, with a baby – no, his baby – cinching onto his hips, like a large crab. He looks back at her, stops whatever he's doing, just looks, their souls conspiring. He walks towards her and gives her a hug. 'I'm so happy you're here. We weren't sure you'd be able to make it, what with work and everything. Thank you.'

She can't believe she's hearing his voice, a sound as real as thunder, as familiar as the toaster popping up. Yet the formality in his tone makes her feel like breaking down. She'd always fitted perfectly inside those arms. And she resents his polite reserve now, thanking her for her time, as if she's an accountant, here to run up the tax he still owed on breaking her heart. The baby in his arms – Dora – smacks him in the face, wedging a few of her fingers straight into his mouth, which he removes playfully, pretending to eat them up, making her squeal with delight. She'd seen photos of her, of course: Noah's dark complexion layered over Dylan's cheekbones, merged with the Wyn nose, lifted slightly at the tip – her own nose. She swallows the saliva building under her tongue and allows herself the painful thought: what would their baby have looked like?

'This is Dora, Inny,' Emma tries, tugging her gently out of the daydream.

'Of course it is. Dora. Aren't you lovely? Gosh, and you have so much hair.' She hates each benign word that trots after the last.

Noah tells her she was born with most of it and this assaults her with the visual of him in the delivery room with Dylan, the crowning of an entirely new person. Who would change everything.

'I brought her a gift.' She looks down, surprised to still be holding it.

'That's really generous.'

'Well, you don't know what's in it yet.'

'Let's have her open it.' He walks a little further into the garden where there's a picnic blanket, puts Dora down and she starts sucking on the wool tassel. 'Here, Dora,' he says. 'Look! What's this your aunty Ines has given you?'

She kneels on the blanket, feeling the presence of Emma beside her as she watches him with his daughter, seeing how happy it makes him.

Ines tears at the paper, opening her mouth in faux-surprise and crunching it in her hand to make a sound Dora seems to like. The white soft toy emerges, a mouse with pale pink paws, held open as if to offer an embrace, and a pink rope for a tail that goes straight into Dora's mouth.

'Her teeth are coming through. She likes it,' he adds, smiling again, gratefully.

She knows then that Dylan is in the garden, can sense her, feel her gaze. Not wanting to be caught scrabbling on the ground she stands up, and as she rises to her feet her sister is by her side.

'You came.'

They stare at one another then, she and her sister. The inflictor of all this pain, a conduit to a violet-coloured love that lit up the darkest corners of her childhood. Trying to make sense of the mess they are still learning to live with.

'Your daughter is lovely.' Ines scrunches up her nose involuntarily, feels the tears wet her eyes. They haven't seen each other since before Dora was born. 'She looks just like you, and she has our nose.' She laughs at herself then, gently pressing the back of her hand to her mouth.

'Would you like some cake?' Dylan asks.

'No, no, I can't stay long. I'm back on set tonight. I just wanted to drop in and meet her.'

There was still so much more to say to each other. Maybe one day they would.

'Can we just have a quick photograph together?' Emma calls over a friend and hands him the camera, directing them all to the only sunshine-lit corner on the lawn.

And Ines feels the low hum in her body, the savage cadence that comes with her sisters. Lilah and Sunny squabble as Emma's friend repositions them gently by their shoulders. Gwen reaches for her hand and discreetly squeezes it, firm and just the once. Emma pushes the hair out of Aimee's face and there's sweetness in the gesture. Noah is holding Dora, chin lifted to the camera with pride, Dylan next to him, sucking in her soft tummy, brave enough now to let him glide his hand around her lower back. And in the years that would follow, Ines would look at this photograph and be reminded of the excruciating pain she would still feel from that day, of the sting that would never really leave but, with hope, could ease a little in time, tended by a family who would have to find their way back to a future and a new version of love that could be found within it.

Acknowledgements

I extend my deepest gratitude to the editors who worked across this novel: Lily Cooper, whose vision and foresight led to its commissioning; Tallulah Lyons, who stepped into Lily's role and guided the process with confidence and precision; and Kit Nevile, whose conviction carried this book through to publication.

To the team at Hodder, who were pivotal in bringing this book to life and believed in it from the beginning. A special thanks to Helena Fouracre in marketing and Becky Mundy in publicity for their calm and creative approach, which makes all the difference.

I am deeply grateful to Sofia Hericson, the cover designer, and Valeria Duca, the gifted artist whose painting was used.

Thank you to my agent, Kate Evans at PFD, a steadfast presence and a force for good. I am especially grateful for her patience in tackling the unenviable task of agenting an agent.

To the early readers who gave invaluable feedback. Thank you, Nicole Bergstrom, for enduring multiple early drafts with kindness and encouragement; Mickey Bourne for your thoughtful insights and care, which enriched this work; Romilly Morgan, for bolstering my confidence in this story; Aislinn Arrigo for her positive enthusiasm and energy; and Nikesh Shukla, for sharpening the narrative with his faultless editorial instincts.

To my family, I am endlessly grateful for your continued faith in me. To Mark, for your love and for your boundless care and support.

Finally, to you, the reader: thank you for dedicating your time – the most precious resource of our modern age – to this book.

'An intelligent, moving and darkly comic debut . . . taking us deftly from serious explorations of trauma to riotously funny scenes of modern life'
Sunday Times

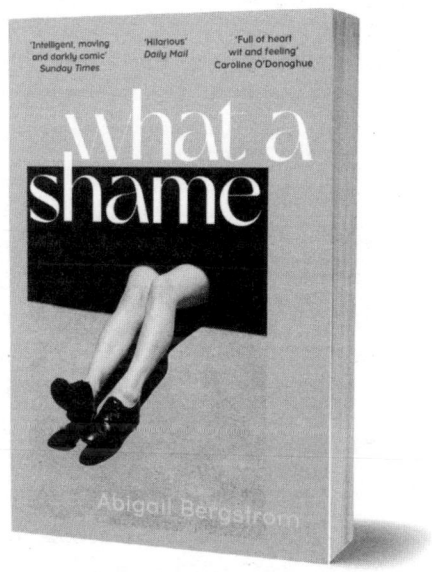

There is something wrong with Matilda . . .

Perfect for fans of Dolly Alderton and Holly Bourne. Get your copy now!